RALPH COMPTON

All work and no play
makes a man deadly....

VIGILANTE DAWN

D0035338

A RALPH COMPTON NOVEL BY MARCUS GALLOWAY

SIGNET

$6.99 U.S.
$7.99 CAN.

ISBN 978-0-451-47069-0

5 0 6 9 9

S > EAN

COLD VENGEANCE

Comforted by the weight of the guns in his hands, Jarrett brought both pistols up and thumbed back the hammers. The man on horseback was about twenty yards in front of him. He most likely would have gotten a clear shot at him by now if his horse hadn't been getting more and more spooked by the flames that were spreading to consume the bunkhouse.

Walking forward, Jarrett pulled his triggers again and again. The stolen pistols bucked against his palms, spitting death into the killer in front of him. Even as the man fell from his horse, Jarrett continued to fire. He circled around the horse, pointing the guns down at its owner as the hammers slapped against one spent round after another.

"He's done," Edgar said.

When he felt a hand on his shoulder, Jarrett spun around so quickly that he knocked one pistol against the older man's shoulder. Edgar hopped back and raised his hands. He still held the rifle but pointed it at the light purple sky as he said, "Easy, boss. It's just me."

Jarrett nodded.

"Looks like there was just the two of them left behind," Edgar said. "We'd best get out of here, though."

Jack was nearby as well, bearing the weight of his friend without the slightest bit of exertion. Stan's eyes were open and he walked like a drunk while taking in the sight of the body lying on the ground. "What the hell is this?" he asked in a stupor.

Tucking the guns under his belt, Jarrett replied, "It's a good start."

Ralph Compton

VIGILANTE DAWN

A Ralph Compton Novel
by Marcus Galloway

A SIGNET BOOK

SIGNET
Published by the Penguin Group
Penguin Group (USA) LLC, 375 Hudson Street,
New York, New York 10014

USA | Canada | UK | Ireland | Australia | New Zealand | India | South Africa | China
penguin.com
A Penguin Random House Company

First published by Signet, an imprint of New American Library,
a division of Penguin Group (USA) LLC

First Printing, November 2014

ISBN 978-0-451-47069-0

Printed in the United States of America
10 9 8 7 6 5 4 3 2 1

THE IMMORTAL COWBOY

This is respectfully dedicated to the "American Cowboy." His was the saga sparked by the turmoil that followed the Civil War, and the passing of more than a century has by no means diminished the flame.

True, the old days and the old ways are but treasured memories, and the old trails have grown dim with the ravages of time, but the spirit of the cowboy lives on.

In my travels—to Texas, Oklahoma, Kansas, Nebraska, Colorado, Wyoming, New Mexico, and Arizona—I always find something that reminds me of the Old West. While I am walking these plains and mountains for the first time, there is this feeling that a part of me is eternal, that I have known these old trails before. I believe it is the undying spirit of the frontier calling me, through the mind's eye, to step back into time. What is the appeal of the Old West of the American frontier?

It has been epitomized by some as the dark and bloody period in American history. Its heroes—Crockett, Bowie, Hickok, Earp—have been reviled and criticized. Yet the Old West lives on, larger than life.

It has become a symbol of freedom, when there was always another mountain to climb and another river to cross; when a dispute between two men was settled not with expensive lawyers, but with fists, knives, or guns. Barbaric? Maybe. But some things never change. When the cowboy rode into the pages of American history, he left behind a legacy that lives within the hearts of us all.

—*Ralph Compton*

Chapter 1

Flat Pass, Wyoming, 1884

Some men had families. Others had their work. While most folks had both, they could never love them the same. Early in his life, Jarrett Pekoe made his choice and never looked back. He loved his kin with all his heart, but all of his sweat, blood, and soul had been poured into the Lazy J Ranch. It was a small operation. From careful planning, hiring on the best hands, and building partnerships spanning several states, his ranch didn't need to be large to make a profit. It had taken years to make certain he was the only rancher driving his herd to some of the most selective buyers, and now Jarrett could reap his reward.

It was a cool spring day and the sun was high in the sky as Jarrett rode the perimeter of his land. Although his official task was to make sure the fence had been repaired in three spots that had rotted away, he barely kept one eye on the wooden rails. His gaze wandered along the horizon, savoring a comfort that could only be granted by contented solitude. Years ago, he'd been a hired hand who needed to make the rounds without taking a moment to lift his eyes from where they needed to be. When he'd ridden as a regulator at the Hard Luck spread up in Montana, his days were filled with chasing rustlers and rounding up strays. Naturally plenty of other men working the same jobs at those same places took time to indulge in simpler pleasures. These days, they were still at those jobs while Jarrett had clawed his way up to being the man who slept in the big house on his own patch of land.

Just as a smirk had gotten dangerously close to becoming a smile on his face, Jarrett spotted a portion of fence that didn't quite meet his standards. He immediately pulled back on his reins and climbed down from his saddle.

"Easy, Twitch," he said while patting the white nose of his otherwise brown gelding. "Just checking to see if I need to tan anyone's hide when I get back."

Judging by how much the horse shook his head and shifted on his feet, one might think the animal was worried that it was his job on the line. Of course, that very thing was how he'd earned his name. All of the fidgeting in the world, however, wouldn't have dimmed Jarrett's view of the horse he'd ridden since his regulator days in Montana.

Knowing his horse didn't need to be tied up, Jarrett approached the fence and placed his hand on the top rail. He gave it a shove, gripped it with both hands, and put his whole body into it as he shook the sturdy posts. When he kicked the lowest rail, he scowled down at the length of wood.

"I suppose it'll do," he grumbled. As he climbed back into his saddle, he was still thinking of new ways to improve the fence's longevity so even fewer repairs would need to be made in the future.

All fanciful thoughts from a few minutes ago were gone as Jarrett continued his ride along the fence. That sort of single-mindedness came easier to him without needing to concern himself with a wife and children of his own. If he was going to succeed the way he wanted, he would need to devote himself fully to the cause. He couldn't do that if he was also pulling the weight of a missus and young ones. Of course he knew plenty of ranchers who raised a whole mess of children on their land. Those men also needed more hired hands to keep their heads above water. More important, they had to be content with taking a lesser part in the growth of their ranch. If Jarrett was going to do something, no matter what it was, he wasn't going to do it halfway.

Jarrett's clean-shaven face was almost always set into firm, straight lines. His light brown eyes weren't cruel, but there wasn't a lot of forgiveness to be found within them. The only thing about his appearance that was consistently unkempt was his hair, and that was only because it made more financial sense to cut it himself with a razor instead of paying some barber in town to clip it while yammering on about the weather. As soon as he'd spotted the pair of riders coming his way, Jarrett sat tall in his saddle and stared out at the approaching men with all the authority of a sea captain surveying his crew.

The men riding toward him were two of Jarrett's regulators. Matt and Pete were good workers and mostly trustworthy. Although they tended to partake in a bit too much liquor for Jarrett's liking, they had proven themselves on more than one occasion, which was good enough for him. Pete was the taller of the two and Matt had enough whiskers on his chin to evenly cover his face, his partner's face, and a good portion of Jarrett's. All of those whiskers weren't enough to hide the uncomfortable frown he wore when he caught sight of the Lazy J's owner.

"Howdy, Mr. Pekoe!" Pete hollered.

Waiting until he was close enough to respond without shouting, Jarrett asked, "You men on your way back to the bunkhouse?"

"A bit early in the day for sleepin', sir," Matt said.

After giving his partner a quick swat, Pete added, "Thought we might get a bite to eat before taking a ride into town."

"So that means your work is done for the day?"

"More or less. All that's left is some bits of repair work and then taking our turn at patrolling the perimeter to make sure none of them vagrants show their faces again."

Jarrett nodded. Even though the vagrants in question had only managed to steal one horse for less than a day before being tracked down, he wasn't about to give them a chance to take another run at the place. Still, his men had put such a scare into those two filthy thieves that he doubted they'd return anytime soon. "You two have the night patrol, right?" Jarrett asked.

Matt nodded. "Yes, sir. We should be back from the saloon in plenty of time to—" The next swat he received from the man beside him was almost hard enough to knock him from his saddle.

Before Matt could say another word, Pete said, "We don't intend to get drunk, Mr. Pekoe. Just thought we'd play some cards and have a bit of fun in town. That's all."

While Jarrett might not have been one to drink much liquor himself, he wasn't the sort who would harbor bad feelings against those who did. For the purposes of keeping his men on their toes, he kept his expression severe and waited a few heartbeats before nodding. "You'd best be riding your patrol and have enough of your wits about you to see a jackrabbit bolt from its hole or there'll be hell to pay."

"Naturally, Mr. Pekoe," Pete said while tapping one finger against the rim of his hat.

Neither of the two men was much younger than Jarrett himself, but they treated him with an earnest respect. Jarrett repaid that by not treating them like anything less than the men they were. "Tell you what," he said. "I had a look at a portion of fence that you two were responsible for repairing."

"We were just headed back that way," Matt said. "We patched it up, but I didn't think it was sturdy enough, so we're just about to finish the job."

Having already spotted the tools, lumber, and bag of nails being carried by the men, Jarrett dug into a pocket while saying, "I guessed as much already." He then tossed a silver dollar to each man. "Do the job right and there won't be any need to pay me back."

They smiled and caught the money in callused fists. "We're good for it, Mr. Pekoe!" Pete said.

"I know. You see anything else while you're out here?"

"Matter of fact, we did. There's a wagon coming in from the east."

"There is?"

"Yes, sir. Weren't you expectin' company?" Pete asked.

"Yes, but not for another day or two," Jarrett replied. "How many were in the wagon?"

When Pete looked over to him, Matt said, "Couldn't say for certain. There was two in the driver's seat and at least one horse riding alongside, but they were a ways off and taking their time in getting here."

"Any children with them?"

"Maybe."

Furrowing his brow a bit, Jarrett asked, "Could it be another damn salesman?"

"After the way we chased the last two off this property, I sure doubt it," Pete replied with a laugh. "That wagon we just saw has probably been riding hard for a good, long while. The team was tuckered out. A blind man could have told you that much."

Slowly Jarrett's smile returned. "Then that could be Norris."

"That your brother?" Matt asked.

"It sure is. And it's just like him to try to get here early to give me a bit of a surprise."

"You want me and Pete to ride out to greet them?"

"No," Jarrett replied. "You said they were coming in from the east?"

"That's right."

"Then I'll go see them myself. If Norris worked this hard for a surprise, there's no good reason for me to spoil it."

"So, you're all right with us two heading into town?" Pete asked. "After we finish with that fence, of course."

"Sounds like a plan. You two have a good time and try not to fall off your horses on your way back."

Unaccustomed to seeing their employer in such good spirits, both of the hired hands waved to Jarrett and snapped their reins to ride away before he added some other bit of hardship to their workload.

Jarrett not only snapped his reins as well, but tapped Twitch's sides to coax a little more speed from the gelding. The horse was all too happy to comply since he always seemed more comfortable when his hooves were churning through the dirt and the wind was in his face.

After riding for about a quarter mile along the fence, Jarrett turned north and rode for a short ways more. With every second that passed, Jarrett's grin became wider. Pulling back on his reins, he stopped less than fifty yards away from the spot where a wide road pointing toward Nebraska met up with a gate in the Lazy J's fence. Jarrett reached into his saddlebag and dug around for a pair of field glasses. When he found them, he brought the glasses to his eyes and peered through the lenses. The magnified view might have been somewhat marred by several scratches on the glass, but he saw more than enough.

"You sure are taking your time, little brother," Jarrett said to himself. He then panned the field glasses away from the wagon he'd found until he spotted another horse keeping pace with the wagon while maintaining a healthy distance from it. Jarrett squinted through the lenses but was unable to make out much of the rider. "Scott's getting bigger," he mused. "I imagine he insisted on riding in on his own. Thought for sure Grace would be the one to scout ahead."

On a hunch, Jarrett kept searching the horizon. Before long, he found the other silhouette he'd been looking for. "There you are," he said.

The sun was just bright enough to cast a glare on everything below. Although it was the same ball of brightness that shone down on the rest of the world, it seemed to cast longer shadows in Wyoming than anywhere else. If he lived closer to Old Mexico, he surely would swear that it was hotter and he'd heard more than a few men from Montana tell him how their sun resided in a wider sky than the blue expanse that could be found over any other part of the country.

Having lived in Wyoming for years, Jarrett rarely pondered such things anymore. The harder he strained to get a better look at his approaching guests, the more he wanted to curse the sun for being too damn bright and his glasses for being too damn old. When his horse stomped the ground with one front hoof and shook its head hard enough to jostle the man on its back, Jarrett sighed and said, "You're right. I already know it's them." While putting the field glasses away, Jarrett scratched his horse behind the ear. "My nieces and nephew are getting big. Before you know it, I'll be hiring them on as hands for a summer or two. Then maybe one of them will want to work here for good."

He flicked the reins to point the horse's nose away from the fence and start moseying toward the road that led all the way to the center of the ranch. "Last time we saw Grace, she was nothing but a sprout with pigtails in a wrinkled dress," he said fondly. "And Scott was knee-high to a grasshopper. Ain't even seen the baby yet, but that's about to change."

Jarrett took a quick look over his shoulder. The wagon in the distance was picking up enough speed to kick up a cloud of dust, and the horses accompanying it were drawing in closer. Surely the young riders were getting a few final instructions from their father.

Knowing how much Norris enjoyed his surprises, Jarrett had intended to ride all the way back to the house so he could play his part as the oblivious host. He made it less than a hundred yards before bringing Twitch around in a sharp about-face turn. "Eh, to hell with it," he said. "Just because Norris is the baby of the family, that doesn't mean he gets to have all the fun."

Chapter 2

In any family, being the youngest child had its advantages. The Pekoe clan wasn't any different. Raised on a small Iowa farm, the children were doted on by their mother and worked harder than a rented mule by their father. Jarrett's older sister lived with her husband in Virginia, and the next one in line was Kyle, who'd died of a fever in the winter of '78. That had left Jarrett to maintain the family name in business and Norris to provide a few more branches of the family tree. Even if Norris had only contributed a few kind words at the occasional family picnic, their mother would have put him up for sainthood.

Surely Norris had put some small amount of thought into how he would announce himself while making his grand entrance at the Lazy J. No matter what idea he came up with, even if he'd cobbled it together in less time than it took for a nut to fall from a tree, Norris would expect it to be received with an abundance of enthusiasm from anyone within eyeshot. Jarrett took no small amount of pleasure from the thought that he was popping his brother's bubble before it had gotten much of a chance to float. It did the baby of the family some good to be treated like the rest every now and then.

Jarrett amused himself with these thoughts after having opened the gate and positioning himself in the middle of the road directly behind it. He'd planned to stay there, staring at his brother to let Norris know that he wasn't the only one who could arrange a surprise. The wagon rolled toward him, but at a snail's pace. Both of the children rode their horses at least five yards away from it on either side and were keeping their distance. There was no possible way any of them could have overlooked the fact that Jarrett was waiting for them, and yet nobody had shouted a word to him.

Not one excited holler from Grace or Scott.

Not a single brotherly taunt from Norris or even a wave from his brother's wife.

After a few more seconds of the strange silence, Jarrett started to worry. Perhaps someone was sick. Maybe there had been harsh words passed between members of the family. One of them might have been injured during the ride. The longer Jarrett considered the possibilities, the more gruesome and terrible they became. Finally he forced them out of his mind completely.

"Enough of this," he said as he snapped his reins. "Guess I'll have to get a look for myself."

As he rode closer toward the wagon, Jarrett realized how impatient he'd gotten in a relatively short amount of time. The wagon wasn't really moving that slow. It was just being pulled by tired horses and driven by what was most likely a tired man. Within the space of a minute, he was able to make out the faces of Norris and his wife. Even from a distance, Jarrett could tell his brother was not his normal self.

Jarrett got such an uneasy feeling from the look on his brother's face that he pulled back on his reins a little early so as not to draw any of the ire that was brewing on the faces of both Norris and his wife. Norris pulled his reins as well to slow the covered wagon before plowing straight over their welcoming committee.

"Imagine my surprise!" Jarrett said cheerily. "You all are early."

The only responses he got were heavy breaths from the wagon's two-horse team and the creak of the wheels as they rolled to a stop. Norris had a rounded face and cheeks that would perpetually make him look five to ten years younger than he truly was. His sandy brown hair might have been thinning a bit in front, but the rumpled way it framed his face still had a boyish quality. Whenever Jarrett thought about his brother, he pictured Norris laughing, shouting, or giving some other overly emotional display. That was a far cry from the weary visage he wore on this day.

"How was the ride?" Jarrett asked. "Did you run into any bad weather?"

Norris shook his head as if in response to a voice that only he could hear.

Shifting his eyes to Norris's left, Jarrett wasn't surprised to find a vaguely sour expression on his sister-in-law's face. She never did like Jarrett very much, and the only time she'd done more than simply tolerate his presence was on her wedding day. After that, she'd endured the occasional visit only slightly better than before, which Jarrett had always assumed was for the children's benefit. She wasn't an ugly girl. Her thick black hair was always well brushed and couldn't be contained by the bonnet she wore. A thin face gave her something of a mousy quality, which Jarrett had never found appealing in anyone.

"Good to see you, Jen," Jarrett said to her. "You're looking well."

She scowled silently at him, which really wasn't much different from her usual greeting.

"So," Jarrett said, "did you take a shortcut or did you just whip those horses to within an inch of their lives?" Since Norris and Jen merely looked nervously at each other, he asked, "Where are the kids? Perhaps they'll be more conversational." Turning toward the sound of hooves beating against the dirt, he shouted, "That you, Scotty? You must've grown a foot since the last time I've seen you!"

"Jarrett," Norris sighed. "I . . . I . . ."

"Well, now! He finally speaks," Jarrett chuckled. "And here I was thinking the little woman had taken your tongue out."

The brothers had weathered plenty of hard times together. They'd seen each other through as many trials as triumphs, but in all those years Jarrett hadn't seen this particular expression on his younger sibling's face. "What is it, Norris?" he asked.

Norris grew increasingly anxious as his children's horses approached the back of the wagon. "I'm sorry, Jarrett. Truly I am."

The bottom had never fallen out of Jarrett's stomach so quickly. Although it was his nature to assume the worst of most any situation, he rarely thought those worries would come to pass. When he got a whiff of something terrible drawing closer to him and his kin, it was all Jarrett could do to compose himself. "What's happened, Norris? Tell me."

"They got to us yesterday," Norris explained. "I tried to shake loose of them before bringing them here, but . . ."

Twitch was getting increasingly nervous and for a change Jarrett himself couldn't blame him. Rather than try to rein in the animal, he allowed it to back up a few steps from the wagon. That little bit of extra space allowed him to get a better look at one of the riders that had been accompanying his brother. Norris's son and daughter had both been taller than most anyone else their age, but the person holding the reins of this approaching horse was definitely no child.

"Who the hell are you?" Jarrett asked. "Where are Grace and Scotty?"

The man in the saddle had a slender build, which seemed even more so owing to his slouched posture and slumped shoulders. His skin resembled starched sailcloth that had been draped on a wire frame. He gripped his reins tightly in one hand while the other hung within a few inches of a holstered pistol. Grinning beneath a mustache consisting of irregularly spaced hairs scattered unevenly on his lip, he said, "They're just fine. Don't you worry none about that."

Scowling at the stranger, Jarrett said, "You didn't answer my first question."

"Don't get yer feathers ruffled. How about we all get on the other side of that fence so we can have a word like civilized folk?"

"Don't give orders to me. This is my spread and these are my kin. Tell me who the hell you are before I send you away."

"Send me away? Now, that ain't no way to treat a guest."

As those words were spoken, the second horse that had been traveling alongside Norris came around the back end of the wagon. This one had a slender build as well but made himself look even slighter by hunching over. Once he sat up fully and put on his hat, he looked to have a build similar to Jarrett's and was at least eight years his junior. He drew his .45 without so much as a how-do-you-do.

Calming Twitch with a few subtle gestures and a nudge from one foot, Jarrett placed his hand on the gun holstered at his side. Unbeknownst to him, Norris had climbed down from the driver's seat to approach him from behind.

"No," Norris said. "Don't draw that pistol."

"I want an explanation," Jarrett said. "Right now."

Chapter 3

"Just simmer down, Jarrett," Norris said. "Let me explain."

Jarrett wasn't about to take his eyes off the two riders when he told his brother, "You're not the one that needs to explain himself."

"You'd best think twice before touching that gun again," the second rider announced. "Or this little visit is gonna get bloody."

"Shut up, Dave," the first rider said.

Even though the second rider outweighed his skinny partner by a considerable amount, he deferred to him without a struggle.

"Where are the children?" Jarrett asked in a voice that was drawn tighter than a bowstring.

"They're fine," Norris replied. "They're both fine."

Finally looking away from the two strangers, Jarrett glanced at his brother when he asked, "You sure about that?"

"Of course I am."

Comforted by the truth he saw in that familiar face, Jarrett shifted his focus back to the strangers. "Tell me who you are."

The skinnier of the two riders shifted in his saddle to

place his hand a bit closer to his holstered weapon. "We," he said, "are the men in charge of this for the time being. That makes you the folks who will listen to what we say and do what we tell you to do."

Because Twitch needed so much encouragement, the horse was finely attuned to a complicated set of Jarrett's movements. All it took was a little nudge to get the horse slowly walking toward the skinny rider.

"I don't want any trouble," Jarrett said.

"Good," the skinny man replied. "Neither do we."

Another nudge steered Twitch so the skinny rider was between Jarrett and the second stranger.

"If it's money you're after, I'll give it to you," Jarrett said to him.

Clearly the younger gunman was getting anxious. He pulled his reins one way and then another to keep a clear line of sight fixed on Jarrett. "Damn right you'll give it to us," he snapped. "You ain't got a choice."

Turning to shoot a warning glare at his partner, the skinny gunman barked, "Dave, I told you to shut the hell up and that's what you'll—"

The instant the gunman's eyes were on Dave instead of him, Jarrett tapped a heel against Twitch's side. The gelding lurched forward with a start, giving Jarrett a bit of added momentum as he straightened both legs in the stirrups to send him flying at the closest stranger. Jarrett stretched out both arms and grabbed whatever he could of the skinny man's clothing. They collided in a tangle of flailing limbs. The other man's saddle horn gouged Jarrett in the ribs and took the breath from his lungs.

The two of them couldn't have struggled atop that horse's back for long, but Jarrett felt each moment stretch into an eternity. He guessed he was lying sideways across the stranger's saddle but couldn't be absolutely certain. It was all he could do to hang on to the other man to keep him from getting to his gun and keep himself from falling off. Jarrett lost the second battle fairly quickly but managed to win the first by dragging the stranger down with him.

They landed hard on the ground. Jarrett hit first, but the other man didn't drop on top of him because one of his feet was still caught in a stirrup. Scrambling to get his legs beneath him, Jarrett reached for his holster and flipped away the leather thong that had kept his Colt revolver from slipping out during the fall.

"Drop the pistol!" Dave shouted.

Still wobbly on his feet, Jarrett took a moment to get his bearings. His hand was still pressed against the .38 at his side and he wasn't exactly anxious to remove it.

Dave glowered down at him from his horse, taking aim over the top of his firearm. "I said drop it!"

This wasn't Jarrett's first scrape where guns had come into play, but it had higher stakes than any other fight of which he'd taken part. For that reason alone, he steeled himself with a quick breath and dropped to a knee while making a quick grab for his Colt. Dave was either surprised by the move or reluctant to fire out of fear of hitting his partner, because Jarrett somehow managed to draw the .38 before getting burned down in the process.

Jarrett pulled his trigger without taking a moment to aim. If he'd been an experienced gunman, he might have actually hit something. As it was, the only thing his bullet did was burn a trail into the sky.

"Jarrett, stop!"

That plea came from Norris, but Jarrett was too deeply invested in what he'd started to pull back now. Dave had swung down from his horse to position himself in a spot better suited to taking a clear shot. He fired once, sending a bullet whipping past Jarrett's head toward the wagon. Terrified screams came from within the canvas cover, letting him know that the children were alive and well enough to know what was going on.

It had been pure instinct that caused Jarrett to glance toward the wagon. He caught sight of a young girl looking out, and when he snapped his gaze forward again, he was staring straight down the barrel of Dave's pistol.

Jarrett's entire world ground to a halt.

"All of you," the skinny gunman said through a series of heavy breaths. "Just take a breath and stop this right now."

Dave gritted his teeth while steadying his aim. "This one's too much trouble, Clay. He'll just take another run at us."

"No. He won't. Ain't that right, hero?"

Jarrett's heart was slamming with too much force against his battered ribs for him to form an answer.

"Turn around," Clay said in a voice that was already steadier than it had been a moment ago.

As much as he didn't want to do anything the gunmen said, Jarrett heard a muffled whimpering that convinced him otherwise. Rather than turn his back to Dave, he took a few shuffling steps so he could get a look at the wagon while keeping the younger gunman at the edge of his field of vision. He had to fight to maintain his composure when he saw that frightened little face he'd glimpsed not too long ago.

"Grace?" Jarrett gasped. "Honey, are you all right?"

The girl was indeed taller than the last time he'd seen her, but the terror etched into her eyes as she was held tightly by the skinny gunman made her seem small and all too vulnerable. Clay now stood behind her and slightly to one side. One of his hands was clamped over her mouth and the other held a pistol, which he pointed at her temple.

"Let her go!" Norris demanded.

Jen screamed from the driver's seat, too frightened to move and now horrified by what she might find if she did.

"Shut up!" Dave barked. "You know better than to speak 'less you're the one that's spoken to!"

Jarrett didn't have to see his brother to know what he was thinking. It was what any man would be thinking when he saw his family threatened.

"Everyone settle in before things get worse," Clay said. Looking to Jarrett, he asked, "When are your men going to come this way again?"

"This is a small spread," Jarrett explained. "I don't have a lot of men working for me."

"We know you've got regulators riding your fence line. Either tell me when to expect them or I'll cut my losses here, starting with this one," Clay said while jamming the barrel of his pistol even harder against Grace's head.

Jarrett struggled to come up with another course of action, but he simply couldn't find it. Reluctantly he said, "They're repairing a section of fence south of here."

"How many more are there?"

"Three, but they're not all armed. Some are just hired hands. There's no need to hurt anyone."

"They may not be armed, but you are," Clay said. "Do what my partner kindly asked you and drop that pistol."

Every inch of Jarrett's body wanted to let go of the Colt and do anything else that would result in Grace being released from that killer's grasp. He knew nothing of these men, but he'd already seen enough to be certain they would have no problem doing something as cowardly as shooting an innocent child to get whatever the hell it was they wanted.

And yet there was one thing that kept Jarrett from doing what he'd been told. "If I let go of this gun," he said, "that just means you'll take another prisoner to do with as you please."

"In case you haven't noticed," Clay said, "we can already do what we please."

"For Pete's sake, do what they want!" Jen shouted. She must have been climbing down from the driver's seat, because Dave took a few long steps in that direction while pointing his gun at her.

"You wanna die?" Dave snarled.

"You want me to believe we'll live if I help you?" Jarrett said before he had time to stop himself.

As Jen sobbed into her trembling hands, Norris reached out to his brother and said, "Don't do this. It won't help."

"Listen to him, hero," Clay sneered.

"There's more than just these two to worry about," Norris continued.

Jarrett's eyes snapped toward his brother. "How many more?"

"I don't know."

"You haven't seen them?"

"Damn it, why won't you ever listen to me?" Norris said with mounting urgency. "You think I'd just stand by and let these two animals hurt my family?"

"No, but you were alone until now," Jarrett said. "Not anymore. If we're going to put an end to this, it's got to be here and now before—"

Dave thumbed back the hammer of his pistol while snarling, "I'll end it, sure enough."

"No!" Clay said in a voice that hit everyone in the

vicinity of that wagon like a sharp jab. "Not yet. Whatever you do, hero, this little girl dies first. Understand?"

Those words ignited a spark within Jarrett that burned through almost everything human within him to leave nothing but animal instinct and feral rage. Perhaps spotting that inside him, Clay shifted his aim with a simple flex of his wrist. The gun in his hand barked once and spat a single round through the meat of Jarrett's thigh like the talon of a passing hawk. He felt a burn through that leg, but the grazing scratch wasn't nearly enough to put him down.

"Please, Jarrett!" Norris begged. "Do what they say!"

Just then, Jarrett saw something in the icy depths of Clay's eyes.

Reluctance.

Clay might have been a killer, but he didn't want to kill Grace. Jarrett was certain enough of that to want to keep fighting. His desire grew even stronger when he heard a voice carried to him on the wind from the direction of the ranch.

"Mr. Pekoe?" Matt hollered. "We heard the shot. You all right?"

Matt and Pete were riding back along the perimeter on the other side of the fence. They'd responded to the gunshot as they would on any number of occasions when such a signal had been used to call for a hand.

"Get the others!" Jarrett shouted desperately. "These men are trying to kill us!"

He couldn't have hoped for a better sight than when Pete urged his horse to take off at a run toward the road leading to the center of the ranch and Matt reached for the rifle kept in the boot of his saddle. Pete only made it another couple of yards before a rifle shot cracked through the air, hissed past the wagon, and knocked him from his saddle.

Jarrett couldn't tell if Matt had seen the other man fall or not. In the end, it didn't matter. The next bullet from the rifleman in the distance snapped Matt's head straight back and sent him to the dirt.

"No!" Jarrett shouted. When he drew his next couple of breaths, he expected to feel a rifle bullet punch through him as well. Some part of him felt it was only right that he tasted the same lead that had claimed both of his men.

"You've pushed this far enough," Clay said. "You wanna push it further or should we all conduct ourselves in a more civilized manner?"

It wasn't in Jarrett's nature to give up. It also wasn't in his nature to put good people at risk. Realizing he simply didn't have any other options, he let the Colt slip from his hand. "Whatever money I got," he said to the gunmen, "it's yours."

Clay nodded solemnly. "Money's just the start, but it's a good one. Now let's get a look at this ranch of yours."

Chapter 4

Once Jarrett handed himself over to the gunmen, events passed by in a rush. His Colt was taken from him. He was roughly searched for any other weapons by Dave, who found a hunting knife hanging from his belt and claimed it before doubling Jarrett over with a solid punch to his gut.

"That's for being such a pain in the ass," Dave snarled.

As much as he wanted to fight back, Jarrett had already been shown the futility of that train of thought. Besides, he didn't have enough wind left in his sails to do much by way of damage, so he remained bent at the waist until he was pulled upright and shoved toward his horse.

"You get any ideas," Dave said while taking the Winchester from Jarrett's saddle, "and the lead will fly."

"So you keep saying," Jarrett groaned.

"You think I'm foolin' about?"

"No."

"Good," Dave said. "Now get on that horse and introduce me to the rest of your men."

"Why? So you can slaughter them like you did Matt and Pete?"

"I didn't slaughter nobody. If'n you'd like me to start, then I'd be happy to oblige."

"Tell me why you want to see the rest of my men."

The wagon was only a few yards away, and from there, Clay said, "Just put the man's mind at ease, Dave. It ain't like he's in a spot where he can do anything about it. It'll make the rest go that much quicker."

Unlike the younger gunman, Clay didn't have to threaten Norris or his family with every other breath. The deadly promise lurked below each word just as surely as sharks circled beneath calm waters of the sea.

Jarrett hung his head and climbed into Twitch's saddle. The gelding shifted as he always did, giving his rider a little dose of familiarity to let him know that not everything in his world had come undone.

"You're gonna show me the rest of your men to keep them alive," Dave said. "We can either round them up all at once or hunt them down one at a time. The more you make us work, the worse things'll be."

"I understand."

"Good. Now get moving."

They rode across Jarrett's land, touring the Lazy J while he made introductions as if Dave were a new hand that had been hired on through the summer. When each of the three remaining workers showed Dave the bunkhouse, they were knocked on the back of the head with the butt of a pistol and tied up. In what was surely a show of dominance as well as some kind of perverse thrill, Dave even made Jarrett help in dragging his own men to the back of the bunkhouse where they wouldn't block the doorway. The process took just over an hour and when it was through, Jarrett wound up in front of the main house watching the wagon come rolling up to within a few yards of the porch. On any other time, such a sight would have brought a smile to his face. This day, however, it filled him with dread.

"I was hoping you might have gotten away," Jarrett said as he helped Jen down from the seat atop the wagon.

She gripped his hand with desperate strength and still nearly toppled on her way down. "There's nowhere to run," she said in a shaky voice. "Lord only knows how many more of them are out there."

Jarrett could still only see the two gunmen. Clay had a hold of Grace's wrist, but at least he was no longer pointing a gun to her head.

Norris was at the back of the wagon doing his best to coax his son into the open. "Come on, Scott. You can't stay in there forever."

"I need to protect Autumn," the boy replied from within the wagon.

"We all want to protect her. Now bring her out here to me, son. Come on now."

Dave was tying the horses to a post near the house, and when he drew a breath to yell something toward the wagon, he was silenced by a sharp expression from Clay.

Without having a stranger bark at him, the boy poked his nose into the fresh air. His face was wet with tears and he held on to a bundle of blankets as if it were the most precious package in known creation. He was a small boy with his father's eyes and his mother's thick dark hair. If that hair remained as curly as it was now, he would have no trouble whatsoever in attracting female attention when he got older. Jarrett got hardly a glimpse of the pudgy little face wrapped up in all those blankets and couldn't have been more grateful for it. The baby was quiet and blissfully unaware of what was happening around her. Where Jen had seemed on the verge of fainting away just a few moments ago, she regained all of her vigor when she saw her youngest two children.

"Come here, Scott," she said while hurrying around to the back end of the wagon. "Let me get a look at you."

The boy approached her as if they were the only souls left in the world. Jen lowered herself to the young boy's level so she could wrap her arms around him and gently squeeze Autumn between the two of them.

"Aw." Clay sighed. "Ain't that just sweet?"

Jarrett couldn't decide which would bother him more: if the outlaw's words were a sarcastic mockery or if they held genuine sentiment.

When he approached Clay, Jarrett didn't give a damn how anxious Dave seemed to get. Ignoring the pistol in the younger outlaw's hands, he addressed the skinnier of the two when he asked, "What are you going to do with them?"

"Who?" Clay asked. "Those two little angels?"

"Yes," Jarrett said through clenched teeth. "They've been through enough without you tossing them in with the others."

"I suppose you'd prefer they not be tied up as well?"

Hoping to refrain from saying things like that where they could be heard by his niece and nephew, Jarrett quickly replied, "That's right. It's not like either them or their mother can pose much of a threat."

"I suppose not. Still, however they're treated, it depends on you."

"Perfect. If it's up to me, then let them all go."

Clay let out a laugh that shook almost every inch of his bony frame. When he caught his breath, he said, "Tell you what. If you got any better suggestions, I'd like to hear 'em."

"There's plenty of room in the house," Jarrett said.

Looking at the structure situated more or less at the

center of the Lazy J, Clay scowled as if he'd just bitten into a rotten piece of fruit. "That really ain't much of a house. I thought there'd be something a lot bigger, to be honest."

"I have three bedrooms of good size. Two have doors with locks and windows that are too small to be of much concern."   •

"Sounds like a fine sales pitch," Clay scoffed. "So long as it's accurate."

"I know every inch of that house," Jarrett assured him. "I did build it, after all."

"All right, then. I'll bring the girl upstairs myself. If the rooms are like you say, then I can lock her in so she's nice and comfortable. If not, then I'll tie her up so she'll never remember what comfortable is."

When Clay started to reach for Grace again, both Jarrett and Norris moved to intercept him. The outlaw pulled the gun from his holster and had it ready to fire in a flicker of motion. The look in his eye left no room for doubt that he would kill the next man who took a step forward.

Despite the gun being pointed at him or the intent of the man holding it, Norris looked Clay dead in the eye and said, "If you harm one hair on that girl's head, I swear I'll—"

"You'll what?" Dave snapped.

Before his partner could make the threat he'd surely been cooking up in his head, Clay motioned for him to stand down and returned Norris's intense glare. Quietly, calmly, Clay said, "Go on, Norris. Tell me what you'll do."

Hearing the gunman address his hostage in such a coolly familiar way was jarring. Since it was plain to see that no words would have much effect on him, Norris choked back whatever ones he'd been planning to say.

"Yeah," Clay growled through a sly grin. "That's what I thought. Dave, watch these good folks while I take the young lady up to her room."

It was physically painful for Jarrett to watch Clay take hold of Grace's arm and escort her into the house. After the two of them disappeared inside, an eerie silence fell upon the entire ranch.

Jen held her baby close with one arm and had the other wrapped around her son's shoulders. Her eyes were trained upon her husband, pleading with him to perform some sort of miracle that would free them all.

Ashamed of his limitations as a mortal man, Norris couldn't bear to look at her.

Dave licked his lips while holding a rifle in his hands.

When Clay emerged from the house alone after an acceptably short amount of time, Jarrett was finally able to let go of the breath he'd been holding.

Clay stood on the porch, looking out at the people in front of him while clearly savoring the power he held over each and every one of them. After a prolonged silence, he clapped his hands together and rubbed them as if he were trying to build enough heat to create a fire. "Well, now," he announced. "Seems you were right about them rooms. Sturdy doors. Windows might be a bit too big for my liking, but that ain't much of a worry. If any of you try to creep out of any of them, one of my men posted outside will pick you off like pigeons."

"So does this mean we can stay in the house instead of in the barn like a bunch of animals?" Jarrett asked.

Dave chuckled. "I don't know. I kinda like the barn idea."

"You want in the house so bad?" Clay said. "Then you can stay in the house. Or close to it anyway. Don't get too comfortable, though. There's plenty of work to be done."

"Might help if you told me what work you're talking about."

"First of all . . . you know any good knots?"

Neither of the brothers responded to that, but the two gunmen got quite a laugh out of it. Everything that had happened that day, combined with whatever had happened before he arrived at the ranch, suddenly became too much for Norris to bear. It didn't matter that he was unarmed. Jarrett recognized the look in his younger brother's eyes as the one he'd gotten when he finally had enough of being pinned down and teased by his siblings.

"No," Jarrett warned when he saw Norris's muscles tense. "Don't."

Norris took one and a half steps toward Clay before a rifle shot cracked through the air to drive a bullet into the ground inches away from Norris's foot.

Even though Dave was the one to draw his .45, Clay had the look of someone who was closer to putting Norris down.

"By all means," Clay hissed. "Proceed."

Norris couldn't allow himself to step back, but he also knew better than to take another step forward.

Putting himself directly in front of Norris and turning him around with a rough shove, Clay said, "Let's get these folks inside before they hurt themselves."

Chapter 5

"You know what's funny?" Jarrett asked.

His words broke a silence that had enveloped him and his brother soon after they were tied up and tossed into the room where they now were.

That had been well over an hour ago. Possibly longer.

Jarrett's voice didn't travel very far. Thanks to the dirt walls and timber support beams around them, the thick wooden planks above their heads, and the dirt floor beneath their feet, any sound seemed more like a muffled presence lingering around their heads or lurking just behind them. Of course, such a peculiar effect could have been caused by the fact that there wasn't so much as a single flickering candle to provide them one bit of light.

"I know you're still here," Jarrett said before too long. He then sighed. "Damn kid brother. It's just like him to find a way out and crawl away like a kitten without taking a moment to consider anyone else."

"Kitten?" Norris grunted from somewhere nearby. "You haven't called me that for a while. That was childish of you. Even when you were a child."

Jarrett smiled. Even though there was no way for it to be seen, the expression could be heard in his voice when he said, "You used to make those little mewling sounds. Remember?"

"I was seven."

"Meow, meow. You'd do it when someone asked you a question and you didn't want to answer. Or if you wanted to get on Mother's good side without having to lift a finger."

"I had to do something," Norris said. "Just to be noticed. Between you and Catherine getting praised for every little accomplishment you made, I didn't have many other options."

"You did plenty," Jarrett said. "Apart from the mewling."

"Sure I did. You and Catherine just did it all first."

"You sounded ridiculous. Meow, meow."

"Oh, for Pete's sake, will you let it go?" Norris said. "Aren't there more important matters at hand right now?"

"Sure. We just can't do much about them at the moment."

Silence wrapped around them again. The angered breaths coming from Norris's section of the dark room quickly abated. After that, he said, "You used to torture me with that."

"With what?"

"Calling me kitten. It's something you'd call a little girl."

Jarrett laughed quietly. "I know," he mused. "Got under your skin something fierce. Why do you think I kept doing it?"

Although it might have been the rustle of movement against the boards over their heads, Jarrett was fairly certain he heard his brother trying to suppress a laugh. "When I'd finally escape from you or Catherine, I'd find a quiet spot and think of ways to get you both back."

"Under the porch," Jarrett said. "Or behind the hay bales in the barn. That's where you'd scamper off to, right?"

More silence for a short while.

"Yeah," Norris finally replied. "How'd you know?"

"I followed you there when you got away from me. I meant to keep at you, but it seemed better to let you simmer down. Also, if you had a place of your own you wouldn't pester us for a while."

"I appreciate that," Norris said as if he'd just been given that particular gift. "I did a lot of good thinking in those spots. Nice memories."

"Well, don't get too sentimental. It was Catherine's idea. I wanted to lurk outside one of those little hiding spots of yours and scare you out of your shoes when you finally poked your head out."

"Sounds about right. You never passed up a chance to give someone a fright." Norris drew a deep breath and let it out. "I don't recall you mentioning this house had a cellar."

"I didn't want to be locked up in here," Jarrett said.

"Good plan."

Since his brother no longer sounded like a watch that had been wound too much, Jarrett asked, "So, what happened?"

"What happened where?"

"What do you think? What happened during the ride here? I'm guessing those gunmen who decided to pull their weapons and turn this visit into a nightmare aren't friends of yours."

Norris sighed as he was dragged out of his pleasant memories and back into the much darker present. "You'd be right about that. We set out from the bluffs just over a week ago. Made it out of Iowa and into Omaha on the first day. I had some trading to do."

"Still trying to get that courier route cinched in?"

"Yeah. It's been coming along well too. All I needed was to shake a few important hands a bit farther west and I'd get exclusive transport contracts from two good-sized merchants."

"Not bad for a two-man operation," Jarrett mused.

"Learned from the best, big brother."

When Jarrett felt a grin slide across his face, he reflexively lowered his head and kept himself from making a sound. It was never a good idea to let the youngest child get too full of himself.

"Anyway," Norris continued, "I met one of those bastards while I was in Omaha."

"Which one?"

"The skinny one. Clay Haskel."

"Never heard of him," Jarrett said, mostly as a way of thinking out loud.

"Neither had I. He introduced himself as another courier. More like a messenger actually. Carrying letters and such in between businesses who want something faster than the post office."

"Someone should tell them about the telegraph. Hell of a wondrous invention."

"Also requires someone to send and receive the messages," Norris pointed out. "There's no foolproof way of knowing if the man on the other end of that wire can be fully trusted or not."

"Ah," Jarrett sighed. "I see you're talking about something other than shipping manifests or conversational letters."

"That's right."

"Is that the sort of business you're in now? There's a lot of money to be made in catering to rich men who have secrets to keep."

"All rich men have secrets to keep," Norris replied. "That being the case, I'm not interested in helping them with their dirty laundry. All that would really do is help them get richer."

Jarrett chuckled while shifting his weight. "Sounds like something Pa would have said."

"Believe it or not, he passed on a thing or two to someone other than you. I had to wait until after you left home to get it, but it was still there." As Norris continued speaking, his voice sounded even more relaxed. "I didn't think much of it when I met Clay in Omaha. A few days after we left to keep moving west, I ran into him again. It was near a little hole of a town where we stopped for supplies. He tipped his hat and that was it."

"Sounds innocent enough."

"Yeah . . . well . . . it wasn't. The next day, he and that other one caught up to us while we were on a long stretch of nothing in western Nebraska."

"Sounds like most of western Nebraska," Jarrett said.

"Scott was out on his own horse. He'd been champing at the bit to scout ahead. I saw him farther up the trail and there was another man on a horse right next to him. Clay told me in no uncertain terms that all he needed to do was give a signal to that man and he'd shoot my boy."

Jarrett stewed in the darkness, clenching his fists until he felt his fingernails dig deep into his palms.

"At first, I just thought he was robbing us," Norris continued. "Then he started asking me about where I was going. Somehow he knew about you already. Damned if I know how. Perhaps he asked one of the men I stopped in to see along the way."

"Could have been," Jarrett said. "I've done business with plenty of folks out that way."

"Well, it became obvious that he wasn't out to rob us. Him and that other one made themselves comfortable with me and the family and forced us to keep heading here."

"Did you try to get away from them?"

"Of course I did!" Norris snapped. "I'm not still some little child anymore, you know."

"That's not what I meant."

"I know. Sorry. I tried. Jen tried. Hell, even the kids tried, but if one of us slipped too far away, another one of us was rounded up and . . ."

"And what?" Jarrett asked, even though he wasn't completely certain he wanted to know the answer.

"Let's just say it was unpleasant enough to make a point and loud enough for that point to be delivered. And before you ask, they didn't touch Grace or Jen. Not in that way. It was perfectly clear that simply running wasn't an option unless all of us could go and be real quick about it. Anything less and we'd get hurt. I took a few beatings, but that didn't bother me much. I suppose that's one thing growing up with you as a big brother was good for. Gave me a real tough hide."

"Well, someone had to toughen you up," Jarrett said. "Are your hands and feet tied?"

"No, Jarrett. I'm just sitting here because I like this cellar," Norris said. "And before you ask the next brilliant question, the answer is yes. I have been trying to pull loose."

"What I meant to ask was if you're tied *to* anything."

"Hang on," Norris said as he started grunting with effort. "Trying to . . . reach back . . . and feel."

While his brother did that, Jarrett continued gathering whatever bits of information he could in regard to his own situation. He'd been tugging and pulling his arms and legs to get an idea of how secure his bindings were. He didn't have to wriggle very much before reaching the limit of his range.

"Think I'm tied to a post," Norris finally said.

"Don't you remember being tied to one? Those two must have had a lantern with them when they brought us down here."

"I recall getting my wrists tied after making the rounds over every damn inch of this property."

"So do I."

"Then I remember Dave making some remark about Jen. After that . . ."

"Right," Jarrett said. "After that is when you told him exactly what you thought of him . . . what you thought of both of them, in fact. That's when you were knocked on the back of the head."

Norris let out a prolonged sigh. "That explains the fresh ache in my skull. To be honest, I've been knocked back there so many times lately that I've almost stopped noticing. That's how those killers would put us to sleep every night before we arrived here. Been having head-aches every minute of every day. Forgetting simple things. That doesn't explain why you can't remember be-ing dragged down here, though."

"I was knocked out too," Jarrett said. "Not long after you, in fact."

"What for?"

"For trying to make them two pay for putting you down."

"Really?" Norris asked. "That's touching . . . in an odd sort of way."

"What are brothers for? I just came around a little bit ago. Been sitting here catching my breath for a spell."

"I've been awake for a while too. But while you were

resting, I was listening for footsteps, voices, anything to let me know what those men are doing up in the house or how many of them there are."

"What'd you figure out?" Jarrett asked.

"Sounded like they were arguing about something earlier."

"About what?"

"Don't know," Norris said. "I'd guess one of them was angry with Clay, and it wasn't Dave. It was someone else's voice."

"Could be the man with the rifle."

"There's more than one rifleman."

"That's what Clay told us," Jarrett said. "That doesn't make it so."

"Well, whoever it was stormed off and the others have been talking about him ever since."

"What have they been saying?"

"I can't tell," Norris replied. "I couldn't hear much through this floor. Whatever it was, I'd say it's something that might point to a fight brewing between those men."

Rather than take credit for building such a sturdy and solid house, Jarrett asked, "How could you tell so much if you couldn't hear exactly what was being said?"

"When you've grown up with the big brother and sister I had, you get real good at hiding in dark places and listening to how the tides are turning in the outside world."

"I suppose so. About that—"

"Stop right there," Norris cut in.

"Why?"

"You were about to apologize. I can tell. There's no need for it. I was lucky to have you two for a brother and sister."

"I suppose we all turned out fairly well. As good as can be expected anyway." Jarrett smiled again. "How many of them did you count?"

"More than two."

"That's helpful."

"So what now?" Norris asked.

"We keep trying to get loose and listen for something that may be even more helpful."

"Those men are here for a reason. If they'd just wanted to take whatever money I had or even if they'd wanted my herd, they could have taken it and been on their way by now."

"Not necessarily," Jarrett said. "A herd isn't something you just pick up and carry off. It takes men who know what they're doing, supplies for a long ride, and a buyer at the other end. They could very well have had the last one lined up before Clay played his hand, but the rest requires some time."

"With us tied up and them roaming this place like they owned it, I'd say they've got plenty of time to do whatever they please."

"We'll just have to see what we can do about that." Now that he'd been awake for a bit longer, Jarrett had a lot more of his wits about him. The more breaths he took, the harder he was able to strain against the ropes binding his wrists. The more he strained, the deeper those ropes cut into his flesh. The deeper they cut, the more it hurt, and the more it hurt, the sharper his thoughts became.

Just as Jarrett's mind was becoming so focused that he nearly forgot about anything other than the ropes sawing through his wrists, Norris asked, "So, what was funny?"

"Huh?"

"When you first started talking, you mentioned something being funny. What was it?"

Grateful for any excuse to stop struggling for a moment or two, Jarrett said, "Oh, right. When I was riding out to greet you as you first arrived, I was thinking how the sun here in Wyoming felt different from the sun anywhere else. I was grateful that, no matter how bad things got, I would always have that simple pleasure. And now here we are, locked up in the dark."

Silence.

"Isn't that kind of funny?" Jarrett asked.

"No," his bother said drily. "How about we just stay quiet for a spell?"

Chapter 6

Whoever had tied those knots sure knew what they were doing. No matter how much Jarrett struggled, all he had to show for it was bloody wrists and sore ankles. Norris had taken to pulling against the post to which he was tied, creating a muffled thumping sound that slowly faded into the back of Jarrett's mind.

After what could have been hours or the better part of a day, the door to the cellar creaked open and a small bit of flickering light spilled into the cramped space beneath the house. The sputtering little candle flame that was carried down there was enough to strain Jarrett's eyes as though he'd been staring up at the sun that had so recently drifted into the conversation between him and his brother.

"How you boys doin' down here?" Clay asked once he reached the bottom of the steep stairs leading to the dirt floor.

Norris was quick to respond. "Why don't you cut these ropes so I can show you firsthand?"

"That's quite all right. Just thought I'd poke my head down here to see if you'd like anything."

"I'd like to know what you want here," Jarrett said.

"Didn't I just tell you?" Clay replied with a chuckle.

"Whatever you're looking for, I can help you find it. This is my ranch, after all. If you've been trying to get anything from my men, I can make your job a whole lot easier. They're good men, but they don't know where the money is kept."

Clay held a candle in one hand and kept the other resting on the grip of his holstered pistol. "You sure are fascinated with all this money you're supposed to have," he said while stepping behind the post where Norris was tied. Every move he made shifted the flickering light source in his hand to make shadows dance across barrels of sugar, stacks of spare lumber, and a row of shovels propped against one wall. "It's all you keep going on about. Suppose that should be expected from a successful businessman like yourself."

"Spare me the sweet talk," Jarrett said. "Just get me and my brother out of this damn cellar."

"You hungry?" Clay asked in a purposely slower manner. "You need something to drink?"

"How about a trip to the outhouse?" Norris asked.

Hunkering down to his level, Clay replied, "Not just yet."

When Norris lunged forward at him, Clay didn't even flinch. Knowing exactly how far his prisoner could go, he'd placed himself just a few inches beyond that range so he could watch the ill-fated attempt to lash out.

"You finished?" Clay asked after Norris allowed himself to slump backward again.

"Not even close," Norris replied.

Clay nodded smugly and then turned toward Jarrett. "You're coming with me."

"Gonna have to cut me loose first," Jarrett replied.

"Dave!"

Responding like an obedient dog, Dave hurried down

the stairs when he was called. Without another order given, he circled around behind Jarrett's back and sliced the ropes securing him to the post. Half a second later, Jarrett felt a rough hand grab him by the collar to haul him to his feet. He'd barely gotten his balance when the same knife that had cut his ropes pressed against his throat.

"Do I gotta tell you what happens if you decide to play the hero again?" Clay asked.

"No," Jarrett said. Even the subtle shake of his head was enough to drag his neck back and forth against the blade. No blood was drawn, but it wouldn't take much for that to change.

"All right, then. Bring him up."

When Jarrett felt a shove from Dave, the blade at his throat was drawn in just a little tighter. Turning only his eyes to look at his brother, he said, "Remember what we talked about."

"I will," Norris replied. "Watch yourself."

Before Jarrett could say anything else, he was being forced up the stairs. The fresh air felt good against his face, and the inky black sky was a comfort to eyes that had been in darkness for so long. Even though Jarrett was well aware that he'd lost track of time, it felt a lot later than he'd anticipated. There was a cool dampness to the wind that brushed against his cheek, which spoke of the hours just before dawn.

Clay walked a couple of paces ahead of them. As soon as he'd emerged from the double doors built into the ground that led into the cellar, he circled back around toward the house in an easy stride. "Remember them offers you made?" he asked. "In regards to the money."

"I don't have much," Jarrett said.

"From the way you were talking before, it seemed like

you've got plenty. Considering the bind your family's in, now ain't exactly the time to change your story."

"I do have money here. It's just not enough to warrant all of this."

"I'll be the judge of that. Where is it?" Clay asked.

"In the house. I've got an office on the first floor."

"We been there," Dave snarled from directly behind him. "Didn't find no money."

"It wouldn't exactly be safe if it was out in the open, now, would it?" Jarrett sneered.

"No," Clay said from the front of the short procession. "It sure wouldn't."

They were inside the house by now. Before they took more than three steps through the front door, Jarrett could tell the gunmen had been busy. Tables were overturned. Chairs were broken. Even the few pictures he'd gathered had been ripped off the walls. Considering how little he and Norris had heard from the cellar, most of that damage had to have been done when they were both still unconscious.

It was a short walk down a hall that led the three of them to Jarrett's office. At least, it had once been an office before the room was turned upside down by careless hands. The only thing in there that wasn't tossed onto the floor or overturned was the desk, and that was only because the piece of furniture was too heavy to be moved more than an inch or two from the spot it had been in since the house was built. Jarrett was shoved roughly forward and released from Dave's grip, only to stumble over a pile of ledgers.

"Time to get that money you've been promising," Clay said.

Dave was quick to add, "And it had better be enough to keep us from goin' upstairs to finish what we started with them two womenfolk."

"What did you start with them?" Jarrett asked.

"Shut up and do what ye're told!" Dave said.

"One of them is just a girl, for Pete's sake!"

Stepping forward to grab his partner by the shoulder and roughly pull him away from Jarrett, Clay said, "They're both fine. You have my word."

"That doesn't mean a damn thing to me," Jarrett snarled. "I want to see them."

"You will. After we have the money."

"No. I want to see that they're all right or you might as well shoot me right now before you get one cent of that money."

Dave drew his .45. "Don't tempt me," he spat.

"You want to see the women?" Clay asked. "Fine. Tell Dave where to look for the money so he can get it while I take you upstairs."

"It's in the desk."

"I already looked in the desk!" Dave roared.

"Look again."

Dave slammed a fist against the solid desk and stalked around it as if the mass of polished wood were one giant egg that needed to be cracked. As he yanked at each drawer in turn, the gunman grumbled a steady line of obscenities to himself.

Clay kept his hand on his holstered pistol and stood to one side. "Come on," he said to Jarrett. "Let's go visit them ladies."

Walking past him, Jarrett made his way back down the hall toward the bottom of a narrow staircase. "You really got a talent for getting under Dave's skin," Clay said from directly behind him. "That's the sort of thing that may come back to haunt you."

"I couldn't care less about that."

"Can't say as I blame you considering the circumstances. And just between you and me, I enjoy watching him fret too."

The second floor wasn't as disheveled as the one below it, which was mainly because there were fewer items to toss about. A single little table near the top of the stairs was still upright, although it did shake a bit when Dave threw something heavy against a wall in the office.

"Where are those other men of yours?" Jarrett asked.

Clay surprised him with a quick answer. "Keeping an eye on the men we got tied up in the bunkhouse," he said.

"And after this, you'll turn them loose?"

"Those who want to go. Sure."

"What's that supposed to mean?"

"You want to play guessing games?" Clay asked. "Or do you want to get a look at these two fine ladies?"

The tone in Clay's voice was enough to make Jarrett reach for the nearest door. Whether that was the intention or not, he couldn't open the first one quickly enough. It was the door to one of the smaller rooms that he'd been using mostly to store clothes and old trunks. When he pushed the door open, he found Jen tied to a cot that was rarely used. He wasn't about to ask permission before rushing into the room and peeling down the scarf that was wrapped tightly around the bottom portion of her face.

"Are you all right?" Jarrett asked in a hurried whisper. "What did they do to you? Are you hurt?"

"I'm all right," she said in a shaky voice.

Jarrett examined her by carefully turning her head and checking her arms for any bruising. Before he could do much more than that, Clay said, "You got your look. Now come on."

"What's happening, Jarrett?" she asked. "Where's Grace? What about Norris?"

"Norris is all right. He's been kept with me."

She nodded. "And Scott? The baby? Have you checked on them too?"

"Not yet, but I will."

"You're bleeding. What have they done to you?"

He could have been bleeding from a shallow cut on his neck or from one of the gashes on his scalp, but Jarrett wasn't about to waste time in checking to see which had caught her eye. "I'm fine," he said.

"What about the bullet wound on your leg?" she asked.

Until that moment, Jarrett had forgotten about the nick he'd gotten when he was introduced to Clay and the others. He reached down to his thigh and felt several cloths had been tied around his leg. There was a bit of pain, but it was fully eclipsed by his circumstances. "They bandaged me up," he said.

Jen nodded. "Good."

"I'm going to check on Grace right now."

"Don't let anything happen to her," she pleaded.

"I won't."

"Swear to me you'll keep her safe. Whatever happens to me, I don't care just so long as my children are safe."

"I swear."

She nodded again, appeased for the moment but far from tranquil.

When he stood up, Jarrett turned to face his captor. "Where are you keeping the children and the baby?"

"I guessed you'd want to see them as well," Clay said as if he were soothing a wailing infant. "They're up here too."

Jarrett nodded and stepped into the hall. He was taken to the other two rooms in short order. Grace was being held in the next bedroom that was used for the occasional guest who came to visit the Lazy J. Scott and Autumn were comfortable in Jarrett's own bedroom. The conversations he had with Grace and Scott were short, but he got a chance to relay the same basic information he'd given to their mother. "That's plenty good enough," Clay said. "Time to get back to work. Sounds to me like Dave isn't having any better luck now than when he tried the first time."

"I suppose he wouldn't," Jarrett said while looking down at the baby's face. Autumn's expression was so peaceful that he felt he could escape through her for just a moment. That moment was all he needed to gain the strength to keep plodding forward even if he didn't know where he was headed.

"That's a real sweet baby," Clay said.

Jarrett straightened up, turned to face him, and saw that the outlaw had already drawn his pistol. "Don't say another word about these children," he warned, "unless you're telling me you let them all go."

"Not quite yet, hero. Get moving."

"What's the matter?" Jarrett asked as he started marching toward the door. "Losing some of that confidence?"

"No. I've just found that men in your position tend to gain a bit of confidence once they've gotten a look at them they care about. Sometimes they need to be reminded who holds the reins. That is," Clay added, "unless you want these little ones to watch me blast a hole clean through you?"

Jarrett glanced back into his room to find Scott watching with wide, terrified eyes. "Don't fret," he said to the boy. "This man's just blowing smoke."

Although the boy nodded, he wasn't about to be put completely at ease so quickly. When Jarrett started walking again, he did so at his own pace. It was the smallest of victories but felt good all the same.

"Feeling better?" Clay asked.

Jarrett didn't even dignify that with an answer.

As he walked back down the hall, Jarrett looked for an opening that could be exploited to earn his freedom. When he got to the stairs and started walking down them, he thought of a few different things he'd like to do. Setting those plans into motion, however, meant putting his family in even more jeopardy. That was simply something he wasn't about to do.

"I know what you're thinking," Clay said as they reached the first floor and made their way back to the office.

The moment he felt a hand rest on his shoulder, Jarrett shook it off.

"You did the right thing," Clay went on to say. "That run you took at me before when we first got here . . . that was natural. Expected. Doing it again would've only gotten you hurt. And them ladies upstairs . . . the boy too . . . they would've been hurt worse."

"So you keep saying," Jarrett snarled.

Long before he could see inside the office, Jarrett could hear Dave struggling with the desk. It did him a little bit of good to hear frustration building to a boil within the gunman. Even though it hardly seemed possible for the office to be put in any worse condition than when he'd last seen it, Dave had managed to do just that. The previous mess had been jumbled even more, leaving Dave standing in the middle of it like a rabid dog that had just ripped through its muzzle.

"He's lying through his teeth!" Dave said while leveling a finger at Jarrett. "There ain't nothing hid in that desk. There's nowhere left for me to look!"

Jarrett strode right past the fuming outlaw and stepped around his desk to stand in the spot where his chair would normally have been. Reaching down beneath the middle section of the desktop, he felt for the head of a nail that was a hair's width from being flush with the bottom of the surface. It was actually a recessed switch that he pressed inward and slid toward him. The simple yet hidden latch came loose and allowed him to slide out a thin drawer that was almost as wide as the desk itself.

"There's your damn money," Jarrett said.

Dave was speechless. His jaw hung open as he looked over to Clay and then back to the desk. Both of the gunmen approached the desk as Jarrett stepped aside to allow them to see what had been uncovered. Spread out to fill every bit of space within the wide, shallow drawer were several small stacks of hundred-dollar bills, an array of gold and silver coins, and the deed to the Lazy J.

Chapter 7

Once again, Jarrett found himself in the dark.

It was only his familiarity with every inch of his home that saved Jarrett from breaking his neck when he was shoved down the stairs leading into the cellar. Once Dave followed him with a lantern in hand, he rewarded Jarrett's feat of dexterity with a sweeping kick to the back of his knees that dropped him to the floor. The gunman wasted no time before tying Jarrett up once again and securing him to the same post where he'd awakened not too long ago.

"Thanks for the money," Dave said before pounding his fist into Jarrett's side. "And this is just because I feel like it," he added before driving another punch into the same spot.

"Leave him be!" Norris said as he strained against the ropes that held him in place.

After thumping a boot against Jarrett's lower body, Dave took a few steps toward Norris and snapped his head toward him as if he were teasing an animal in a zoo. "You don't want none of this, boy," he said.

"Come closer so I can be sure of that."

Dave might not have been the sharpest knife in the kitchen, but he knew better than to take Norris up on his offer. Instead he chuckled and climbed the stairs. The little bit of light from the lantern he'd been holding disappeared as the cellar door was dropped into place.

"How you doin'?" Norris asked with a tired sigh.

Jarrett struggled to sit fully upright but could only make it to a lazy slouch with his back against the post and one leg stretched out in front of him. Since nobody could see him even if he did manage to regain his posture, Jarrett allowed himself to slump. "I been better," he replied. "What about you?"

"Better than you."

Despite the pain in his side, Jarrett still allowed himself to enjoy a laugh with his brother.

When he caught his breath, Norris asked, "Did they actually take you to see Jen or the children?"

"Yes, and they're all fine."

"Honestly?"

"Yes," Jarrett replied.

"Would you tell me if they weren't?"

"Why would I hide it?"

"Because you know what it would do to me if I lost them." Norris pulled in a deep breath and tried to play off a sniffle as though he were clearing his throat. That trick hadn't worked when he was a kid, and it didn't work now.

Jarrett let it pass without confronting him about it, though. "They're scared," he said. "Tired. But that's about it."

"The baby?"

"Actually she's sleeping like she doesn't have a care in the world."

Norris let out a little chuckle. "Now I know you're not just trying to make me feel better. That girl could sleep through a windstorm. She has slept through a few big storms, in fact. What about your men? Did you get to see them as well?"

"I didn't want to push my luck," Jarrett explained. "I only offered to help them so I could check on Jen and the little ones. Actually I was surprised I got to see as much as I did. Besides, if my men were in any immediate danger, I'm sure Clay or that other one would have been quick to tell us about it."

"I suppose they were busy greeting those others that came along."

"What others?"

"The ones that arrived a bit after you were taken out of here," Norris replied. "I heard a bunch of horses outside as well as a good number of voices I hadn't heard before. Thought for certain you would've noticed something like that."

"I was a bit distracted by handing over everything I own. How many men arrived?"

"At least three. Could have been more."

Just then the cellar door was pulled open and heavy feet thumped down the stairs. Jarrett hadn't been expecting to see anyone for a while, so the sudden entrance caused his entire body to flinch in surprise.

Dave strode down the stairs and once again went through the motions of cutting the ropes wrapped around one of the support posts. This time, however, he freed Norris instead of Jarrett. Still standing behind the post, Dave kept his knife in an easy grip while slamming the heel of his boot between Norris's shoulder blades. "Get up those stairs," he grunted.

"Where are you taking him?" Jarrett asked.

Norris motioned for his brother to stand down and said, "I want to see my family and then I want to see the men who work for my brother."

Without a moment's hesitation, Dave replied, "Sure."

"And I want food for all of us," Norris added.

Dave was impatient as always but nodded while shoving Norris forward. "I'll scrape something up for you."

Norris continued with his list of demands as he was pushed up the stairs and outside. Jarrett couldn't hear much more than that because the cellar door was slammed shut to leave him in the shadows. For the next several moments, he sat still so he could focus all of his attention on whatever sounds he could detect through the heavy wooden barrier between him and his brother.

There were definitely more men outside apart from Norris and Dave. Jarrett didn't have to listen for very long before he picked up the grating tone of Clay's voice as well as a few others that didn't strike him as familiar. Norris shouted something at them, which was met by a tense silence.

"Give 'em hell, little brother," Jarrett whispered.

A wind blew through the property, scraping unseen hands against the outside of the cellar doors.

There were a few more voices: icy calm and barely loud enough to be heard.

Then . . . a gunshot.

Jarrett's heart sank. His eyes snapped open and darted back and forth, even though there was nothing for him to see in the all-encompassing shadows.

Another shot was fired, followed by a third. Each one made Jarrett even more certain that they were being fired from no more than a few paces away from the cellar's entrance.

"Norris!" he shouted.

Jarrett waited for a response, listening for any sound that might possibly be his brother's voice. Outside, there was plenty of movement and none of it had anything to do with the wind.

"Norris! What's happening out there? Answer me!"

First one horse thundered away and then another followed. Their hooves pounded against the ground in a drumbeat that Jarrett could feel through the post and all the way down to the soles of his boots. A third horse rode off in the same direction as the first two. Men's voices rose into the night with sharp hollers and cries. After a few more seconds, an even deeper rumbling sent tremors through the dirt surrounding Jarrett on almost every side.

The herd was being moved.

As the world beyond the cellar churned without him, Jarrett was left with nothing else to do other than pull and struggle against his ropes with everything he had. When he was testing their limits the first time, he'd bloodied his wrists enough to make the rope slick. That was before he'd been brought out to see Jen and the children. When he was brought back, the ropes had been replaced.

Jen and the children.

Just thinking about them made Jarrett struggle harder. The sound of more gunshots in the distance could have been his fears wreaking havoc with a clouded mind. Outside, more horses galloped in different directions and men shouted back and forth. A woman screamed. It could just as well have been the high-pitched voice of a child, but the difference was inconsequential. Either option tied Jarrett's innards into knots.

It wasn't until the pain shooting through his shoulders and wrists became unbearable that he realized he'd been thrashing against his restraints like a wild, enraged beast. When the cellar door was opened, he saw it through a murky haze that seemed to fill his entire head like smoke.

"You didn't think I forgot about you, did you?" Clay asked as he ambled down the stairs.

Jarrett opened his mouth as if he was going to howl like a demon. Instead he barely managed to form the words "What did you do to my brother? Cut us loose! *All of us!*"

So far, Clay had barely shown more than a hint of emotion. This time was no different. He drew his pistol, thumbed back the hammer, and took aim, all with the same expression he might have worn if he was pulling on his boots. "You've been real helpful, Jarrett. Time to part ways."

Jarrett thought he might have seen something else beneath the gunman's surface, possibly some hint that he was something more than a skinny edifice. The instant Clay narrowed his eyes, Jarrett tucked his head down low and to one side.

A plume of smoke exploded from the barrel of Clay's gun, accompanied by a roar that filled the cellar as well as every inch of Jarrett's head.

He was knocked brutally to one side.

Jarrett's back smashed against the post behind him.

Everything faded into murky, muddled silence.

Chapter 8

Jarrett's senses were dimmer than a candle with a wet wick. As he tried to pull himself up from the cool dirt floor, he learned that his muscles weren't in much better condition. He drew a breath, only to feel a pain so intense that it crumpled him quicker than a swift punch to the stomach. Since he'd had more than his share of those recently, he'd become something of an expert in that area.

Shifting his weight to one side, Jarrett attempted to prop himself up. The jolt of pain stabbed all the way through the back of his head and neck, threatening to knock him out. He wasn't certain if he'd been unconscious after being shot, but wasn't about to allow himself to fade away again.

His eyes snapped into focus and his body became still. He'd been shot.

That piece of information came back to him after being lost amid the confused turmoil that had enveloped him.

It wasn't difficult to figure out where the bullet had been meant to go. All Jarrett needed to do was lean back to scrape his head where the post behind him had been splintered. Thanks to the darkness of the cellar and his desperate motion at the last second, the bullet intended for his skull grazed his scalp and dug into the post instead. The more he shifted, the more he was reminded of all the other injuries he'd recently collected. "Ow, son of a . . . ," he grunted as his sore ribs made themselves known. If he was going to find out any more, he would need to get his hands free.

One benefit to the current situation was that he had plenty of blood and sweat running down his arms to make the ropes binding his hands very slick. Jarrett clenched his fists, twisted his hands, pulled his arms, and leaned forward until he hit the end of his rope. All the while, pain tore through him like a set of malicious raking claws. The scream that burst from his lungs filled his ears as if it were the only sound in the world. After one more concentrated effort, he flopped forward to pull his wrists free from the ropes that had held him back.

As soon as he could move without being so constricted, Jarrett got to work on the rest of the ropes. He reached for his ankles, feeling for knots or any other weak point that could be exploited. While his hands busily worked, his eyes grew accustomed to the narrow strips of light poking into the cellar between the slats of the door. The rumble of hooves could still be heard but were considerably more distant than they'd been before. There was also the roaring sound of blood rushing through his head like a steady current beneath everything else.

The sound of some horses that were closer than the rest, combined with a few voices from the house above, spurred Jarrett on even more until he ripped away the ropes around his ankles like so much dead moss. He started to climb to his feet but was given a sharp reminder of the wound that he'd been given as Clay's parting gift.

Gritting his teeth against the pain, Jarrett used his right hand to feel the spot where he'd been shot. There was skin encrusted with bits of dirt and blood near the top of his head toward the back. He patted himself down, forcing himself to use the pain as fuel to his fire instead of something that would consume him.

"Thank God," he breathed when he felt no additional wounds. It was a messy situation, but much better for him than if he still had to contend with a piece of lead stuck inside him or a head that had been cracked open like an egg.

Jarrett wasn't a medic by any stretch, but he'd dealt with wounds worse than these. All he needed was something to use as a bandage. Allowing his left arm to hang relatively loose at his side, he reached for the front of his shirt, gripped it tight, and tore off a wide strip of cotton. A bit more of it came off than he'd anticipated, leaving his shirt a ripped mess. After wadding the shredded material he'd taken into a ball, he pressed it against his wound and held it in place.

From what he could tell, the bleeding wasn't nearly as bad as it could have been. The wound hurt, but he'd already come to embrace pain as a crutch to keep him moving. Holding the wad of cotton in place, he forced himself to stand up. That effort, something so simple on almost any other day, took nearly everything Jarrett's body had to offer. The hardest part was getting his wobbly legs to support his weight. From there on, it was just a matter of falling forward instead of down.

The dirt floor seemed particularly uneven as he made his way to the steps. Jarrett climbed one and then another, reaching up with a shaky hand to push the door until it fell to one side. Almost immediately, his eyes were set to watering and his lungs were filled with a thick, acrid fog. By the time he'd fully emerged from the cellar, Jarrett had pulled enough of the foul taste into his mouth to recognize its source. He turned around while taking a few more staggering steps as the full scope of what was happening made itself all too clear.

The Lazy J was burning.

Not just the house at the middle of the property, but every structure that he could see was either consumed by flames or reduced to a blackened husk. The house was directly in front of him and filled his entire field of vision with a blazing spectacle of fire licking from every window, spitting smoke in all directions. If his head had been clearer, he could have more clearly heard the roaring of flames instead of just a continuous muffled growl. Even his own cries as he shouted the names of his brother's family were swallowed by the nightmarish haze filling his mind.

His first thought was to charge inside and make his way to the second floor. If he burned to death somewhere along the way, then so be it. At least he could live with himself for having tried, but the door was already completely blocked by flames and fallen debris. Jarrett had taken all of three steps toward the smoking outline of the entrance when the house's roof collapsed in on itself. The sight before him was so terrible that it seemed unreal as, bit by bit, the home he'd built fell down. Some insane part of him still considered charging inside to get upstairs until the second floor ceased to be.

It was just gone.

In a rush, his hearing returned. The first thing to register in Jarrett's mind was the groaning of lumber splitting apart and collapsing into a pile. His legs carried him backward away from the burning house as his arms came up to protect his face from the wave of heat that rolled over him. In those moments, Jarrett was certain he was experiencing the final pains of his life. Something caught his heel with a jarring impact and everything tilted to one side.

When he hit the ground, he realized he was still alive. Considering the amount of pain he was in from his wound, his burning lungs and nearly every joint in his body, that wasn't exactly a blessing. Clenching his jaw, he rolled onto one side to climb back to his feet. No matter how much anguish was coursing through him at that moment, his instincts wouldn't allow him to simply lie in the dirt and be swept away with the rest of the ash.

Jarrett's next several breaths were like hot tacks scraping at him from the inside and he hacked them up amid seizures that twisted his chest and shoulders. Closing his eyes, he felt water pouring from them to stream down his face. When he cleared them using the back of one hand, Jarrett got a look at what he'd tripped over while backing away from the fire.

"Norris?" he croaked through a ragged throat. "Oh God," Jarrett said while grabbing his fallen brother's collar. "Norris, can you hear me?"

Norris had been almost completely covered by dirt, gravel, and blackened detritus that had blown in from the fire. The debris clung to his skin, making him look less like a man and more like just another charred lump stuck to the ground.

"Come on," Jarrett said as he shook his brother. "Please say something. Anything at all."

But Norris was gone. For anyone to have survived the grievous wounds Norris had in his head and chest would have required a miracle. It took several seconds for Jarrett to even acknowledge those wounds, but once he did, he knew his brother was no more. He set Norris down and looked at the burning remains of what had been.

The next building in sight was the bunkhouse. While there were plenty of flames to be found there, most of them were licking up along the roof or creeping around one corner like a demonic hand closing into a fist. Jarrett pulled himself up and started walking in that direction. Not only did it feel good to see something other than his house and dead brother, but the movements became easier with every step he took.

When he heard voices coming from within the bunkhouse, Jarrett broke into a run.

The front of the building was where the majority of the blaze was concentrated. Just stepping too close to the door was enough to make Jarrett recoil as if he'd accidentally touched the front of a stove. Not only was there a side door, but it was on a portion of the structure that had barely been touched by any of the flames.

"Stan!" Jarrett shouted. "You in there?"

"Stan's here!" someone said from within the bunkhouse. "But he keeled over. I think the smoke got to him."

Jarrett recognized the voice as belonging to another one of his hired hands, an older fellow from Kansas named Edgar. By the sound of it, Edgar was well inside the bunkhouse, which meant he wouldn't be hit if the side door was kicked in. Jarrett did just that so he could charge inside before the fire spread.

The interior of the bunkhouse was filled with smoke that swirled within a wide-open space. Essentially the structure was one large room with rows of cots and chests lined up along both side walls. All three of the remaining men on Jarrett's payroll were tied to support posts near the back of the bunkhouse in a fashion similar to how he and Norris had been tied in the cellar. Their hands and feet were secured and one end of that rope kept them from getting more than a few feet from their posts. The man Jarrett had first called for was the strongest of the bunch. Unfortunately Stan was on his side and not moving.

"Thank Christ you're here!" Edgar said. He was a slender fellow with skin that looked like old leather. Having spent almost all of his life herding cattle and doing every odd job imaginable on a ranch, he was anything but a frail old-timer. "Where's Matt or Pete?"

"They're gone," Jarrett said as he approached the three men.

"They got away?"

"No."

The flicker of hope that had showed in Edgar's eyes was snuffed out. "Oh. I see."

"This place is burning," Jarrett said. "You men need to get out of here. Can you carry Stan between the two of you?"

"Sure, but ain't you coming as well?"

Untying the knots was a lot easier when Jarrett could see them and use both hands. As soon as he got Edgar's hands free, he shifted his attention to the third man being held prisoner there. Jack was a good worker with a strong back who never caused any trouble. Part of why he was so easy to work with was because of his even temper, but mostly it was because he was mute.

"You hurt, Jack?" Jarrett asked.

The other man shook his head.

After years of working with him, Jarrett could tell plenty about what was going through Jack's head just by reading his expression. He didn't need one bit of that experience to know what was happening when he saw the other man's eyes go wide and his mouth drop open. Jarrett followed Jack's line of sight to see movement outside the bunkhouse.

The front door had fallen halfway off and now hung by only its lower hinge. Through the thickening smoke, he spotted a figure on horseback gazing inside.

"You men reconsider my offer?" the man asked.

Jarrett didn't recognize the voice. "What offer?" he whispered to Edgar.

The older man was almost finished untying Stan. "He wants us to come along with them rustlers to help manage the herd. Promised a real sweet payday if we accepted. We told him to go to hell and that's when he lit the place on fire."

"Stay here."

Jarrett didn't wait to see if his order would be obeyed or not. He stooped down to pick up one of the ropes that had been tied around Jack's wrists and walked straight toward the door.

"Hey, not so fast!" Edgar said.

The man outside leaned a bit lower and shouted, "Don't worry none. I'm not going anywhere just yet. You might want to hurry up and give the word, though, if'n you want to keep from getting real hot real quick."

Stepping to one side, Jarrett ignored the crackling flames gnawing at a growing hole in the roof to send chunks of wood falling onto a group of cots across the aisle from him. The beds closest to the door and the ones in the very back were always the most popular among his workers. Pete's was the bunk that Jarrett went to and he pulled open the chest near the foot of the cot. As he rooted through a mixture of clothing and other random possessions, he didn't even think about the man who'd owned them. His mind was focused on a single purpose and his hands didn't stop moving until he found something tucked between two folded shirts. The boot knife wasn't exactly what he'd been hoping to find, but it would serve his purpose well enough.

"So, the three of you come to your senses or not?" the man outside asked.

"Yeah!" Jarrett shouted.

"All right, then. We'll see about that."

The smoke was growing thicker inside the bunkhouse, but the front door was open and several of the windows had shattered. A hot wind drifted in from the south to stir gritty air within the large structure. Because of that, Jarrett could see just enough of the man outside to tell he was climbing down from his saddle. Jarrett approached the door, jerked the knife from its scabbard, and tossed the leather casing aside.

"You men won't regret this," the man outside said.

Jarrett marched straight to the front door, ignoring the flames to his left, the creaking of the lumber above him, and the smoke that threatened to suffocate him on the spot. He simply held his breath and quickened his pace to a run as he climbed through the window next to the door and threw himself at the man who was tying off the reins to his horse.

That man wasn't familiar to Jarrett, which didn't slow him down in the slightest. Jarrett came straight at him while swinging the boot knife with everything he had. His first slash caught the man across the chest, tearing shirt and skin alike. The next one gouged into the man's shoulder, cut straight down, and sliced across the first bloody gash that had been made. He wore a gun at his side. Two of them, in fact. Jarrett only noticed them because the man's hands were within inches of them, but he was too surprised to skin either of the weapons.

"Who . . . the hell are you?" the man asked.

He didn't know.

He truly didn't know.

For a moment, he and Jarrett simply stood there, gazing at each other in sheer disbelief.

"You got him!" Edgar said from somewhere behind Jarrett. "That's the one that's been coming around kicking the hell out of the three of us and you got him."

"No," Jarrett said. "Not yet."

The surprise on the gunman's face was wearing off. He blinked the rest of it away so a mean grimace could take its place. "You're the asshole that owns this spread," he growled. "Clay said—"

Jarrett had barely moved. It had been simple to take the knife in his hand, drive it into the other man's belly, and put an end to his killing days. When the gunman's hand finally did move, it was to grab the knife that had stuck him. Jarrett did the worst possible thing in that situation for him by removing the blade in a swift, sideways arc.

The gunman dropped to his knees, gulping like a grounded fish as he flopped onto his side.

"Th . . . there's another one," Edgar said.

Looking over to him, Jarrett asked, "What's wrong with you? Are you hurt?"

Edgar stood there with one of Stan's arms draped over his shoulder. Jack stood on the other side to support Stan by his other arm. Both ranch hands seemed more taken aback by the scene in front of them than they were by the burning buildings around them. "No," Edgar replied before too long. "Not hurt. I just . . . I didn't think . . ."

"He was here to watch you men burn," Jarrett said.

"I know, but . . ." Suddenly Edgar's head shifted so he could look at something past the horse that was pulling nervously against the reins tied to a post near the bunkhouse.

Jarrett looked over there as well to find another man on horseback. This one, he did recognize. That rider was one of the men who'd been leaving his house when Clay brought Jarrett in to retrieve the money hidden inside the desk. Judging by the expression on the rider's face, he recognized Jarrett as well.

"You?" the rider said. He didn't wait for an answer before pulling the smoke wagon that was holstered on his hip.

As soon as he saw the gunman reach for his weapon, Jarrett dropped to one knee so he could arm himself as well. Since the killer he'd stabbed was beyond the need of any mortal possessions, Jarrett helped himself to both of the pistols he wore.

"I'm here," Edgar said breathlessly. "I can cover you."

Jarrett barely took notice of the old ranch hand as he struggled to retrieve the dead man's guns. When the killer fell, he'd landed in an awkward heap. Working from a peculiar angle, combined with the leather straps holding the guns in place, Jarrett was unable to get himself heeled before the man on horseback fired his first shot.

After what felt like an eternity had passed, Jarrett pulled one of the guns free. The second one came loose soon after, which was when he took a moment to see what Edgar was doing. The older man stood beside the dead gunman's horse and had removed a rifle from its boot.

"Stay here," Jarrett said.

Edgar nodded and cringed when another shot was fired. "You don't have to tell me twice."

Jarrett stood up. Comforted by the weight of the guns in his hands, he brought both pistols up and thumbed back the hammers. The man on horseback was about twenty yards in front of him. He most likely would have gotten a clear shot at him by now if his horse hadn't been getting more and more spooked by the flames that were spreading to consume the bunkhouse.

The first shot Jarrett fired was mostly just to steel himself for the next one. He sent it flying through the air as the mounted gunman did the job properly by taking an extra moment to aim. Unfortunately for him, someone else had beaten him to the punch. The distinctive sound of a rifle shot came from behind Jarrett, giving him the chance to follow up.

Walking forward, Jarrett pulled his triggers again and again. The stolen pistols bucked against his palms, spitting death into the killer in front of him. Even as the man fell from his horse, Jarrett continued to fire. He circled around the horse, pointing the guns down at its owner as the hammers slapped against one spent round after another.

"He's done," Edgar said.

When he felt a hand on his shoulder, Jarrett spun around so quickly that he knocked one pistol against the older man's shoulder. Edgar hopped back and raised his hands. He still held the rifle but pointed it at the light purple sky as he said, "Easy, boss. It's just me."

Jarrett nodded.

"Looks like there was just the two of them left behind," Edgar said. "We'd best get out of here, though."

Jack was nearby as well, bearing the weight of his

friend without the slightest bit of exertion. Stan's eyes were open and he walked like a drunk while taking in the sight of the body lying on the ground. "What the hell is this?" he asked in a stupor.

Tucking the guns under his belt, Jarrett replied, "It's a good start."

Chapter 9

"We shouldn't be here," Edgar said.

The sun had breached the eastern horizon and hung low in the sky, casting the early morning in a bright yellow-and-orange light. Although the flames had eaten everything they could, smaller fires were still scattered among the remains of the Lazy J. One of the smaller buildings, a shed used to store tools and such, was nothing more than a pile of cinders that were still hot to the touch. Jarrett sifted through them, kicking aside larger chunks of scorched wood before driving his hands into the smoldering remains. "If you want to go," he said as a few embers hissed against his hands, "then go."

"It's not what I want," the old ranch hand replied. "It's not what any of us want. It's what we got to do. It ain't safe here."

"The fires are out."

"That's not the kind of safe I mean."

Stan stood nearby, rubbing the back of his head. "He's right. Them rustlers could come back."

"Why would they?" Jarrett asked. "There's nothing left for them to steal."

"That's right," Edgar said. "There's nothing left. Ain't no reason to stay here."

Finding what he'd been searching for, Jarrett pulled a shovel from the ash. Its blade was charred and the cracked remnant of its handle was scorched, but there was enough left for it to still be a viable tool. "My brother's here. My family's here."

"No. They ain't. They're gone." Pulling back a step when Jarrett wheeled around to face him, Edgar added, "And they wouldn't want you to stay until someone comes along to send you to meet 'em."

"I'm not going to just leave him lying there," Jarrett said. "If you don't want to help, then get off my land."

Jack stepped forward to take the shovel from Jarrett's hand. He used it to scoop away the blackened cinders until he uncovered another shovel and a pickax. Having found those two things, he handed the first shovel back to Jarrett, gave the second shovel to Stan, and kept the pickax for himself.

"Oh, for cryin' out loud," Edgar grumbled as he started kicking aside some more of the ashes. As soon as he found something he could use to lend a hand with digging, he hurried to catch up to the others in a small patch of empty land about sixty yards from the house.

That piece of land had always caught Jarrett's eye. After completing the last part of his house, he thought he might expand his business by building on that land. He'd had big plans for those couple of acres. Perhaps he might add a chicken coop or a pen for some hogs. He could hire on a blacksmith and put his shop there so he was even more self-sufficient. Now those plans had all been whittled away until only one course remained. He and his three workers rolled up their sleeves and started digging graves.

First, they laid Norris to rest. Then, while Jack and Stan kept digging, Jarrett and Edgar picked through the rubble of the main house. Part of its frame was still standing, but it was just a skeletal reminder of what had been. Most of the first floor was buried beneath the second, which was consequently almost lost beneath the roof. As they went through the blackened mess of shingles, wooden beams, and broken furniture, neither man had much of anything to show for it.

"Maybe this ain't such a good idea," Edgar said.

"If those gunmen haven't come back by now," Jarrett replied, "they're not going to."

"I'm not talking about that. I mean . . . what exactly do you expect to find in here?"

"I . . . they were . . ." Jarrett looked down at the mound of rubble under his boots and thought about the loved ones that had been trapped inside that house when it burned down. He knew he wanted to put them to rest, but actually finding them was something else. Finally he said, "Yeah. I suppose you're right. Still, I can't just leave them."

Edgar rubbed his lower back and propped his shovel on a shoulder. "When I lost my wife and little boy some time ago, the preacher gave me a whole lot of platitudes and advice. He meant well, but it wasn't nothin' I hadn't already heard. I'm sure you've heard the same things yourself once or twice, so I'll spare you the sermon. I'll just remind you that you ain't leaving them. They've already moved on."

Slowly Jarrett climbed down from the rubble. "We need to ride to the east gate. Matt and Pete were killed out there. At least we can give them a proper burial."

"They was good boys. I'll go with you."

Even though the stables had burned down along with most everything else, the rustlers hadn't gotten all of the horses kept there. A few of them had bolted and escaped into the night amid the chaos of the fire and the moving of the herd. Those horses had returned to the fields near the stables, looking at their former home and idly watching the men they'd come to know.

When he saw one of those horses standing by itself with its head bowed, Jarrett smiled. "Come here, boy," he said as he approached the gelding.

Twitch's brown coat was dusted with so much ash that the white patch on his nose had turned gray. The horse scraped his hooves against the dirt and shook his head nervously, but he allowed Jarrett to approach and eventually rub his neck. After a bit of that, the gelding calmed down.

"That's it. You up for a little work?" Jarrett asked.

Twitch might have preferred an easier alternative, but he didn't object to Jarrett climbing onto his back and grabbing him by the mane. They rode out to the fence and traced it back to the spot where the road met up with the eastern gate. It took a bit of searching for Jarrett to find the bodies of his two workers, and by the time he did, Edgar rode along to help load them onto the horses' backs.

"Damn shame about these two," Edgar said. "I hope whoever did this gets strung up to a high branch for what they done here."

"It'll take more than hopes to see that through," Jarrett said grimly.

"What are you doing?"

Stooping down, Jarrett dug through some of the bushes growing against the fence. When he stood up again, he held a pistol in one hand and a rifle in the other. "Those boys won't need these, but I will."

"Maybe sooner than you think. Take a look."

Jarrett had just spotted the silhouette past the fence

line. It was a single man on horseback standing just as still as the rocks and trees around him. Cursing himself for riding out before finding his saddle or the bags containing his spyglass, Jarrett dropped the pistol so he could grip the rifle in both hands. "Get down," he said to Edgar.

The old man was quick to drop and sat with his back against one of the fence posts. "You think it's one of them gunmen?"

"If it was a neighbor, he'd probably be riding up to introduce himself."

"Probably. What should we do?"

"If things get too rough," Jarrett said while checking to make sure the rifle was loaded, "start shooting."

"If I get a clear shot, I'll—"

"Any chance you can hit that bastard, just do it. Don't worry about me."

Edgar sputtered something out of frustration, but Jarrett wasn't listening to him. He was too busy climbing over the fence.

As soon as his boots hit the ground on the other side, Jarrett brought the rifle to his shoulder. "You there!" he shouted. "If you're looking for your friends, they already left. It's just us here!"

"Jarrett," Edgar hissed from his hiding spot. "That may not be such a good idea. If they thought you were dead, it might be best to just let them keep thinkin' it."

"Too late," Jarrett said. "If you want to go, just go."

The old man poked his nose out from behind the fence post to get a look at what lay beyond. So far, the horseman in the distance was holding his ground. While that might have suited Edgar just fine, it didn't satisfy Jarrett in the slightest.

"Come on!" Jarrett said as he fired a rushed shot that

didn't come anywhere close to hitting anything. "You enjoy picking off men from a distance? Here's your chance!"

The rider's horse stirred as lead whipped through the air in its vicinity, but it was obviously no stranger to such a thing. The man in its saddle was even less disturbed by the gunshot.

Jarrett levered in a fresh round and then sent it flying. "I said *come on!*"

That one must have gotten a little closer to its mark, because both horse and rider reacted to it. Settling his horse with a few tugs on the reins, the rider brought his own rifle to his shoulder and took quick aim. He fired a shot before Jarrett had a chance to voice one more taunt.

"That's it!" Jarrett said as a mound of dirt was kicked up several inches away from his left boot. "I'm not afraid of you." He fired again. "You hear me? I'm not afraid!"

When Jarrett fired his third bullet, the horse in his sights reared up and churned its front legs through the air. He lowered his rifle a bit so he could get an unobstructed view if the rider fell from his saddle. Instead the horse dropped back down onto all fours and turned away from the fence.

"Come on, you coward!" Jarrett shouted in a voice that strained his throat to the point of burning.

Whoever the rider was, he didn't seem interested in a fight. Jarrett glared at him with the same intensity he would have had if the man was two feet in front of him. Edgar kept his distance, holding his tongue until his employer tucked the rifle in tight against his shoulder and carefully sighted along the top of the barrel.

"Hold on, now!" Edgar said.

"Shut up," Jarrett snapped.

"You've made yer point. Now back away."

"Why?"

"Because for all you know, that's just someone coming round to check on all the commotion or the smoke from the fire. Maybe he knows something about the herd! Anyone that wasn't locked up when they were taken has got to know which way they went."

"It's a good-sized herd of cattle," Jarrett replied. "It won't be difficult to catch up to it."

"Fine. Then we'll do it and tell the law about what happened." By now, the older man had worked his way up to where Jarrett was standing. When he spoke again, his voice was lower and deliberate. "We're still licking our wounds, boss."

"Which is why we can't afford another fight in close quarters."

"Go to the law about this," Edgar pleaded. "Sheriff Rubin will put together a posse and there's no reason he won't let you go along with them."

Jarrett stared at the distant rider through his rifle's sights. So far, the other man was just getting his horse to calm down fully after the near misses that had been fired at him. As if sensing he was being so closely scrutinized, the rider straightened in his saddle and looked back at Jarrett.

"I can take this one down right here," Jarrett said. "Right now."

"That could very well be the sheriff. Putting a bullet in him wouldn't be a smart thing to do under any circumstances."

"The sheriff would have announced himself."

"Then maybe one of his deputies. The point is that you don't know who that is! Ain't there been enough senseless killings for one day?"

Jarrett leaned his head to one side so he could work

out a kink amid the wet crunch of tight joints. "Killing one of those bastards isn't what I'd call senseless."

"But . . ."

"Yeah," Jarrett said as he let out his breath and lowered the rifle. "You're right. I don't know for certain if that's one of them or not."

Edgar had been holding a breath as well. When he let it out, he needed to rest a hand on Jarrett's shoulder for support. "You really had me goin' there, for a moment. I thought you was gonna shoot that man from his saddle without even gettin' a look at his face."

"So did I."

"With everything that happened, it's understandable. Just seein' Pete and Matt the way we found 'em got me riled up as well."

Jarrett couldn't take his eyes off the rider. When he saw the glint of sunlight off glass near the other man's head, he knew he was being studied through a spyglass or something similar. "If that sheriff was good for anything, he would have been here already."

"Then let's go have a word with him." Stepping forward, Edgar raised a hand over his head and waved it back and forth. "That could still be him or one of his men right now!"

When the rider turned his back to them and headed away from the Lazy J at a full gallop, Jarrett said, "I doubt that's any lawman, but I think I'll be seeing him again real soon."

Chapter 10

Matt and Pete were brought back to the house and put into the ground with all the proper respect and reverence that the four exhausted men could muster. A few solemn words were spoken over the short row of graves, but Jarrett hardly paid any attention. His eyes remained fixed on the mound of dirt covering his brother. Always at the edge of his field of vision was the heap of rubble marking the spot where his brother's family would remain. Once the words were spoken, Jarrett just wanted to collect as much of his things as he could and put that smoking hell behind him.

Apart from Twitch, only two more horses could be found wandering the Pekoe lands. The rest had bolted for calmer pastures, which wouldn't be hard to find. Stan took one while Jack and Edgar doubled up on the other. Jarrett had offered to carry one of them on his horse's back, but none of the men were comfortable with Twitch's ever-changing moods. They rode the two miles into town and made their way down Main Street. As soon as he caught sight of the sheriff's office, Jarrett steered toward it.

"If it's all the same to you," Stan said, "I'll head down to see the doctor."

"After that, I'd say drinks are in order," Edgar added.

"We've got more important matters to tend to," Jarrett said.

"We should all see the doctor," the oldest of them insisted. "That should be at the top of the list."

"I'm fine," Jarrett replied. "The rest of you were in good enough shape to do a full day's work digging them graves, so that means you don't need any doctoring."

"We also got the hell knocked out of us," Stan said. "Some of us more than once. I was plenty happy to help back at the ranch, but my head feels about ready to split in half. And as for you," he added while looking at Jarrett, "you even caught some lead."

"Just got grazed is all," Jarrett said. "I've had worse cuts from splitting logs and won't hear another word about it."

"Suit yourself. We're gonna see what the doctor has to say."

Jarrett turned away from them and continued toward the sheriff's office. "Fine. Once that's over, you'll have a word with the sheriff to tell him whatever he needs to know."

"If he wants to talk to us," Stan said, "you'll know where to find us. Either at the doctor's or at the Chip."

"Go on, then. But if you're needed and you're too drunk to answer me, all I have to say is . . . God help you."

"Are you threatening me?"

Jarrett pulled back on his reins to bring Twitch to a stop. Glancing over his shoulder, he said, "Just consider it a fair warning."

Before the tension between those two could get any worse, Edgar stepped in by saying, "Ain't nobody threatening no one. We're all just tired after being put through hell. Both of you is right. Someone needs to talk to the sheriff and we sure could all use a stiff drink. The boss will tend to the first while the rest of us see to the latter. After both things are done, we'll all feel a whole lot better. Don't you men agree?"

Stan was quick to voice his approval, but all Jarrett could manage was a grunt and a nod before steering Twitch back to his original course. The ranch hands spoke among themselves as they turned a corner onto Prosser Avenue, where both the doctor's office and a few of Flat Pass's saloons could be found. Jarrett continued along Main Street, stopped at a small building with a star painted on the front window and tied Twitch to a post near a half-full water trough.

The times he'd been to see Sheriff Rubin could be counted on one hand. Only one of those had been in an official capacity, and that was just to pay a fine to get one of his former ranch hands out of jail. The rest had been simple efforts to foster goodwill with the local law. It never hurt to be on a lawman's good side, and now Jarrett hoped some of his efforts would pay off.

"There you are, Mr. Pekoe!" the sheriff said. "I was just about to pay you a visit." He was a couple of inches shorter than Jarrett and fancied himself as being cast from the same mold as Wild Bill himself. In the years Jarrett had known him, Sheriff Rubin had always worn his hair long with a mustache to match. Although he didn't wear a sash about his waist like the gun-toting legend, he did wear his pearl-handled .45 on proud display. "Saw some smoke coming from the direction of your ranch," he said while getting up from his desk to shake Jarrett's hand in an overly strong grip. "Hope that had nothing to do with you or your spread."

"It did, Sheriff."

Rubin slowly circled back around his desk and placed his hands on top of it. "You lose anything?"

"The ranch is gone," Jarrett said with hardly any inflection in his voice. "Burned. Herd's gone. Stolen. My family . . ." He swallowed hard as his eyes turned icy-cold. "They're gone too."

"Good Lord," Rubin said. "What happened?"

"Rustlers came. They followed my brother onto my property, held his family hostage, and killed a few of my men."

Those words struck Rubin and he quickly asked, "Which ones?"

"Two good fellows named Matt and Pete. I don't know if you remember them, but—"

"Yes. I remember."

"After they were killed, I was taken hostage and robbed. Sometime during the night," Jarrett continued, "I was knocked out. When I came around again, my ranch was in flames and the herd was being moved away."

"They left you?"

"I got away. Killed two of them, but the rest were gone."

The sheriff opened one of his desk drawers to pull out a bottle that was less than half-full of whiskey. He took two glasses from the same drawer and poured some into each one. "I hear a lot of terrible things in this line of work," he said while handing over one of the glasses. "But this is one of the worst. Take this. I imagine you need it."

Although Jarrett had already heard enough about how much he needed a drink, he took the one that was being offered so he wouldn't have to hear any more. Tossing back the whiskey, he let out a loud breath as the liquor went down. It had to have been one of the finest, smoothest drinks he'd ever had. It rolled through his insides like a warm glow that went all the way down to his toes. When he set the glass down, the sheriff was finishing his own drink.

"Mighty fine stuff, ain't it?" Rubin asked.

"It is, actually."

"Calms the nerves. Now, please, have a seat."

Jarrett needed to set himself down onto that chair more than he'd needed the whiskey. The moment his weight was off his feet, he felt the entire day's exertion soak into his bones. "The herd is moving," he said. "It's gotten a head start on us, but it won't be hard to find."

"Do you even know which way it's headed?"

"West. Possibly southwest."

"That leaves a wide margin of error."

"You expecting to have trouble finding an entire herd of cattle, Sheriff?"

"No. I just want to have a real good idea of where I'm going before heading out of town on a—"

"Don't," Jarrett snapped. "Please, don't say it'll be a wild-goose chase."

"I wasn't going to say that, Mr. Pekoe. I was going to call it a manhunt, which is what it will be. Organizing a posse is no small affair, and I want to make sure it's done right. That's all."

"So you will be pulling men together to hunt these animals down?"

"First things first," the lawman said. "In the morning, I'll take a ride out to your spread. What is it?"

"The Lazy J."

"Right. Me and one of my deputies will ride out to the Lazy J and have a look at what was done."

Jarrett's hands curled into fists. "But I already told

you what was done! My family was slaughtered! My home was burned to the damn ground! Good men were killed and you need to go take a look at it all for yourself before you'll do anything? What's the purpose of that? To get a close look at some fresh graves?"

"It's the law. As a keeper of the peace, I can't go charging off on a blood hunt just because one man told me to do so. If what you told me is true, and I got no reason to doubt that it is, the punishment will be swift and necks will most likely be stretched. Before that kind of thing takes place, I need to see what happened for myself. I understand that may not set well at the moment, but you've got to see the good sense behind it."

Reluctantly Jarrett nodded. "I do, Sheriff. Why don't I take you out there right now so we can at least get this wheel turning as soon as possible?"

"Because even if we did walk out that door and ride straight to your land, we wouldn't be able to see much of anything in the dark. You look like hell. I'd suggest you see a doctor to make certain you're able to take part in any posse. Riding on one isn't an easy thing, you know."

"I didn't think it would be."

Rubin stood up. "These men you told me about sound mighty dangerous. They're not likely to come along quietly when we find them."

"Most likely not."

"That means there's going to be a fight coming."

Standing up and meeting the lawman's eyes, Jarrett said, "I'm not about to back away from any fight with these men."

"On the contrary, I'm sure you're itching for it. Isn't that all the more reason for you to be patched up and well rested when it happens?"

Jarrett nodded.

"And I can assure you it's favorable to have the law on your side if any more shots are to be fired."

"That's why I came to see you, Sheriff."

"And that's why I need to ride out and have a look for myself at what happened to your spread," Rubin said. He put the bottles and glasses back in the drawer where he'd found them and walked around his desk. "You have my word, Mr. Pekoe. The men that did this to you and yours will answer for it. It's just my job to make sure this sort of thing is done properly."

"I still want to come along with you."

"I'd like you to ride with me when I take that look at your ranch. Show me everything I'll need to see."

"On the posse, I mean," Jarrett said.

Sheriff Rubin put a hand on his shoulder. "You have my word. If you're in good enough condition to ride come morning, and if I see what I'm sure I'll see at that ranch, you'll be the first one I ask to join me to see that justice is done."

"That's all I wanted to hear, Sheriff. Thank you." When Jarrett started to turn toward the office's front door, he was stopped by a grip that tightened on his shoulder to hold him in place.

"Now I want your word on something."

"What's that?"

"No matter what decision I make, you'll abide by it," the sheriff said. The tone in his voice made it clear that he was giving an order rather than making any sort of request.

"Aren't you in the business of enforcing the letter of the law?" Jarrett asked.

"Yes, sir, I am."

"Then we won't have any trouble."

"And make no mistake," Rubin said. "Your business

is wrangling cows. Striking out on your own in this matter isn't a good idea. I'll have you know that vigilantes see the same punishment as any other man who takes up a gun for the wrong reason."

"When I take up a gun, it'll be for the right reason."

"Good," Rubin said. "Then we won't have any problem."

Looking down at the hand that still gripped his shoulder, Jarrett asked, "You gonna let me go so I can see the doctor?"

"There," Rubin said as he relaxed his hold. "Clean yourself up and get plenty of rest. Speaking of which, do you have a place to stay for the night?"

"I'll find one."

"Good. If you come up short, come right back here and I'll set you up with a cot." When Jarrett glanced toward the short row of three jail cells at the back of the room, Rubin added, "Don't worry. I won't lock the door."

"Much obliged, Sheriff," Jarrett said with a tired grin. "But I think I'll try a hotel first."

Chapter 11

The doctor in Flat Pass was good enough at his job but not much of a night owl. Everyone in town knew to stick to his regular hours unless there was dire need to interrupt his sleep. A retired army field medic, Dr. Nash still rose before the rooster's call as though he were hearing reveille every morning. Jarrett knew this just like everyone else in Flat Pass, which was why he was none too eager to pound on Nash's door at this late hour.

When the summons was answered, Jarrett was given a quick once-over. "What on earth happened at that ranch of yours?" Nash asked.

Knowing the doctor wasn't looking for details, Jarrett only told him the parts that were relevant to his current state of health. As he spoke, his jeans were peeled away so Nash could get a better look at the wound on Jarrett's thigh.

"Looks like you caught the worst of it," Nash mused as he poked and prodded Jarrett's battered scalp. "Your other three men were in here and they were mostly anxious to get out again. I've treated children that weren't as fidgety."

"I won't keep you any longer than I have to."

"Much appreciated," Nash said while washing off the wound. "Most people around here don't seem to realize or care how much I value a good night's sleep."

Rather than irritate the doctor any more than he already was, Jarrett simply stayed still and nodded while Nash did his work.

"You're lucky," Nash said. "If the bullet that did this had been a few inches to one side, you would have been in real bad shape. Dead, most likely."

"I did my best under the circumstances."

"All you need is some stitches and you'll be right as rain. Try to take it easy, though, and give yourself a chance to heal properly."

"I will, Doc," Jarrett lied.

After sewing him up with all the tenderness he'd show to a ripped tent, Nash cleaned Jarrett up and sent him on his way. Just to be safe, Jarrett made sure to ask if he'd be all right to ride the next day.

"You can ride out right now," Nash replied. "The sooner, the better as far as I'm concerned."

"Thanks, Doc," Jarrett said. "Appreciate the help."

He was waved off and shown brusquely to the door.

From there, Jarrett walked up Prosser Avenue to the part of town that was liveliest after suppertime. Flat Pass wasn't exactly known for its saloon district, but there was enough liquor being poured to keep the locals happy. Two of those locals, Jarrett soon discovered, were very happy indeed.

"There he is!" Stan said as soon as he saw Jarrett walk in through the front door of a place called the Buffalo Chip. Walking to meet him halfway between the bar and the door, Stan opened his arms and wrapped them around his employer. "I thought you weren't gonna show," he said in a gust of breath that stank of cheap whiskey and even cheaper beer.

"What can I say?" Jarrett replied. "When you're right, you're right. You said I needed a drink and you were right."

Stan slapped him on the arm and then roughly dragged him to the bar. "Of course I'm right! I may not know a lot about much, but I know much about . . . uh . . . I mean I know something about much of it and that's whiskey!"

"Whatever you say," Jarrett chuckled.

The Buffalo Chip was supposedly named for the bison painted on all of the poker chips used at the card tables and faro layout. Since most of the saloon's regulars were trappers, hunters, or cowboys, the less savory definition of the term wasn't exactly a secret. The place always seemed to have an unpleasant smell to it, which was why Jarrett rarely patronized it. Whether it was because of the liquor the sheriff had given him or the blood that had dried inside his nose, he wasn't overly concerned with the odor that night. Edgar and Jack were waiting for him at the bar to hand him a drink as soon as he got there. Jarrett took the glass and immediately poured its contents down his throat.

"You have a word with the law?" Edgar asked.

"I did."

"And?"

"And," Jarrett replied, "we're heading out on a posse in the morning." It wasn't the whole truth, but it was close enough.

"See?" Edgar beamed. "I told you the sheriff would come through. Hey," he grunted as the rest of Jarrett's words made it through the haze filling his brain. "*We're* heading out in the morning? As in *all* of us?"

"You wouldn't be interested in riding on the posse to hunt down the murderers that burned the Lazy J?"

"I . . . don't suppose I gave it any thought. To be perfectly honest, I was just happy to be able to kick my heels up for one more night."

"What he's tryin' to say," Stan said as he ambled up next to Edgar, "is that he's too damn old to ride on a posse."

Edgar didn't much care to admit it, but he wasn't about to refute the statement either. He merely winced and gave half a shrug.

"What about you?" Jarrett asked.

"You want me on a posse?" Stan replied. "After all I did was get myself knocked out and tied up the last time we crossed paths with them rustlers?"

"That's right."

Stan grinned widely. "Why, that would be just dandy. And I ain't sayin' that because I'm drunk. If there's a bunch of men riding out to bring a fight to them bastards, you can count me in." Turning to look over his shoulder, he said, "What about you, Jack? Care to ride on a posse come mornin'?"

The ranch hand leaning against the bar might have been short on words, but he was never short on action. He answered Stan's question by raising his beer mug and nodding.

"There you go," Stan said. "Two out of three ain't bad."

"No," Jarrett replied. "Not bad at all."

The four of them spent a good portion of that night at the Chip, whittling away at the line of credit Jarrett had there. When thoughts of what had transpired at his ranch crept in too far, he bought another drink and downed it as quickly as he could. It didn't take much whiskey for him to figure out that the only way to block out so much pain altogether would be to drink himself into oblivion.

There was no way Jarrett was about to do that.

Not yet anyway.

He had too much to do in the morning.

Chapter 12

Rooms at the Chip were small and cheap. Mostly they were only used as closet space to store men who were too drunk to walk out of the place on their own steam. Thanks to the last bit of credit on his account, Jarrett was able to provide a cot and four walls for himself and each of his men. When he opened his eyes after a few hours of nightmare-filled sleep, Jarrett was raring to go. He went to each of the other rooms he'd paid for, gave the cots a few swift kicks, and dragged two of the three men downstairs.

"I'm comin', I'm comin'," Stan groaned. "Does it have to be so damn early?"

"We're riding out to the ranch first and then the sheriff will pull together the posse."

"You mean he still has to go to the ranch first? He'll just have to come back here afterward, you know."

"So?"

"So that means we can get some more sleep. Come get us when the posse's ready to ride."

As much as Jarrett wanted to drag both of them to their horses, he knew that would just take longer and be more effort than just taking the ride out on his own. He went to the sheriff's office, where Rubin and one of his deputies were already saddling up their horses.

"I was just about to come and collect you," the lawman said. "I hear you and your men had a wild night with some of the girls at the Buffalo Chip."

"Did you? Must've been one of the others, because I don't recall anything like that," Jarrett said.

"No matter. You ready to go?"

"I'll lead the way."

The ride from town to the Lazy J was so familiar to Jarrett that he could have made it with his eyes closed. It wasn't a long way under normal circumstances and seemed even shorter this time with Jarrett leading the other two at full speed. Smoke still hung above his property in a thin black cloud. The stench from the fire filled Jarrett's nostrils, and bits of ash drifted through the air to sting his eyes. All the whiskey or beer in the world wouldn't have been enough to wash that taste from Jarrett's mouth, and when he breathed it in again, the horror of it all came rushing back.

"I can already tell there was a fire," Sheriff Rubin said.

"Ain't no herd about either," the deputy added. "On any spread with a herd on it, you can usually hear them by now."

Jarrett didn't know the younger man's name and didn't much care. Right now his only concern was that the lawmen stop wasting time and get on with hunting down the men who'd put that smoke into the air in the first place.

"I'll take your word for it," the sheriff said. "Your ears were always better than mine."

"House is this way," Jarrett said as he rode through the gate and down the road that cut straight across his property. "What's left of it anyway."

The three of them took their look-about and saw the scorched remnants of Jarrett's home. They spotted the freshly dug graves and then circled back around to head back into town. Jarrett didn't say a word until they approached the sheriff's office again. He was barely able to draw a full breath until the ranch was well behind him.

"So," Jarrett said as he climbed down from Twitch's back, "you see enough?"

Rubin and his deputy dismounted as well. Hitching his horse to the post near his office's front door, the sheriff said, "That sure does verify your story. At least about the fire."

Jarrett's eyes narrowed. "What about the killings? Did you need me to dig up the bodies to convince you?"

"No need for all that. I'm convinced. I'll put the word out right now and as soon as I get enough men we'll head out after the animals that burned your place to the ground."

"Good. When do you think we'll ride out?"

"Shouldn't be more than a few days," Rubin said.

"A few days?"

"Depends on how long it takes me to collect enough men for the job. Remember, there's your herd to think about, so we'll need men who know how to do a job like that."

"I've already got men for that," Jarrett said. "My men. We've handled plenty of herds."

"Do they know how to handle themselves in a fight? Things could get rough."

Without hesitation, Jarrett said, "They can handle themselves. They know what they're up against. Between your men and mine, that makes at least five. You have more than one deputy, right?"

"I do, but someone's got to stay behind to watch the town. There are other folks in Flat Pass apart from you, Mr. Pekoe."

Biting back the urge to answer that with a quick punch to the face, Jarrett said, "I know that. I'm just saying the longer we wait, the farther away those killers can get."

"You told me it wouldn't be hard to track an entire herd, right?"

"Yes, I said that but—"

"Then one day or two won't make a difference," the sheriff said.

"How many more men do you need?" Jarrett asked.

"At least one or two more, I'd say."

"Fine. I'll help find someone."

Rubin stretched his legs and showed Jarrett a patronizing smile. "If it's all the same to you, why don't you rest up and get those stitches looked at? Forming a posse is my job, so just let me do it."

Reaching up to his head, Jarrett felt the rough patch where some blood had dried. He hadn't felt the stitches in his thigh tear at any point during the ride, but the wound also hadn't stopped aching either. Ignoring the bloody spot, he said, "If I find someone, I'll bring him to you."

"It'll need to be someone other than one of your cowboys," the deputy said. "We got enough of them, so we'll need someone who can handle a gun."

"Yeah, I understand," Jarrett said.

The younger deputy, perhaps feeling territorial or merely flexing his muscles, stepped forward while glaring fiercely back at him. "Maybe it'd be best for you to stay out of this altogether. Put your affairs in order and such."

"Put my affairs in order?"

"Yeah. Don't you need to pay a visit to the undertaker?"

This time, Jarrett reacted before he had any chance to

think twice about it. He swung his right fist in a quick arc that caught the deputy squarely in the jaw and sent the younger man staggering backward. His other fist was on its way to the deputy's face as well but didn't get a chance to land before the other man charged at him.

Only momentarily taken off his guard when the deputy's shoulder thumped him in the torso, Jarrett planted his feet and then drove his elbow straight down into the deputy's shoulder. The younger man let out a grunt before shoving him back to get some space between them.

"Stop it!" the sheriff said. "Both of you!"

When the deputy swung at his face, Jarrett managed to duck beneath it. He wasn't quite fast enough to dodge the next blow, which was an uppercut that clipped his chin and stood him up straight.

"I said *stop!*"

Like any other man in his early twenties, the deputy had to prove his point until it was driven into the ground. He bared his teeth and pounded a fist into Jarrett's stomach to force all the air from his lungs. Only then did he step back and raise his hands a bit. "Fine," he said. "I'll stop."

"What about you?" Rubin asked as he looked over to Jarrett. "You through?"

Jarrett caught his breath and spat some blood onto the ground. He approached the deputy and made sure the young man's eyes were on him when he punched the young man in the midsection as if he meant to drive his fist all the way out through his spine. Nodding while moving away, he said, "Now I'm through."

"You're through all right," the deputy swore.

Stepping between both men, Sheriff Rubin held a hand out to Jarrett and physically pushed his deputy back. "You're both done, you hear me? Both of you!"

"But he hit me first!" the deputy said. "I'm a lawman and he swung first!"

"I saw what happened, Tom," the sheriff said, "and you had it coming. Look me in the eye and tell me different."

The younger man shrank back half a step but quickly regained the snarl on his face. Jabbing a finger toward Jarrett, he said, "Watch your step, rancher."

Jarrett rubbed his jaw and smiled back at the deputy. Although he wasn't trying to taunt the younger man, seeing the frustration on his face was definitely a pleasant sight.

"Get inside and get the supplies ready for us to ride out on that posse," Rubin said to his deputy. "And you," he said while shifting his attention to Jarrett, "just keep your mouth shut."

Once Tom had stepped inside the office and shut the door, Rubin let out a long sigh. "It's like dealing with my sister's kids," he sighed.

Since he wasn't about to apologize for his actions, Jarrett simply put them behind him by saying, "I'll find that other man to ride with us. Even if I don't, I want to head out no later than tomorrow."

"Tomorrow would have been the earliest we could go," Rubin pointed out.

"No. The earliest would be right now. I'm the one that'll be tracking that herd and I say the trail will just get too cold if we wait much longer than that."

"Fine. Fine. Between the two of us, we should be able to scrape up at least one more man. If both of us find one, all the better. Just don't get a swelled head about what happened here just now," the sheriff added while sweeping his hand over the patch of ground where Jarrett and Tom had traded blows. "You step out of line, no matter who runs off at the mouth first, and I'll see to it that you're in one of my jail cells while that posse is riding. You got me?"

"Yeah."

Still grumbling angrily to himself, the sheriff turned on his heel and stomped into his office. When he slammed the door shut, he rattled the front window within its frame.

Once he was alone, Jarrett turned away from the office and allowed himself to let out a breath and wince in pain. He'd been in his fair share of fights, but the bumps and bruises piled up a whole lot worse now compared to when he'd been closer to Tom's age. It wasn't until that moment when he noticed how many folks had been drawn to the scuffle between him and Tom. It wasn't a large crowd, but the half dozen or so locals standing nearby were enjoying the show.

Now that the display was over, the crowd began to disperse. Jarrett was given a few approving smiles from some within the crowd who must have had similarly low opinions of Tom before they too wandered away. Jarrett had started walking down Main Street when he saw one of the members of that crowd was still watching him.

Already feeling a little embarrassed that his confrontation had inadvertently taken center stage, Jarrett looked directly at the stranger and asked, "Something I can help you with?"

The stranger had features that looked as if they'd been blasted by years of desert winds. He was somewhere in his late thirties and judging by the thick stubble on his chin, might have sat in a barber's chair on fewer than a dozen occasions in that span of time. The only move he made in response to the tersely worded question was to angle his head slightly and spit a wad of tobacco juice to the ground. After studying him for a moment, Jarrett decided he wasn't likely to get much more from the stranger, so he started walking once again down the street.

"I saw what happened with you and that deputy," the stranger said.

Without breaking his stride, Jarrett replied, "You're hardly the only one."

"You ask me, that kid had it coming." The stranger spat once more and added, "That and maybe a bit worse."

"Well, if you want to give it to him, he's right in there."

Every two or three steps Jarrett took, he could hear the solid knock of boots against the boardwalk on the other side of the street. He looked back to find the stranger keeping pace with him using longer strides. When it became clear that the stranger meant to keep following him, Jarrett crossed the street to stand in front of him. The man was wearing a pistol on his hip, which might have made Jarrett think twice about confronting him a week ago. After what had filled the last few of his days, he was hardly impressed by such a thing.

"What is it?" Jarrett asked. "You another deputy?"

The other man cracked half a smile. "Not as such."

"Then what do you want?"

"First off . . . I want to let you know I heard about what happened to your ranch."

"I imagine everybody's heard about that by now," Jarrett said.

"It's a real shame."

"Yes. It is."

Obviously not one for making speeches, the stranger lowered his head just long enough to collect his thoughts. Then he lifted his gaze again and said, "I also heard some of what was being said between you and the sheriff. There's a posse that's gonna be formed?"

"That's right."

"I'd like to ride on that posse."

Jarrett looked the other man up and down. "Can you handle a gun?"

"Yes, sir."

"Things may get rough."

"I heard the talk," the stranger replied. "I can handle rough."

"Why do you want to ride along with us?"

"What's it matter? Look, if you don't want me to come, then I won't."

"No," Jarrett said quickly. "That's not it. I've just never recruited men for this kind of thing. I figured there were questions that needed to be asked. Honestly we can use all the help we can get."

"That's what I figured."

"What's your name?"

"Lem Beauchamp."

"Ever shoot a man, Lem?"

"I reckon I have."

"All right, then," Jarrett said. "You're hired."

Chapter 13

If there was more time, Jarrett would have liked to give the lawmen some distance for a while to let them cool off. But time was something that was in short supply and slipping away all too quickly. Jarrett did take a short while to visit the bank to make a withdrawal and then met Lem outside so they could both march straight back into the sheriff's office. Judging by the looks he got from the men in there, things hadn't even started to cool down between Jarrett and Tom.

"What is it now?" Sheriff Rubin asked impatiently.

"I've found someone else to ride with us," Jarrett said while motioning toward the man who'd followed him through the door. "His name is Lem Beauchamp."

"Never heard of him."

"What does that matter?"

Pressing both hands flat upon his desk to support his weight as he stood up, Rubin said, "If I'm to ride with another man through dangerous territory and give him my blessing under the letter of the law, I want to know something about him."

"Any other provisions you want to tell me, Sheriff?" Jarrett sighed. "Perhaps you'd like me to find someone of a certain height or eye color?"

The sheriff gritted his teeth and circled around his desk. His gaze swept over Lem from head to toe, lingering just a bit longer when he saw the .44 Smith & Wesson holstered at his side. "You know how to use that pistol?"

"Good enough," Lem replied.

"Ever ride on a posse?"

Lem nodded. "Joined up with Marshal Callow in Missouri some years ago. Ran down a gang of bank robbers with him. Year after that, I hunted down a man who killed his wife and mistress in Kentucky."

"Who was in charge of that posse?"

"Sheriff by the name of Bob Whittaker."

"Never heard of any of those men either." Turning toward the other lawman in the room, Rubin asked, "Any of those names strike you as familiar, Tom?"

"Nope," the deputy replied.

"Anyone else, Mr. Beauchamp?" Rubin asked. "Anyone I might have heard of?"

Lem drew a long breath and shook his head. Before he could say anything, Jarrett stepped in and announced, "This is ridiculous. You asked me to find a volunteer for the posse and here he is. Now, not only do you want to know him personally, but you're gonna hold it against him because he did work for other lawmen you don't know? How many other lawmen are in this country? Hundreds? Thousands?"

"I take your point, Jarrett. No need to push the matter," Rubin said. "We could be gone awhile," he said to Lem. "That be a problem?"

"No," Lem said.

"Then I guess you're on the posse. Doesn't pay much."

"Fine."

"All right, then. We ride out tomorrow, bright and early. You and Mr. Pekoe can meet us here. Until then, I suggest you get your affairs in order . . . somewhere other than here."

"Or within eyeshot of me," Tom added.

"Shouldn't be a problem," Jarrett said. "Come on, Lem. I've got a line of credit at the dry goods store just down the street. I'll see to it you're properly outfitted."

Both of them left the sheriff's office. The moment he shut the door, Jarrett could hear the two lawmen discussing something. By the sound of it, neither of them was very happy.

"They don't want to ride out anytime soon," Lem said in his dry, scratchy voice.

"I got that impression myself."

"There a reason for that?"

"Probably," Jarrett said. "As to what it is, I don't know for certain. Could be they're just lazy and don't want to undertake a ride like this. Could be they're scared. These rustlers are killers, after all."

"Yeah," Lem said. "I heard as much."

"I don't really care what their reasons are. All that concerns me is that we find those rustlers and bring them to justice. Having a lawman and some others along with me will just make it easier."

"And if those men don't come?"

Jarrett had been walking along Main Street heading toward a short row of shops. Stopping to look directly at Lem, he asked, "Why wouldn't they?"

"None of them seemed too eager to leave town."

"Like I said before," Jarrett said distastefully, "they're lazy or scared."

"That could be a bad mix. Especially if things come down to a shooting fight."

"They're still lawmen."

Lem made a noise that sounded like a muffled cough.

It wasn't until Jarrett saw the wry grin on the other man's face that he realized Lem was actually laughing. "What's so funny?" Jarrett asked.

"You talk like pinning a badge to a man's chest makes a difference in who he is or what he'll do when things get rough."

"Doesn't it?"

Lem laughed one more time, although it was kept even deeper inside than his first attempt. Rather than question him any further, Jarrett forged ahead with his main purpose, which was to get ready for a long ride.

Being the owner of a prosperous ranch for a good stretch of time, he'd fostered good relationships with several local merchants. With his ranch being nothing but a pile of ashes anymore, he had to do his best to convince other businessmen to honor his credit. The Buffalo Chip's account had been paid in advance, but Jarrett didn't expect the other merchants in town to be as generous.

Their first stop was Mabry's Dry Goods. Jarrett had done almost all of his purchasing at that store ever since the Lazy J became a functioning ranch. As always, Dell Mabry sat behind the front counter. Part of his round face was hidden behind the cash register and the rest was covered by the newspaper he was reading.

"Howdy, Dell," Jarrett said with a wave as he walked inside. "Looking to buy some supplies."

Although the store's owner was quick with a smile, his face soon darkened as he said, "Hello, Jarrett. Sorry to hear about what happened. Is it true what they say about your brother and his family?"

"Yes," Jarrett replied since he wasn't ready to say much more than that on the subject. "The sheriff's forming a posse to hunt down the men that made off with my herd. Care to sign on?"

Dell chuckled and patted his ample belly. "I'd only slow you down."

"I don't know about that. Me and Lem here are riding out in the morning, though. Any chance we can get our supplies here on my account?"

Although Dell winced at that, he nodded slowly. "Under the circumstances, I'd say so. Any notion of when the Lazy J will be rebuilt?"

"Not yet."

"Well . . . under the circumstances . . ." Dell made a face as if he were consoling a boy who'd just buried a beloved pet. Finally he made a decision and nodded. "Your account is still open."

"I appreciate that," Jarrett said.

"Come see me when you get back from that posse and we'll discuss making any necessary changes to our arrangement."

"I'll do that."

Jarrett and Lem gathered up the barest of necessities for a prolonged ride. They checked in with Dell, got another meek nod, and were on their way. Once outside with their bundles in hand, Lem said, "He was mighty concerned about his money."

"That's his business," Jarrett replied while stuffing his supplies into Twitch's saddlebags. "What would you expect?"

"Maybe a little compassion."

"We got plenty of it, and I won't turn my nose up at it, you hear?"

Lem nodded. "I was just talking, is all. Ain't never had someone show much kindness to me in that regard. Didn't know quite what to expect."

"I'm new to this as well," Jarrett said. "Let's just see if we can get the rest of what we need."

All that remained was for Jarrett to buy some feed and a bit more canned fruit. They had to go to two more stores for that and Jarrett was treated in a manner similar to what he'd experienced at Dell's place. The shop owners knew what had befallen the Lazy J and pitched in what they could to help Jarrett in his time of need. It was a bittersweet afternoon. While Jarrett was plenty thankful to have friends who would help him however they could, it stung his pride to have to cash in on pity rather than what he'd earned by the sweat of his brow. In the end, however, he got the supplies he'd needed and the posse was set to carry on.

"I'd say that about does it," Jarrett said after tossing some bags of grain over Twitch's back.

"Not yet," Lem said. "We got one more stop to make."

"Where might that be?"

Lem looked down the street and nodded toward the corner. The only things there were a dentist's office, a bookstore, and a little shop with a sign that bore a picture of a disassembled pistol on it.

"Looking for something to read while we're on the trail?" Jarrett asked.

"Not quite."

"Since it doesn't seem like you've got a toothache, that'd mean you want to purchase a gun?"

"Could come in useful," Lem said.

"Don't know how much credit I can get at that place."

Lem started walking. "Let's find out."

This time, Lem was first to step inside. Jarrett was right behind him. He recognized the man who stood behind a glass-topped display case, but just barely. "Hello. I'm Jarrett Pekoe. I own the Lazy J."

The man behind the case was somewhere in his sixties with a scraggly mop of thinning gray hair sprouting from his head and a beard to match. His hands were thick with dark calluses that pegged him as a blacksmith. "Heard about the fire," he said. "Damn shame."

"Sure was. We're headed out on a posse and—"

Having already stepped up to the display case, Lem tapped his finger on the glass and said, "That one, that one, and . . . that one."

The old man raised his eyebrows and reached inside the case. "Not a bad eye for weaponry," he said. "Although I can make a suggestion if you'd prefer a better overall pistol."

As soon as the old man placed the first gun on top of the counter, Lem picked it up and began taking it apart. Jarrett knew how to clean his weapons and put them back together again, but he'd never seen someone do the job so quickly. It was almost as if Lem were simply moving his hands over the gun as it fell apart on its own accord.

The old man seemed to be equally impressed. "Know your way around a Smith and Wesson, I see," he mused.

Lem was too busy examining each piece of the gun to respond. After picking up the individual parts, he set most to one side and a few to the other. From there, he moved on to the next pistol the old man brought out from the case. The same process was repeated and both piles of parts grew larger. When he was done with that one, he asked, "What about the third?"

"I don't normally like anyone handling the merchandise unless they put down some sort of deposit." When the old man saw Jarrett approach the case, he raised a hand to hold him back. "But in this case," the merchant said, "I'll make an exception." He retrieved the third pistol Lem had pointed out and set it on top of the case. "Always a pleasure to see a man in his element."

So far, Lem had yet to take his eyes from the hardware in front of him. His gaze remained steady as his hands moved with equal parts speed and precision. Once that third gun was fully disassembled, Lem focused his attention on the smaller of the two piles he'd made. His pace slowed a bit, but his eyes became even more intense as he carefully examined every piece.

Jarrett could do nothing but watch. Even with his limited knowledge of weaponry, Lem's display was impressive. The old man, on the other hand, was enthralled.

Piece by piece, Lem put together a pistol from the parts he'd taken from the other three. They'd all been .44 caliber Smith & Wessons that looked similar enough to Jarrett. Since they'd been taken apart so quickly, he couldn't tell much more than that. Lem hefted the weight of the pistol that he'd put together and started examining it even more closely.

First, Lem held it sideways and then he turned his wrist so he could sight along the top of its barrel. He opened his hand, allowed the pistol to dangle by its trigger guard from one finger, and twirled it with a barely visible flick of that wrist. He lowered the pistol, snapped it up again, and thumbed the hammer back. The action was so smooth that the metallic click could barely be heard.

"Damn fine work," the old man said. "May I?"

Lem handed over the pistol so the old man could examine it. In less than half the time that Lem had taken, the old man went through a few motions of his own and smiled. "Balance is better," he said. "How'd you manage that?"

"Balance is nothing but redistributing weight," Lem replied.

That sounded like a sarcastic response to Jarrett, but the old man didn't seem offended in the slightest.

"The cylinder feels smoother," he said while rolling it against his palm.

Lem nodded. "Made for one model but fits better in another. Couldn't tell you why."

"I'll remember that." The old man handed back the pistol. "You going to buy that or do you plan on putting them all back together?"

"I'll take it."

"Naturally you'll have to pay something for them other two as well," the old man said while motioning to the remaining pile of parts. "It's not like I can rightfully sell them in this condition."

Lem set the pistol down so he could draw the one from his holster. As soon as that gun cleared leather, Jarrett's heart leaped into his throat. He didn't know quite what to do if things took a turn and froze in place. That held him off just long enough to remain silent as Lem turned his gun around to hand it grip-first to the old man behind the display case. "I can offer this in trade," he said.

Seemingly unaffected by the draw, the old man took the pistol and looked it over. As he went through his examination, he emptied its cylinder into his palm. "This'll go a ways toward covering it," he said, "but not all."

"I own the Lazy J," Jarrett said.

The old man's eyes snapped over to him. "What's left of it, you mean. Sorry if that sounds harsh, but . . ."

"No, I understand," Jarrett replied. In fact, it was good to be dealt with on his real merits instead of pitied. "I still have assets. Land and such. Some equipment that wasn't lost. Also, we're riding out on a posse to reclaim my herd. Once I get that back, I'll have even more funds to draw from."

"Normally I don't put much credit in promises," the old man said. "But it seems you're in fairly capable company and I imagine you'll come back from that posse in one piece. I'd say that stretches far enough to cover the remaining cost."

"Plus some ammunition?" Lem asked.

The old man nodded. "Plus some ammunition."

Lem took the pistol he'd created and eased it into his holster. Then he and Jarrett took a few boxes of ammunition each. It wasn't enough to fight a war, but they could make their presence known in a few good fights. Once they were outside the shop, Jarrett let out a breath. "That was some impressive work," he said. "Maybe we don't need to wait for the sheriff to drag his sorry hide out on a posse."

"Having the law with us will be a help."

Jarrett imagined it would indeed make things easier. If only just barely.

They went back to their horses, loaded the ammunition into the bags along with the rest of the supplies they'd gathered, and climbed into their saddles. After they'd ridden a short way down Main Street, Jarrett asked, "Where are you staying?"

Lem looked over at him without saying a word and then looked back to the street in front of him.

"Come on, now," Jarrett said. "I've never seen you around here and none of the men who own any of the stores we visited recognized you either. Since you would have had to do business with at least one of those fellows on occasion, I'd say you're newer to Flat Pass than you'd let on."

"Already told you as much."

"I guess so. What brings you here?"

Lem looked over at him. "Weren't you listening when I spoke to the sheriff?"

"Yes, but he didn't care about much more than the shortest possible answer to his questions."

"And you care more than that, huh?" Lem asked. "Is that some sort of sentiment or are you just nosy?"

"I at least care if you have a place to stay and a hot meal. I doubt we'll be living in luxurious accommodations while on the trail of those rustlers. The least I can do is provide a good start to the ride."

"What about the sheriff and his men? Do they get the same hospitality?"

"He likes that jail of his so much," Jarrett replied, "let him sleep in it. I prefer a hot bath poured by a smiling woman."

Lem chuckled at first and then let out a genuine laugh. "Guess it pays to be a Good Samaritan."

Chapter 14

When Jarrett put a roof over Lem's head, he went all out. Not only Lem, but Jack, Edgar, and Jarrett himself all used up one last favor from the owner of the Snelling House Hotel. Despite the unfortunate moniker, it was the best hotel in town and was known particularly for serving a breakfast that was big enough to stuff any man's belly. Stan was offered a room as well but turned it down.

"I might as well keep my cot at the Chip," he'd said to Jarrett. "I won't be able to walk all the way down to Martha Street anyways."

"Remember what I said about getting too drunk to ride," Jarrett warned. "If you can't stay in your saddle come morning, I'll tie a rope around one foot and drag you behind us."

Stan gave him a salute and walked back to the saloon district.

"He'll be drunk tomorrow," Lem said.

Jarrett shrugged. "More than likely, but he'll stay in his saddle. Being three sheets to the wind never kept him from riding as long he's worked for me."

"You hire drunks?"

"Not as a regular practice, but that particular drunk does his job well enough."

Since introductions had already been made all around, Lem took the key he was given and headed for the stairs. Jack wasn't one for small talk, but he could scribble faster than anyone Jarrett knew. He went to the front desk, wrote something on the side of a register page, and turned it toward the clerk.

"Oh yes," the clerk said after reading the note. "We have bathtubs available on the third floor. I'll have some hot water sent up there."

Jack took his key and climbed the stairs to his floor.

"I was gonna ask for laundry service," Jarrett said, "but with such a long ride ahead of us, it may be better to start off as dirty as where I'll end up. Shorter distance to fall."

The clerk gave them each a key and then excused himself to tend to some other manner in the kitchen.

"I . . . wanted to have a word with you," Edgar said.

Jarrett quickly told him, "No need to thank me for the room. You've always done a good job for me, so consider it a gift. Unfortunately you'll have to be on your own once I leave."

"That's not what I meant." The old man pulled Jarrett away from the stairs and into a small parlor where breakfast was served every morning. Glancing nervously toward the stairs, he opened his mouth to speak but closed it again when he heard movement on one of the upper floors.

"What's wrong?" Jarrett asked. "You seem spooked."

"Ain't you?"

"Honestly I'm not really feeling much of anything at the moment. If I did, I doubt I could see straight."

Edgar cringed a bit. "Yeah. I suppose it hasn't been that long since . . . Good Lord," he said as if he'd been struck by lightning. "Hasn't been long at all since everything happened."

Not anxious to be struck by that same bolt just yet, Jarrett said, "Then you were spooked by something else."

"Right." Once again, he looked toward the stairs. "It's that Lem fella."

"What about him?"

"He seems . . ."

"Spooky?"

"Yes!" Edgar said in a harsh whisper. "Where'd you find him?"

"Actually he found me. He heard about what happened to the J and wanted to help."

"You don't think that's peculiar?"

"Not as such," Jarrett replied. "Especially since I was on my way to start looking for men who might want to help with that very thing. News travels fast in a town this size, and even if a man was too blind to see the smoke for himself, he would have smelled it. Only seems reasonable that a posse would be formed soon after." He was drifting a bit too close to the fresh wound on his soul, so Jarrett backed away a few paces from the subject. "Do you think it was strange he heard about what happened?"

"I guess not. It's just that . . . there's something about him that sends a chill down my spine."

"Then it's a good thing you're not riding with us."

"Come on, now. Don't tell me you think I'd be anything but a burden riding along with some damn posse."

Even though Jarrett agreed with the old man, voicing that opinion would have been a bit harsh.

"There's something about Lem," Edgar continued. "Something I don't much like."

"It's got to be more than that if you pulled me aside like this."

"That gun he wears. It ain't like anything I've seen."

Jarrett nodded. "There's a good reason for that. I was

there when he picked that gun up. Remind me to tell you about it sometime. It was quite the sight."

Edgar was somewhat relieved by that. "So he just got it?"

"From the shop owned by that old blacksmith. Now, that old fella is someone who'll put a scare into folks."

"What about the holster?"

"What about it?" Jarrett let out a sigh.

"I've met a few gunmen in my day," Edgar said. "Killers."

"So have I. And I hope to meet them again real soon."

"I mean before those rustlers came along," Edgar said. "Since before you were born, I was working my way from one ranch to another, and a man crosses paths with all sorts in that kind of life. Many of 'em ain't the sort any decent man should associate with."

"And you think Lem is one of those?"

When Edgar nodded, he did so as if he was afraid even that might be overheard by the wrong set of ears. "You can tell a man like that by the holster he wears."

"Plenty of men wear holsters."

"There are certain kinds preferred by gunmen. Also, when they get enough wear in 'em, you can tell it's seen more than its share of use."

"Right now Twitch seems more levelheaded than you, which ain't a compliment," Jarrett said. "What about Lem's boots? They tell you anything you don't like?"

"Damn it, listen to me! Maybe it's just a gut feeling, but it's there and I ain't crazy."

"Nobody said you were crazy."

"The hell you weren't," Edgar snapped. "I've been around longer than you and I've seen plenty. I've seen more than enough to know that Lem ain't the sort of man you want to be near."

"Under normal circumstances, I'd agree," Jarrett said. "But these circumstances are anything but normal. I've seen killers too and I know for a fact that I don't exactly want farmers at my side when I see them again. This is a posse, not a church social. If Lem knows how to handle a gun, that suits me fine. If he's got the sand to put it to use when the time comes, that's even better."

"What happens if having too many killers in one spot proves to be not such a good thing?"

Jarrett gave the old man a friendly nudge. "Then I'll thank my stars that I'm riding with a bunch of lawmen."

"This is the life, huh?"

Edgar's words echoed within a long room sectioned off by dividers made from red curtains hanging on wooden frames. Between each divider was a space about half the size of a horse's stall, and in each of those spaces was a bathtub with a small table beside it. After having his talk with Jarrett, Edgar decided to indulge in all of the amenities offered by the hotel. Jack had already been sitting in his tub when the old man walked into the room with his bucket of steaming water. The only way Edgar knew he was there at all was the sound of lazy splashing from behind one of the other partitions.

Edgar poured his water into a tub while breathing in the steam that quickly filled the space between the dividers on either side of him. "What are these here?" he mused while removing the lid from a glass jar on the table next to the tub. "Bath salts? Fancy, fancy! Oh, and what is that smell?"

"I think it's lavender."

Edgar was so startled that he dropped the lid onto the jar. "Who's there?"

"I believe Mr. Pekoe introduced us."

"Lem?"

"Yeah. I'd shake your hand, but I'm indisposed at the moment."

"It's all right," Edgar said. "Stay where you are. Seems a mite bit strange. The three of us all getting the same notion in our heads."

"Not really," Lem said. "The only hot water we'll see for a while is what our horses spray on the ground and that ain't exactly gonna clean us off."

The three of them might not have been able to see each other, but they shared a laugh as Edgar dumped his clothes into a heap on the floor and eased into his tub. He let out a prolonged sigh and said, "Maybe I've had it wrong all those years of working cattle drives. I should'a been a banker or some other sort of dandy so I could slow down like this more often. You know the only thing we're missing in these comfortable tubs?"

Without hesitation, Lem replied, "Women."

"You got that right!"

The door opened so someone could step into the room.

Turning toward the direction of that sound didn't help Edgar very much. All he could see was the curtain hanging from the divider on that side as he asked, "That you, Jarrett? Might as well get the whole bunch in here, I suppose."

The person who came in hesitated before answering.

Edgar winced. "Guess not. Whoever it is, I believe there's one tub left. If you prefer a bit more solitude, I'd say we're just about—"

The first gunshot exploded through the room, taking Edgar by complete surprise. When the second gunshot blasted through his divider, the old man slid as far down into his tub as he could. Bringing his legs up, he felt a sharp pain jab through his lower body that shot straight down to his right foot. Edgar reached beneath the water, his hand brushing against jagged edges on one side of the tub.

"Aw no," Edgar groaned as he looked down to see the two holes that had been shot into the side of his tub. Water spilled out through openings that were only marginally plugged by the arm that had brushed against the other side. Ignoring the scraping of his elbow against the spots where metal had been bent inward by the passing bullet, he found a hole in his hip that leaked blood straight into the water.

More shots tore through the room, sending water splashing from multiple damaged tubs. Something heavy hit the floor, followed by the frantic scrape of thrashing arms or legs. Not willing to lift himself high enough to climb out of the tub and feeling his strength drain out through his fresh wound, Edgar slouched down and called out, "I'm hit!"

Nobody answered him.

Chapter 15

It was difficult for Edgar to determine how many people had heard the shots. Surely there were other guests in the hotel, but some could very well have been hiding in their rooms and keeping their heads down. If he'd been in any other spot when the shots were fired, Edgar would have been one of those people. For the moment, all he could do was hunker down in what remained of his hot, bloody water and listen as the steps that had come into the room slowly worked their way forward.

Before long, Edgar became aware of another sound. It was closer than the footsteps. There was a slight rustle followed by the brush of something solid against the floorboards. Just as Edgar looked in the direction of the curtain separating him from the neighboring tub, that rustle grew into something much louder.

Jack let out a raging cry as he leaped out of his stall. From what he could hear, Edgar assumed the bigger man had gotten ahold of whoever had done the shooting. That was confirmed when the divider blocking Edgar's line of sight was knocked down by Jack's falling body. Tripping over backward, Jack became entangled in the curtain, which led to him knocking one shoulder against Edgar's tub. Now that the barrier was down, Edgar could see the man who'd barged in on them.

He was a burly fellow with broad shoulders, a thick chest, and a solid frame. Built like a barrel with tree stumps for limbs, the gunman kept his face hidden behind a filthy blue bandanna. His eyes were wild as he raised the pistol in his hand, thumbed back the hammer, and prepared to punch a few holes into the man he'd just tossed aside like so much trash.

Before the gunman could pull his trigger, Lem flew at him as if he'd been shot from a cannon. Both arms stretched in front of him, Lem collided with the gunman from one side to take him completely off guard. A smaller man would have been knocked down or completely overpowered by the attack, but the bulky fellow behind the mask merely staggered half a step to one side before shifting his weight to answer back. Lem dropped to the floor and scrambled to get his feet beneath him. The rustling Edgar had heard must have been from Lem's stall, because he'd managed to pull on his jeans before making his move. When Lem straightened his knees, he pushed off with both legs to drive his shoulder into the gunman's midsection.

Once again, the gunman remained rooted to his spot. He tried to shove Lem back, but that proved to be difficult since Lem had dug both heels into the floor so he could stand his ground as well. Keeping as close to the gunman as possible, Lem pounded one fist after another into the bigger man's ribs. After at least half a dozen blows, the gunman started to show signs of weakening.

"You hurt, Jack?" Edgar asked.

The mute ranch hand pulled free from most of the curtain, using some of it to wrap around his lower body. Still dazed after his rough landing, Jack shook his head to clear it and then shook it again to answer Edgar's question.

"I'm . . . Look out!"

Jack followed Edgar's line of sight to see what had startled the old man. The gunman was still struggling with Lem, but his pistol was now pointed toward Edgar's stall. Lem also responded to the old man's warning by grabbing the gunman's elbow and shoving that arm upward. When the pistol barked again, it sent its round into the ceiling instead of through flesh and bone. After that, the gunman snarled like a bear and drove one knee straight into Lem's belly.

When Jack stood up again, he looked like something from an old painting of warriors who charged into battle wearing nothing but their clan's colors wrapped around their waists. He also took hold of the gunman's arm, but followed up by slamming a fist into that elbow. The gunman yelped in pain. Since one arm was still being held, he lashed out with the other. Unfortunately for Lem, that arm was closer to him and he caught a wild swing squarely upside his head.

Lem hit the floor hard and sat there for a moment to collect his breath.

Still hanging on to the gunman's wrist, Jack did his best to keep the pistol elevated so no more shots could spill blood. He was a strong man, but the gunman was just a little stronger and the pistol slowly inched its way down.

Edgar might have been hurting, but he knew he would be in much worse condition if he just sat in that tub and did nothing. He hadn't brought a weapon into the bathroom, and there were none lying about. That left him with precious few options, so he climbed out of the leaking tub and grabbed the first thing he could find.

Feeling he was being overpowered, Jack tightened his grip on the gunman's arm, using both hands. The only sound he could make was a strained grunt as the gunman's thickly muscled arm pressed ever downward. A few more seconds was all it would take for that gun to have a real target, so Jack did the only thing he could and sank his teeth into the gunman's forearm.

"Son of a bitch!" the gunman hollered. All his muscle or not, there was only so much he could take before he was forced to relax his grip and let the pistol fall. Inches away from hitting the floor, the gun was caught by Lem's outstretched hand.

There wasn't much time for Lem to steady himself before the big gunman recovered from being bitten. A split second before catching a large boot to the ribs, Lem pulled his trigger to fire a shot up at the gunman. The bearlike man reeled back, clutching his face and hollering with rage. When he lowered his hands, he revealed a long, bloody gash that had been opened from his chin all the way up one cheek. Like any wounded animal, he became twice the threat he'd been a few moments ago. Lem tried to put him down but quickly realized the pistol in his hand was empty.

Jack's grip wasn't even close to strong enough to keep the gunman from drawing his arm back and lashing out with a vicious backhand. The impact of fist against face was loud enough to echo through the room as Jack staggered back. His eyes were vacant as he dropped onto the curtain trailing behind him.

Still enraged, the gunman tore the bandanna the rest of the way from his face and reached for another pistol that was kept tucked under his belt. Before he could get to it, Edgar lunged forward with the jar of bath salts he'd grabbed and tossed every last one of the scented granules into the gunman's face. As soon as all that salt hit the fresh, open wound, the gunman's voice shifted from an angry roar to a higher-pitched wail. All the rage that had been etched into his face was washed away and the only thing he wanted to do was run away.

Sitting on the floor with an empty pistol in his hand, Lem wasn't about to get in the bigger man's way. He quickly scooted to one side before he was trampled under those pounding boots.

At that moment, Jarrett appeared in the doorway, gun in hand and ready for a fight. There was no possible way he could have fully braced himself for what was coming at him, however. To his credit, Jarrett did bring his weapon up a little more than halfway before he was knocked aside and slammed into the wall behind him.

The gunman charged into the hall, bounced blindly off the wall less than a foot away from where Jarrett had hit a moment before, and paused to look around. While he might have gotten a peek at his surroundings, the gunman also got salt into his eyes, which only made him madder. He stormed for the stairs, broke a piece from the top of the banister, and thumped noisily all the way down to the ground floor. By some miracle, he managed to bounce off the walls to keep from falling down the staircase. "Out of my way!" he shouted to some unlucky soul who must have been standing too close to the front door.

There was one final crash as the front door was slammed against the wall, which allowed the gunman to get outside. After that, the hotel was much quieter.

Edgar set the empty jar down and looked over at Lem. "You all right?" he asked.

Lem pulled himself up to all fours and then to one

knee. "Yeah," he said while rubbing a spot on his head. "Least, I think so."

"What about you, Jack? Can you stand?"

The younger man's hand was still tangled up in the curtain that was wrapped around his lower half. After failing in one attempt to get up on his own, he reached out to take the hand Edgar offered him. Try as he might, Edgar was unable to pull Jack up before the other man's hand slipped through his wet fingers. Jack landed on his backside and looked at Edgar with a vaguely disgusted expression.

Edgar looked down to find that he was stark naked and standing there for the world to see. His larger concern was the messy bullet wound in his right hip. Upon seeing the wound, he felt his stomach churn and his head start to spin. "Uh-oh," he groaned. "I think I'm about to . . ." He started to keel over but was caught by a pair of hands from behind him.

"Easy there, old-timer," Lem said. "Let's get you off your feet."

Grunting as he pulled himself up, Jarrett staggered into the room and asked, "What on earth happened? Who was that? I feel like I been rolled over by a steam engine!"

"We know barely more than you do," Lem said. "We were just washing up when that beast charged in here."

"What did he want?"

"Yeah," Edgar said. "What did he want, Lem?"

Lowering Edgar to the floor beside the old man's pile of clothes, Lem straightened up and worked his jaw back and forth. "How should I know?"

Edgar's next breath was stolen from him by a jolting pain from his wound. The more he tried to shift his weight to get dressed, the paler he became. By the time

Jarrett made it over to him, he was almost too wobbly to remain upright.

"Here," Jarrett said. "Let me help you pull some clothes on." Drawing in a few quick breaths through his nose, Jarrett looked down at the old man with even more confusion. "What the hell is that smell? Lavender?"

Chapter 16

The hotel's clerk and owner were both commiserating on the third floor as Edgar, Jack, Lem, and Jarrett all gathered in Edgar's room. Since Edgar was also staying on the third floor, they could hear the clerk and owner bad-mouth them as well as the gunman who'd started the fight that had done so much damage to their bathroom.

"That looks like a nasty wound," Jarrett said as he examined the old man's hip. "We're gonna have to get you to the doctor."

"No!" Edgar said as he lowered himself onto a chair. "He'll just want to take my leg. I'll take my chances with gangrene."

"It's not that bad," Lem said.

"So you think we should just put him to bed?" Jarrett asked.

"No. I say we take him to the doctor. That wound isn't bad enough for anyone to want to saw anything off him. If the doctor in this town is that incompetent, he'll need to get by me to get to him." Looking to Edgar, Lem asked, "Happy?"

"Yes," Edgar replied. "I suppose I am."

When the old man tried to stand back up, Jack came

forward to help him. Edgar's first instinct was to angrily push away the other man, but Jack was barely moved by that and came at him again.

"Let us help you," Jarrett said as he circled around to Edgar's other side.

"I managed to move about on my own during that fight," Edgar groused, "and I can do so again."

Lem stood at the open doorway. "That was when the blood was pounding through your veins like a stampede," he said. "A man can do a lot more at a time like that than he can under regular circumstances. You really want to walk down three flights of stairs and all the way to the doctor's office on that leg?"

Grudgingly, Edgar said, "No!"

Between Jarrett and Jack, Edgar was moved from his room and down the stairs. Lem disappeared somewhere along the way, only to reappear again fully dressed and wearing his gun belt. All four of them shuffled past the front desk. The few others they passed were too shaken by the attack to try to stand in their way.

"This is all your fault, you know," Edgar grunted.

"Whose fault?" Jarrett asked.

Glaring in Lem's direction, the old man said, "Who do you think?"

Walking beside them, Lem recoiled and said, "Me? Why is this *my* fault?"

"Because if you hadn't been so concerned with getting your damn pants on instead of attacking that bastard right away, the whole fight would have been much shorter!"

Jarrett had to turn his head before the cranky old-timer caught sight of the grin making its way onto his face.

They all went outside and nearly walked into the two lawmen who were on their way in.

"Well, now," Sheriff Rubin said. "Look who we have here. Any bit of trouble that comes along, there you men are."

"If the trouble you mean is my life getting burned down," Jarrett said, "then I suppose you're right. Is it against the law to be shot at too many times in one week?"

Rubin held his hands up in a placating gesture. "I spoke out of turn there, Mr. Pekoe. Sorry about that. What's happened this time?"

"Some big fella came in shooting, that's what!" Edgar said. "We was all taking our baths when it happened and he just came right in!"

The other man with Sheriff Rubin was his deputy, Tom. Smirking, the deputy said, "Taking your baths, huh? Were you scrubbing each other's backs?"

"Not in the same tub, you idiot! Aw, what the hell do you care?" Edgar groused. "You ain't interested in catching him anyway."

"You wanna tell us who he was?" Rubin asked. "Which way he went? Anything to let us know where to look for him?"

The four battered men continued shuffling along as the lawmen followed.

"Didn't think so," Tom grunted.

"Tom, go have a word with the folks in that hotel," Rubin said. "See what they have to say about it. I'll help with this bunch here."

"Don't bother with us," Jarrett said. "We can take Edgar to the doctor just fine on our own."

"You sure?" Rubin asked.

"I think the three of us can drag one old man down a street," Lem replied.

"All right, then," Rubin said with a shrug. "I'll go and see what there is to see at that hotel."

Rubin and Tom moseyed off, heading in the general direction of the nearby hotel. After they were several yards away, Edgar grumbled, "That pair was almost as useful as tits on a bull."

"No argument here," Jarrett said.

"You certain you want to ride with the likes of them?"

"They carry badges," Jarrett said. "All they need to do is get close to those rustlers and make it nice and legal for us to put them down."

"What happened to bringing them to justice?" Edgar asked.

"Six of one, half a dozen of the other."

After walking a few more steps, Lem asked, "You need any help pulling this one along?"

"You'll need help pulling my boot out of your rump if you keep talkin' about me like that," Edgar said.

"No," Jarrett said. "I think this is just a two-man job. Why?"

"Those two clowns will barely find the room where them shots were fired," Lem said. "I'll see if I can point them in the right direction."

The only responses to that were a shrug from Jack and an annoyed gesture from Edgar. That seemed to be enough for Lem, so he veered off from the rest of the group and made his way back to the hotel.

The remaining three were within sight of the doctor's office when Edgar spoke up again. "What's got you so intrigued?" he asked.

"Huh?"

"You been looking over your shoulder ever since Lem decided to get himself some sleep."

"You think that's what he's doing?" Jarrett asked.

"Sure. You really think he's concerned about what them fools in badges are doing?"

"I'm curious to see what Sheriff Rubin will say to him. For that matter, I wouldn't mind seeing how Lem takes to getting any lip from that deputy."

When he heard that, Jack made a huffing sound that was as close as he could get to a laugh.

"Oh, you like that, do you?" Edgar snapped.

Jack nodded.

"If I promise to let you know what happens," Jarrett said, "would you mind if I go have a look?"

"Don't be foolish," Edgar replied. "There's already enough of that sort of thing going around."

"I wasn't talking to you."

Jack smirked and used his free hand to motion for Jarrett to go on ahead. He then shifted Edgar's weight so he could carry the old man without any help.

"Looks like you're in good hands," Jarrett said. "Good luck with that doctor. He's a real beaut."

Edgar continued to grumble and complain, which wasn't much of a surprise considering his wound and a less than sunny disposition.

As soon as he broke away from the other two, Jarrett traced his path back toward the hotel. He had made it less than halfway when he caught sight of Lem, who wasn't headed to bed after all. Jarrett ducked into a shadow as Lem ran down an alley and out of sight. Jarrett hung back a ways, but not far enough to lose him as he turned north on Prosser Avenue and then took a sharp turn down a narrow side street. Thanks to Lem being in such a rush and the noise coming from the nearby saloons, Jarrett remained unseen.

Soon Lem was knocking on the side door of a little place called Annie's Carriage House. Although the sign hanging near the front entrance read FINE SPIRITS AND DANCING, everyone in town knew that the only dancing going on at Annie's was in the beds on the second floor. Paying customers looking to avoid being easily seen looking for a dance partner went in through the side door. In all his days of living in Flat Pass, Jarrett had yet to see anyone walking into Annie's through the front.

"I see how it is," Jarrett whispered to himself as he watched the side door open so a woman with dark hair could answer. He was about to turn back around and leave Lem to his affairs when he noticed something peculiar.

While Jarrett was no expert on the matter, he'd visited Annie's more than once. There was a certain way such a thing was handled. It was a fairly simple process where the customer made his intentions known, he was greeted with a smile, and then shown inside. Lem, however, wasn't shown inside. Annie's was located on a small side street off Prosser Avenue, and there were plenty of shadows at this time of night for Jarrett to use to his advantage. He chose one that gave him a better view and settled in across the street from the place where he could watch from a safe distance.

The woman who opened the door in response to Lem's knock carried a lantern in one hand, making her a single source of light in that vicinity. Because of that lantern, Jarrett could tell there was no smile on her face. He couldn't make out every last detail, but the way she carried herself and the clipped way in which she spoke to Lem told him that they were not discussing the usual sort of pleasantries that brought a man to Annie's in the middle of the night.

The conversation between her and Lem was short, if not sweet. It ended with her nodding profusely before backing inside and closing the door. Lem remained outside and when he turned to get a look at the street nearby, Jarrett swore he stood out like a beacon twice as bright as that lantern had been. Although Lem's eyes might have lingered for a few extra moments on the spot where Jarrett was standing, he didn't seem overly concerned with what he saw. His attention was pulled straight back to Annie's when the door in front of him started to open again.

Jarrett considered heading back to the hotel as soon as Lem looked in another direction. He paused, however, when Lem backed away from the door until he all but disappeared into one of the thicker shadows behind him. The door was opened cautiously and since whoever was inside wasn't carrying any source of light, the person remained hidden.

Lem whispered something. It was the rasping, grating sound of a voice that only made it to Jarrett's ears because the commotion from the saloons had died down a bit. Straining to hear what was being said, Jarrett inched forward. His hands snaked out to one side to trace along the wall of the building he was pressed against so he didn't accidentally step into the open. He reached the corner of the wall much too soon to get a clear picture of what was going on across the street.

Because Lem spoke a bit louder this time, Jarrett could hear him say, " . . . here."

"Where?" the person inside asked. By hearing that single word, Jarrett could be certain that other person was a man.

Jarrett squinted in an attempt to focus his eyes enough to see better in the dark. Since he wasn't a bat or a possum, it didn't do him much good. When the man who'd opened the door stepped outside, Jarrett couldn't see much of his face. The man's bulky frame and trunklike limbs, on the other hand, were quite distinctive. Every one of Jarrett's muscles tensed. His hand went for his pistol and he took one step forward. Since another step would bring him out of the shadows at the edge of the building and possibly into plain sight, he reflexively stopped.

The gunman who'd rampaged through their hotel not so long ago moved somewhat hesitantly as he stepped down one of the two small stairs leading from Annie's threshold to the ground. His shoulders were stooped forward and his head jutted out, making him look like an overgrown vulture. "That really you?" he asked in a deep, snarling whisper that carried almost as well as a normal tone of voice.

Lem said something in a tone that was nothing more than a scraping hiss to Jarrett's ears.

Apparently the bulky gunman was just as curious as Jarrett as to what was going on. He stepped forward again and when his right boot crunched against the gritty dirt, he was quickly overpowered.

Lem surged from the shadow in which he'd been hiding, reaching out with one hand to grab hold of the gunman's shirt. Using surprise and leverage to their full advantage, he pulled the gunman off balance while the much larger man was halfway between steps.

The gunman snarled something that couldn't even qualify as speech. He reached for Lem with pawlike hands, prompting Jarrett to step all the way out of hiding before Lem was crushed to death.

In a swift motion, Lem brought his other hand up to hip level while drawing the burly gunman in closer. Two muffled thumps rolled through the air, each of which seemed to hit the big man like mule kicks to the stomach.

Jarrett froze in place. The sounds he'd heard were

vaguely familiar, but not quite. Mostly he was captivated by the sight before him as the man who'd so recently been all but unstoppable now stood gawking down at Lem like a dog that had reached the end of its leash.

Another thump caused Jarrett to flinch.

The fourth made him absolutely certain about what he was hearing.

Gunshots.

"Good Lord," Jarrett whispered. Even though his voice had been so low that even he could barely hear it, part of him was certain he'd just given himself away. No matter how he might have felt about Lem, it was clear that what had just happened wasn't meant for an audience.

For the next several heartbeats, Jarrett fully expected to be discovered. It seemed Lem was more concerned with the open door directly behind the bigger gunman at the moment, which gave Jarrett a bit of time to ease back into the shadows. Lem's gaze did sweep toward the other side of the street, but not before the gunman started to grunt and groan.

Lem whispered something to him again and, miraculously, the gunman found enough breath to respond. The voice coming from that man's gaping mouth was a pale reflection of what it had been before the gunshots. Even Lem had to lean in so he could pick up every word. Slowly he began to nod.

The gunman was crumpling. One hand reached for Lem's sleeve and hung on. When his knees buckled, the big man's weight came forward. Lem held him up for another second or two, which was just enough time to pull his trigger two more times. The barrel of his gun was dug so far into the gunman's belly that no sparks from the shots could be seen. Each of those thumps was a bit louder than the previous ones as both bullets punched out through the other man's back.

Before he was squashed beneath the gunman's considerable weight, Lem pushed one shoulder into his chest and shoved him away. Once the gunman was falling to the side instead of straight forward, Lem released his grip and let him drop. The impact of the gunman's landing was loud enough to be heard all the way down the street in any direction. He even managed to break a piece off the bottommost stair leading to the door into Annie's before rolling onto one side and spitting out his final breath.

Unable to peel away from that wall no matter how badly he might have wanted to, Jarrett watched as Lem calmly reloaded his pistol while dropping to one knee. Once down so he was within a few inches of the fallen gunman, Lem bent down and cocked his head to one side so he could listen for any other sound the gunman might make.

Whatever he heard or didn't hear must have satisfied Lem, because he stood back up and holstered his weapon. Behind him, a dim glow appeared in the half-open door at the top of the two broken steps.

Jarrett could make out a sliver of the same woman's face who'd greeted Lem when he knocked on the door. She pushed the door open a bit, took a cautious look outside, and then shrank back. Lem stood over the gunman, who was now as still as a log that had been lying beside a river for two decades. When Lem turned around to face the woman holding the lantern, the fear in her eyes was easy enough to see from any distance.

"No, Lem," Jarrett whispered under his breath. "Don't you do it."

Lem's hand rested on the grip of his holstered pistol,

reminding Jarrett of the skill that had been shown when the weapon was pieced together as well as when it had been put to use.

"Is . . . is he . . . ?" the woman asked. Her voice was the loudest thing Jarrett had heard since he started watching this scene unfold.

"No need to worry about him," Lem said to her. "He won't be coming back inside."

Although she was still obviously frightened, the young woman said, "Thank you, mister. Thank you."

Lem tipped his hat to her and walked out to the side street.

All Jarrett could do was push himself back against the wall even harder, hold his breath, and pray the shadows were thick enough to hide him.

As far as he could tell . . . they were.

Chapter 17

Jarrett circled back to the hotel using several alleyways and a few unnecessarily long routes. By the time he got to his room, he felt foolish for putting himself through so much trouble. After all, that gunman had wanted to kill all of them and had succeeded in shooting Edgar. While he was uncertain about a few important details, Jarrett couldn't argue with the final outcome of that night. There was one fewer animal in the world and soon that number would be whittled down even more.

After a night of not enough sleep, Jarrett woke up and pulled on a fresh shirt. He checked his supplies one last time and packed them into his saddlebags. When he walked down to have an early breakfast, Lem and Jack were already seated at a table.

"Have you seen Stan this morning?" Jarrett asked as he took a seat at the table.

Jack rolled his eyes and shook his head.

"I could've told you he'd be the last one to get here, and I barely know the man," Lem said.

"Be that as it may, I won't allow him to throw us off schedule."

A stout woman with straight blond hair emerged from the kitchen with plates of steaming food in both hands.

Smiling even wider when she saw Jarrett, she said, "One more for breakfast, I see."

"After the commotion last night, I didn't expect much of a warm reception," Jarrett said. "It's good to be wrong sometimes."

"And it's good to have a little excitement every now and then," the woman said while setting the plates down. One was piled high with scrambled eggs and the other with bacon and griddle cakes. Wincing, she added, "I didn't mean to sound callous. Is your friend doing well? The one that was shot, I mean?"

"He's fine," Lem replied. "Stitched up and resting easy."

"You already checked on him?" Jarrett asked.

Picking up a griddle cake and folding it in half so he could eat it straightaway, Lem said, "I was out and about."

"I'm sure."

The woman stepped over to a nearby cupboard to remove enough plates and forks for everyone. "I just cooked enough for two, so I'll whip up some more after I bring you coffee," she said while handing out the place settings. There was one other guest in the dining room, an older fellow in a dark suit reading a folded newspaper. She glanced over to him and then lowered her voice when asking, "Did you know that man who came in here last night? Was there some sort of feud between the lot of you?"

Matching her excited whisper, Lem said, "We've been chasing him across six counties and he finally caught up to us. Got a price on his head that could buy this hotel three times over."

Her eyes widened into saucers and she clasped a hand to her chest as she gasped, "Really?"

Lem's response to that was a noncommittal shrug. When she looked over to Jack, all she got was a silent cock of his head. Since Jarrett didn't have anything to add, she pressed her lips together and walked away.

"Why'd you tell her something like that?" Jarrett asked.

"She wanted some excitement, so I gave it to her," Lem replied. "No harm done."

"Maybe, maybe not."

Soon the woman returned with a pot of coffee and three cups. She set them on their table before bustling away to tend to the man in the suit as well as another couple who came down for breakfast. Every single one of them was given an excitedly whispered story to go along with the usual small talk she had for hotel guests.

Jarrett and Lem didn't talk much between themselves. Apart from straightening out a few details where the day's upcoming ride was concerned, they spent their time eating as many griddle cakes as they could pack away. After breakfast, Lem and Jack went to collect the horses while Jarrett walked to the Buffalo Chip to get Stan.

It wasn't hard to find him. All Jarrett had to do was step inside the saloon and look for a man who looked as if he'd been propped in his chair and left there after being dragged in from the middle of a raging storm. "Come on, Stan," he said as he walked up to the ranch hand and slapped him on the arm. "Time to go."

"Yeah, I figured," Stan replied. He stood and picked up the saddlebags that had been resting at his feet under his table.

"Did you have anything to eat?"

"Had it last night."

"What about breakfast?" Jarrett asked.

"That's what I mean. Last night, sometime after three in the morning, I had some eggs, ham, and browned potatoes."

"Seriously?"

Stan nodded while shoving open the door and waving to the people who remained in the saloon behind him. "Was gonna have some coffee too, but that would've kept me awake."

"That really wasn't very long ago. Didn't you get any sleep?"

"Sure I did."

"Let me guess," Jarrett said. "You had that last night as well."

"That's right. Just a little while before breakfast."

"Did you have a man come storming in to try to shoot you?"

Stan recoiled and looked over at him as if Jarrett had just tossed a pitcher of river water in his face. "No! Why would you ask something like that?"

"Because we did while we were staying at that fancy hotel not too far from here."

Stan gave a chuckle, which quickly became a wet cough. After clearing his throat, he said, "Sounds to me like the rest of you stayed in the wrong place."

Considering the fact that Stan seemed to be in fairly good condition and had had what sounded like a damn fine breakfast, Jarrett had to agree. They walked down Main Street and rounded the corner that would take them to the sheriff's office. Along the way, they met up with Jack and Lem, who were leading the remaining two horses behind their own, loaded Stan's gear, and climbed into their saddles. After riding down the street a ways, Jarrett looked over to the man beside him and asked,

"Don't you want to know anything more about that man I mentioned?"

"You mean the one who busted in to shoot someone or other?" Stan asked.

"Yeah."

Stan shrugged, removed his hat so he could run his fingers through his hair, and then slapped his hat back in place. "We got a long day ahead of us. I figured on saving that for when I got bored later."

"Fair enough."

The four of them rode to the sheriff's office, where they found a grizzled man in his late fifties sitting outside the office's front door with his feet propped up on a box. He pushed up the brim of his hat with one finger, looked at them, and asked, "You men would be the rest of the posse?"

"That's right," Jarrett replied. "Where's Sheriff Rubin?"

"Supposed to meet you out at the Lazy J."

"Thanks."

"I hear the bunch of you had quite the night," the grizzled man said.

"Sure did," Jarrett said.

The man sitting with his feet up wore a deputy's badge pinned to his chest, but had more of a presence about him than Rubin could ever aspire to. Surely the eyes set deep within that hardened face had seen plenty and wouldn't be easily fooled when they soaked up what each new day had to offer. Setting those eyes firmly on Jarrett, he asked, "You hear about the man they found at Annie's?"

"You mean the cathouse?" Stan asked quickly.

"That's the place."

"I reckon there's plenty of men to be found down there." After making his little joke, Stan laughed at himself and looked around for support. All he got was a tired chuckle from Jack, which seemed to be enough to keep him happy.

Completely unaffected by what passed for humor in Stan's mind, the grizzled man seated in front of the sheriff's office said, "This man was a customer, sure enough. A few of the girls told me so."

"You spoke to them?" Jarrett asked.

He nodded. "Seems the sheriff and his other deputy was too busy to do much of anything. They sure as hell didn't have enough time on their hands to go look at a dead body lying in some dirty alley."

Stan's grin went away real quick when he heard that. "This customer was found dead?"

"Deader than Saint George, as my granny used to say. Big fella too. Say, wasn't the man who stormed into that hotel a fairly big fella?"

Jarrett's eyes flicked toward Lem for the briefest of moments before settling back onto the deputy. "He was. Real big."

"You ever been to Annie's, Mr. Pekoe?"

"Not as a customer," Jarrett said. "Not recently, I mean." Even though he was telling the truth and spoke without sounding overly suspicious, he was almost certain that the deputy could just take whatever answers he wanted from what was written upon another man's soul.

"How was he killed?" Stan asked.

"Shot," the deputy replied. "Up close and personal. Poor gal who found him had to put the fire out that had started in his shirt. Probably came from being so near the gun barrel when it went off."

Jarrett didn't have to impersonate being shocked when he heard that, since he'd turned away from the gruesome sights he'd witnessed before they reached that point. Stan and Jack had lost some of the color in their faces as a testament to what was racing through their heads. Most telling of all, however, was the expression on Lem's face. It wasn't quite as dramatic as the surprise shown by the two ranch hands but seemed every bit as genuine.

"Who shot him?" Lem asked.

After a slight pause, the deputy replied, "Couldn't tell you. Any girls working there weren't about to say. Even if they saw the whole thing spool out in front of them, they were too frightened to be much help."

"Do you plan on hunting the killer down?" Stan asked. "Or were you just gonna sit on this porch and twiddle yer thumbs?"

The deputy's brow furrowed slightly as his eyes darted between all four of the men in front of him. "Never you mind about that," he said. "Shouldn't keep the sheriff waiting." He then used the same fingertip that had pushed up his hat brim to pull it back down again. With that, his part of the conversation was clearly over.

Having been dismissed so completely, the four men on horseback had nothing left to do but ride away. Once they were a safe distance from the grizzled deputy, Lem asked, "You think that dead fella was the same man who shot up the hotel?"

"Could be," Jarrett replied.

"Sounds like a hell of a story," Stan said. "Maybe I should hear it now instead of later."

"I'd like the whole story myself," Jarrett said. "Wish I knew for certain if that dead man really is the one that came after us. It'd make things a whole lot easier."

"Sure would," Lem said. "Too bad there's no way for us to find out unless we want to hunt down one dead body instead of a whole lot of living ones."

"Might as well stay the course," Stan said. "If that fella you're worried about is still breathin', he'll find us soon enough. Now somebody tell me what happened at that hotel."

Chapter 18

Instead of telling Stan about what had happened the night before while riding out to the ranch and then most likely repeating a good portion of it after meeting up with the lawmen, Jarrett and the others focused on simply getting to the Lazy J as soon as possible. Under normal circumstances, Jarrett would have felt a warm familiarity when seeing the sign bearing the ranch's brand at the edge of his property line. The sight of that large J leaning skewed to one side like a tired man resting against a wall had always meant he was coming home. Now it burned Jarrett's eyes just as surely as the irons had burned that symbol into the flanks of his cattle.

Jarrett was more than a little relieved when he saw three men on horseback waiting less than fifty yards inside the fence line. One of them was Sheriff Rubin, another was Tom, and the third was a man Jarrett didn't immediately recognize. Since they were right there, Jarrett wouldn't be forced to ride any closer to the center of his property where he could see the charred remains of his past life while the stench of all that smoke was still fresh in his mind.

Sheriff Rubin raised a hand in greeting and waited for

the other four to come to a stop in front of him. "Glad to see you weren't going to make us wait for long."

"We want to get these men more than you do, Sheriff," Jarrett said. Looking to the tall, lean young man riding next to Tom, he asked, "Who's this?"

"This here is Troy Ackerman," the sheriff said. "He just came in from Cheyenne a few days ago and I've been breaking him in as a new deputy. Figured this'd be a good chance to see how he does when the lead starts to fly."

Ackerman had a long, friendly face, olive-colored skin, and a pointed nose. He reminded Jarrett of any number of men in their early twenties who'd come to work for him as a cowhand or just doing odd jobs around the ranch. He smiled easily and even tipped his hat as he said, "Pleased to meet you." Despite the time it took, Ackerman went over to shake the hand of each man who'd just arrived.

"Seems like an eager kid," Stan said. "What's he doing working for you, Sheriff?"

"Now, what in the hell is that supposed to mean?" Rubin snarled.

Stan scratched his whisker-covered chin as if he'd just now rolled out of bed. "Nothing. Maybe it'll do us all some good to have fresh blood on this ride."

"It better." Still fuming under the collar, Rubin shifted his attention back to Jarrett. "We've been doing a bit of scouting before you arrived and you're right. It won't be difficult to track that herd. They left a trail deeper than the road into town."

"So what are we doing here, then?" Jarrett asked. "Let's get this posse moving!"

None of the lawmen even flinched until they got a nod from the sheriff. From there, they cut across Jarrett's property until they reached the spot where the herd had been gathered and eventually driven to the wide gate at the southwest corner of the fence line. While Rubin and Tom were content to ride in the muddy wake of all that beef, Ackerman took a bit more time to study the numerous tracks that had been left behind. When he snapped his reins to catch up to the other lawmen, he grimaced nervously.

"What's wrong with you, kid?" Tom asked.

"I couldn't get a handle on how many men were driving that herd," Ackerman replied. "I found several sets of tracks left by horses instead of cows, but they all just blend together after a while."

"No need for those kinds of specifics," Rubin said. "Once we catch up to them, we'll see how many there are for ourselves."

"Yeah," Tom added. "You saw the mess they left behind. It ain't like they're gonna be worried about anyone being left to come after them."

Jarrett and the others rode a few yards behind the lawmen. More than anything, he wanted to toss the heaviest thing he could find at the back of Tom's smug head. Judging by the tone of the deputy's voice, however, that was precisely the sort of thing he'd wanted. Men like Tom were all too common. The only thing that made them feel content with themselves was being told they were right or knocking around those who knew they were wrong. Instead of giving him an excuse to have his fight for the day, Jarrett bit his tongue.

"Watch your mouth!" Rubin snapped. "You're talking about that man's family! Have some respect."

Tom was more surprised than anyone else at being dressed down like that by the sheriff. The expression on his face was almost as satisfying as what followed.

"Apologize," Rubin demanded.

Looking over to the elder lawman as if he didn't even recognize him, Tom said, "What?"

"You heard me. Apologize."

After waiting a moment for an explanation that didn't come, Tom shifted in his saddle to look at the men behind him. "My apologies. That was . . . out of line."

Not knowing quite what to do, Jarrett simply nodded.

"There, now," Rubin said. "Now that we're all on good terms, why don't you all tell me what happened back at that hotel? I want the whole story. You've had a chance to think it over, so don't miss anything."

Jarrett started at the beginning and went all the way through to the point where the gunman bolted from the hotel with bath salts in his wounded face. When he was through, he said, "Now I have a question for you, Sheriff."

"Yeah?"

"What did you find when you came around to check on the hotel after everything had calmed down?"

"You saying I sat back until the danger passed?" Rubin asked.

Knowing all too well that at least one of the men near him was capable of taking that bait in any number of ways, Jarrett glared at Lem, Stan, and even Jack. The three of them got his message clearly enough and kept their mouths shut.

"I'm just asking for your part of the story, is all," Jarrett said.

"Ain't much to tell. Not much that you don't already know, that is. Me and Tom showed up on account of the shots that were fired, we had a look around, and all there was to see was the mess that was left behind."

"Yeah, you sure were right, Sheriff," Lem said. "It'd be

a crying shame to accuse the law in that town of sitting on their haunches."

"What would have made you feel better?" Rubin asked. "Have me and my boys magically divine when something bad was about to happen?"

"I think he'd like it if every lawman in the county stood close to him so they could wipe his nose every time he had a sniffle," Tom said.

"That's enough of this bickering," Jarrett cut in before any more barbed comments could be tossed in either direction. "We're not here to squabble like a bunch of women. We're here to follow these tracks to the men that made them. If we're still of a mind to fight when this job is done, I'm sure we won't have any trouble finding a volunteer to throw the first punch."

"I agree," Ackerman said.

Both of the other lawmen looked over at the younger deputy.

Ackerman shrugged. "Well," he said reluctantly, "except for the part about throwing a punch."

"We're wasting daylight," Tom said as he snapped his reins. "Let's get a move on."

Most of the other men were agreeable to that and they urged their horses to pick up the pace. Sheriff Rubin was the only one to lag behind and he waited for Jarrett to ride past him before calling out, "Mr. Pekoe! A moment of your time?"

Jarrett slowed Twitch with a tug of leather straps, causing the horse to fret before huffing a few choppy breaths. "What is it, Sheriff?"

When Tom turned to look back, Rubin motioned for him to carry on. "There was more that happened the other night."

"Then why didn't you mention it before?" Jarrett asked.

"Actually I thought you might have something say on the matter."

"Now, why would you think that?"

Rubin studied him carefully as their horses fell into a quick trot beside each other. Finally the lawman said, "A man was killed last night. Near as we can tell, it wasn't much past the time when the bunch of you were ambushed while taking your baths together."

"They weren't taking baths together. They were just in the same room."

"That ain't the point. What's important is that the man that wound up dead comes awfully close to the description of the big fella who stormed that hotel."

"Is that so?"

"I'd imagine you *know* it is."

Jarrett felt his stomach clench at the certainty in the sheriff's tone. "What makes you so sure?" he asked.

"Because one of my men was left behind at my office this morning," Rubin said. "He would've been the one to tell you to meet us at your ranch and he would have also told you about the dead man that was discovered."

"Right. So he was. But, short of us turning around to head back into town, there's no way of me knowing if that dead man was the same one from the hotel or not."

"I just have one more question for you, Mr. Pekoe. Did you kill that fella who fired a shot at you and your men?"

Although he'd been expecting to be asked that question at some time or other, Jarrett wasn't thinking this would be that time. For once, he was grateful for Twitch's nervous tendencies because putting the gelding back on a straight course gave Jarrett an excuse to divert his attention for a few moments. Although he wouldn't have minded stretching that time out a lot longer, Jarrett didn't want to do anything to make the sheriff even more suspicious. "I would have been well within my rights to shoot him," Jarrett said. "Especially since he was the one who came in with guns blazing."

"And that's what the witnesses at the hotel told me," Rubin said. "What I'm asking is if you tracked that gunman down to Annie's, got him to step outside, and then shot him several times in the chest."

"No. I certainly did not."

"Do you know who would do such a thing?"

"Considering what little I saw of that man, I'd guess there are plenty in this world who wouldn't mind doing such a thing to him."

The sheriff looked over to him. "You're deliberately trying to make this more difficult."

"Am I?"

"The phrase 'pulling teeth' is what comes to mind."

"Look, Sheriff. If you're expecting me to be surprised that someone killed that man the other night, I am. If you're expecting me to be sorry that he's dead, then you're gonna be mighty disappointed, because that just won't happen."

"So you didn't shoot him?"

"No," Jarrett replied.

"And you don't know who did?"

"No."

After studying him for a few seconds more, the sheriff gave him a single, curt nod. "All right, then. I suppose I've got my answer. These tracks here are easy enough to follow, so you and your men try to gain as much ground as you can while I send one or two scouts ahead to see if any of these rustlers split off from the main group."

"I can scout ahead also," Jarrett offered. "I've had some experience in that regard."

"I'm sure you have, but you've got more experience with cattle. Let us see what there is to see, and if we find anything, we can discuss options on breaking off into even smaller groups."

"Whatever you say."

"That's right. What I say goes out here," Rubin said. "Best you don't forget it."

Keeping his face as calm as possible as the lawman flicked his reins to gallop ahead and catch up with his deputies, Jarrett held his breath until the other man was safely away. As soon as there was a comfortable amount of distance between them, he exhaled and allowed himself to slump for a second or two. Jack, Lem, and Stan remained clustered together and turned around to get a look at him after Sheriff Rubin had thundered by.

Jarrett straightened up and steeled himself for his own sake as well as to keep up appearances for his men. After coming up alongside the group, he pulled back on Twitch's reins to keep from leaving them behind.

"Problem?" Stan asked.

"Not at all," Jarrett said. "Let's fan out and watch them tracks to see if any of the rustlers driving this herd split off from the rest."

Jack nodded and led Stan away.

Before Lem could follow suit, Jarrett leaned over to him and said, "Watch your back."

Lem nodded as if he knew everything that Sheriff Rubin had said. "Always do."

Chapter 19

The rest of that day consisted in hard riding and constant vigilance. If Jarrett wasn't watching the ground for signs that he was still on the trail of his herd, he was moving along the edge of those deep imprints to see if he could find a hint that some of the rustlers had veered off in another direction. Jarrett found no indication that any of the men who'd taken his cattle left the herd. That didn't mean it hadn't happened, but the lawmen couldn't find any additional tracks either, so he just had to figure the outlaws had remained in one large group. Considering the fact that everyone at the Lazy J had been left for dead, that wasn't too surprising. Clay and his murderous partners must have thought they had all the time in the world to do as they pleased. That notion stuck like a cold dagger in Jarrett's chest.

When the sun dipped below the western horizon, Jarrett was fully prepared to spur that posse on until the last possible second. That wasn't necessary, however, since the men in the posse continued to ride until they couldn't take another step. A small campfire was put together, a simple dinner was prepared, and they all went to sleep. A short while before sunup, Jarrett woke up first and roused the others from their uncomfortable slumber.

The men gnawed on some jerked beef for breakfast, washed it down with gritty coffee, and got right back to work.

Jarrett's herd might not have been as big as some, but it left behind plenty of tracks to follow. Jarrett and the men followed it so easily that they joked about seeing patterns in the dirt whenever they closed their eyes. Late that morning, before it got too close to noon, Jarrett approached the sheriff while Rubin slowed to speak to Tom.

"Me and the others have been talking," Jarrett said.

"Oh, have you?" Tom sneered.

"Give it a rest," Rubin grunted to his deputy. "What is it, Mr. Pekoe?"

"It doesn't take much to follow these tracks," Jarrett said. "In fact, I'm pretty sure I know where the herd is being taken."

"Let's hear it."

"There's a town less than a day's ride from here. Little speck of a place called Muriel."

Rubin nodded. "I've heard of it."

"It's due south of here, with maybe a slight jog to the west," Jarrett continued. "I think that's where my herd is headed."

"Why that spot and not another?"

"If he was looking to sell cattle, the main routes would have taken them either southeast into Kansas or on a straighter southerly path toward Texas. There are plenty of ranches and buyers along the way, but most of them would be along that same route."

"That's an awful lot to glean from looking at prints in the dirt for a day and a half," Tom scoffed.

Jarrett waited for the sheriff to bring his deputy in line. Although Rubin did shoot the younger lawman a stern glare, it wasn't enough to keep Tom's mouth shut for more than a couple of seconds. Shifting that same glare toward Jarrett, Rubin said, "Tom's got a point. That's a big leap to make."

"There's an easy way to see if I'm right. Let me and one or two others ride on ahead to Muriel so we can see it for ourselves. It won't be a long ride for men on horseback, but a herd of cattle couldn't have expected to get there until tomorrow morning at the earliest."

"And what happens if you and one of those ranch hands you brought along does come across them rustlers?" Rubin asked.

"We can handle ourselves," Jarrett insisted. "If you're concerned, then send one of your deputies along with me. All we need to do is ride ahead, scout that town, and come back."

"Let's say those rustlers aren't there. If me and the rest of the men you leave behind cross paths with them, we'll be shorthanded."

"Only until we get back."

"It's a stupid idea," Tom snapped. "Now go back to studying dirt."

"I should send the two of you out on this errand," Sheriff Rubin groaned. "At least I'd be fairly certain only one of you would come back to give me any more grief."

"And I'd be real damn certain of who it would be to come back," Tom said with all the grit and bravado one would expect from a man trying to prove his worth.

Jarrett wasn't about to lock horns with him over something as meaningless as boastful words. In fact, as he kept silent, he hoped to make the younger man look even worse. His gamble paid off when the sheriff looked to his deputy and said, "Tom, go on ahead and see if Troy found anything."

"What's he supposed to find?"

"If I have to tell you that after all this time, then you might as well turn right around and get back to Flat Pass, 'cause you won't do me a lick of good out here!"

Grunting under his breath, Tom jerked his reins to steer his horse toward the west, which was where Ackerman had gone. He even goaded his horse with added enthusiasm as if that alone would be enough to make anyone watching quake in their boots.

Rubin let out a deep sigh before asking, "What makes you so sure them rustlers would want to go to Muriel?"

"There's a man who lives there who goes by the name of Roland Gein."

"Goes by that name? You think he's got another name?"

"Probably," Jarrett said. "Most likely, he's got a few other names. The one he uses around here is Gein, and anyone who knows him also knows he's the man to go to if you need to sell stolen goods."

"Even cattle?"

"Especially cattle."

"You know a lot about where to sell and, I presume, buy stolen cattle."

"Of course I do," Jarrett said. "Just like someone who buys and sells paintings knows where the forgeries are to be found. A man needs to know his business, and them who work on the fringes of that business are real big parts of it."

The sheriff nodded. "You think this is the best bet as far as where that herd may be going?"

"I do."

"I've heard of a few places where rustlers go to sell off what they stole, but this ain't exactly one of 'em. You sure about this fella?"

Jarrett smirked. "No offense, Sheriff, but any outlaw that stays in one place for long and prospers there is bound to be good at keeping out of a lawman's sight. There are other men in Gein's line of work, to be certain, but he's the one that pays the best and is most trusted."

When Sheriff Rubin turned toward him again, he said, "I don't know whether to admire you or be suspicious."

"Shouldn't you be more suspicious of a man in my profession who didn't know about men like Roland Gein?"

"I suppose so. That still doesn't take away from the concerns I already mentioned. If you do find them rustlers, you'll be outgunned. If those rustlers find us while you're away, we'll be outgunned. Neither one is much good."

"You have my word that I won't be gone for more than a day or so. Just like you should accept that I know how my business works, I'll accept that you know what you're doing. Whether them rustlers find you or you find them, I'm sure you can handle yourself. Besides, it wouldn't be much different if you faced those men now or if you'd gotten a chance to face them when my ranch was put to the torch. Ain't that right?"

The sheriff let the barbed comment roll off his back in much the same way he'd dealt with his deputy's smart mouth. "I understand how anxious you are to ride after these men, Jarrett. If I was in your spot, I'd want the same thing. That's why I not only let you come along on this posse, but let you bring your own boys as well."

"*Let* me come along?" Jarrett said. The words grated on him just as badly when he said them as when they'd been spoken to him.

To his credit, Rubin didn't back down. "That's right," he said. "I let you come along when I should have insisted you stay home and get your head straight. It hasn't been that long since everything went to hell for you."

"You think I don't know that?"

"The wound's still fresh. And like any wounded man with a job to do, you want to keep on moving through the pain. That don't mean it's in your best interest to do so. A man with a lust for blood can do a lot more damage to himself or them that's around him. You should think about that before you insist on riding off on your own."

Forcing himself to simmer down a bit, Jarrett said, "I have been thinking about it, Sheriff. I'm not just charging off half-cocked."

"Really? And did you think about what happens if you're spotted either in Muriel or on your way to it?"

"I told you, we can all handle ourselves. If that wasn't the case, then none of us should be out here."

"I'm not talking about handling yourself," Rubin said. "I'm talking about alerting those killers that we're onto them. Surely they must already be looking for the law to hunt them down. Men like that live every day like that. But if someone like this Gein fella gets wind of a posse on the way or that it's already so close to catching up with that herd, he'll most likely pass word along to those rustlers. After all, how do you think a man in that line of work builds up so much trust with his customers? I guarantee it's not just by setting good prices for stolen cows."

Jarrett hadn't thought about that. Even if he wasn't about to say as much to the sheriff, it was obvious that Rubin could read it for himself just by looking at him.

"You see," Rubin said, "knowing such things about how outlaws work is what I do, Mr. Pekoe. Just like you know things about raising and trading cattle."

"You're right, Sheriff. Sorry to underestimate you."

"I'm not looking for apologies. I'm looking for you to

stay true to your word by doing what you assured me you'd do when I first agreed to let you ride along on this posse. That's follow the orders I give you while we're out here."

Jarrett didn't have anything else to say. He also wasn't about to tuck his tail between his legs to get back in Rubin's good graces.

After a few seconds, Rubin said, "On the other hand, you do raise an interesting point where this man Gein is concerned. You're certain he's known well enough for these rustlers to know about him?"

"If I wasn't certain, I wouldn't want to waste time in riding all the way out to Muriel."

"And what if you do find the men you're after?"

"If I find them, I'll bring you straight to them," Jarrett said. "The benefit here is that we could get a chance to get ahead of those rustlers instead of trailing behind them."

"I know the benefits. Tell me, Mr. Pekoe. What would you do if I refused to sign off on this venture you're proposing?"

"Then I go back to what I was doing and try to think of some other way for us to get this job done even quicker."

If that wasn't the answer Rubin had been looking for, it was sure close enough, because he grudgingly agreed. Jarrett was certain the sheriff would insist on accompanying him personally, but that wasn't the case. Instead Rubin rode ahead to meet his two deputies, who were just now returning to the rest of the group.

Jarrett met up with Jack and Stan, who were riding down the middle of the wide set of tracks left by cattle that had recently trampled that patch of land. It wasn't much longer before Lem came in from searching for diverging tracks to join them as well.

"What was all that about?" Stan asked. "You in trouble or something?"

Jarrett quickly explained the proposition he'd given to the sheriff. When he was through, Stan said, "I've heard Gein's name brought up once or twice, but that's about it. Sounds like you're certain about him being the man to ask, though."

"He's the man, all right," Lem said.

Having never tried to hide his lack of trust in Lem, Stan turned to him and said, "If you knew about a man like Gein, then you should've said something! You think we're all out here for our health?"

"There are plenty of men out there who'll buy stolen cattle," Jarrett said in a voice that he hoped wasn't loud enough to carry. "If I brought up every last one of them, there'd be a dozen places to try and only a handful of us to go there. We're heading toward Muriel because my gut tells me that's the place where my herd is being sold."

"Sounds like it's just one of the most obvious choices," Stan said. "If them rustlers are looking to lie low, I doubt they'd want to be obvious."

"They killed everyone they could back at the Lazy J and tried to kill us," Jarrett said. "For all they know, they succeeded."

"No," Lem said. "They're not gonna think they succeeded. Not completely anyway."

"What makes you so damn sure?" Stan asked.

"Because you killed one or two of them that same night, didn't you? When those men don't come back, someone's going to miss them."

Jarrett laughed as if he was trying to loosen something from the back of his throat. "Do you really think a bunch of murdering bastards like that will be too upset if a few of their number don't come back?"

"Yeah," Stan said. "They'll probably just be glad there's fewer ways to split the money they're gonna get from that herd."

Lem considered that for a moment and then shrugged. "You could be right about that. I'm just saying those rustlers will be on their guard. And if a few of them did ride on ahead to have a word with Gein to let him know they were coming, things could get even more interesting." Seeing the confusion on the ranch hands' faces, Lem added, "Could very well be that someone like Gein might want to protect his investment."

"All right," Jarrett said. "That's something good to keep in mind. Makes me feel smart for choosing you to be the one to go along with me to Muriel."

Chapter 20

It was one of the rare occasions when Twitch wasn't the only overly anxious horse in a group. All three horses making the ride into Muriel were so happy to be allowed to run at full speed that it seemed they were racing each other into town. After being held back to a trot while their riders busied themselves with their search, the horses indulged to such a degree that the ride into Muriel was completed in less time than Jarrett had thought possible.

When they'd first left, Jarrett was hoping Sheriff Rubin might forget about sending one of his deputies along or at least think twice about it. Instead the next best thing happened and Ackerman was tasked with accompanying him and Lem. The youngest of the lawmen was an affable fellow who was too early into his career to care about much more than doing his job properly. He also seemed to be just a bit intimidated by Lem, which could work to Jarrett's advantage. For the moment, however, the three of them were all on the same page, which brought them to their destination all the quicker.

Muriel was a cow town in every sense of the term. Just by looking at the wide streets, the holding pens scattered throughout, and the abundance of granaries and saloons,

Jarrett could tell it was built by ranchers for ranchers. If one part of the town wasn't made to cater to those buying or selling beef, it was tailor-made to draw the money from a cowboy's pocket. Throughout a good portion of the jobs he'd had in his life, Jarrett had been on one side of that coin or the other.

"Is this the place?" Ackerman asked.

Jarrett looked around at the row of stores and stables on either side of the wide dirt lane between them. "What were you expecting?" he asked.

"I don't know. Streets?"

"Streets are generally too narrow for many cows or wagons to be brought through."

"If someone has a herd to sell, they bring it straight into town?"

"You're not from around these parts, are you?" Lem chuckled.

"I've lived in Cheyenne and Kansas City," Ackerman replied. "Bigger towns before that, but not a place like this."

Jarrett looked around and tried to see the place through fresher eyes. There were no boardwalks to be found, and alleys between the buildings were wide enough to be streets themselves. While Jarrett hadn't seen the biggest cities to be found, he'd seen ones large enough to make Muriel seem like a trading post in comparison. "Well, this is the place, all right," he told the young deputy. "Just because the buildings are few and far between, don't think you've seen all there is to see."

"I'm no fool," Ackerman said indignantly.

"Yeah, well, don't say that too loud," Lem said to him. "Could work to your favor for folks to underestimate you as much as possible. Just keep your head high and a mean expression on your face and you should be fine."

"Also, keep the badge where it can be seen, right?" Ackerman said while peeling back the flap of his jacket.

Lem was quick to respond, "No. If this town is home to a man like this Gein fellow, representing the law may not be a good idea."

"Agreed," Jarrett said. "Let's just keep from drawing too much attention so we can get a look around. Come to think of it," he added while squinting at something down the street a ways, "I may have already found something."

"What is it?" Ackerman asked.

"You two just find somewhere to tie the horses while I have a look."

Lem and Ackerman watched him ride ahead. Although the deputy obviously wanted to follow him, he was discouraged by a few words from Lem. Jarrett couldn't hear what was said, but it was enough to convince the deputy to stay put.

What had caught Jarrett's attention wasn't a sight but a sound. With Jarret's having spent so much of his time around herds of cattle, his senses were honed so sharply to them that he could feel the thump of their hooves against the ground from a hundred yards away. His ears picked up on their bovine grunts, breaths, and cries the way a mother could pick up on the discontent of her baby from just a sleepy sigh escaping a little mouth. Such things allowed him to sit at a campfire while on a drive and still know if the herd was at rest or gearing up for a stampede.

The sounds he heard weren't anything close to a panicked group of cattle, but he could at least tell that there were several animals nearby. Since he couldn't see anything more than a few horses tied to hitching posts here and there, his gut told him the animals he'd heard were being hidden. Jarrett followed the sounds down the street to a wide, low building situated between a feed store and what looked to be a barn. As with all of the buildings in Muriel, there was enough space between them for two wagons to roll side by side.

Jarrett tied Twitch next to another horse outside the feed store. From there, he hurried toward the wide building next door and circled around it. Sure enough, there was a sizable lot behind that building where at least two dozen cattle were nudging each other to get their noses into a trough that was just a bit too short to accommodate them all at once.

"Easy, now," he said as he approached the fence surrounding the lot. Two of the cows had spotted him and reflexively shuffled away. Jarrett reached out to place both hands on the fence while leaning over the top of it. "Just want to get a look at ya," he said in a quiet, soothing tone.

Like most cows, these were generally nervous but not anxious enough to do much about it. Jarrett didn't want to get close enough to give them much more of a fright than he already had done, but it seemed he did need to get closer than the fence would allow. The building to which the lot was connected had the look of a stable, but it could very well have been a warehouse of some kind. There were no markings to be found and no lights in the windows. Emboldened by the latter, but wary of the former, Jarrett hoisted himself up and over the fence to land carefully on the other side.

"Easy, girls," he whispered.

The closest cow glanced nervously at him with large brown eyes while taking small sidesteps in the opposite direction. As soon as he was within arm's reach, Jarrett placed a hand on her flank and gave the animal several gentle pats. That, combined with the soft clucking sounds he made, calmed the big animal down enough to focus on feed spilled from the trough instead of him.

If there was a sun shining down on him, Jarrett wouldn't have needed to climb the fence at all. He would have been able to see the brand on the cow's back end from a distance, or tell if there was even a brand at all. He studied the cow's flank for a few more seconds before finding the scars left by the iron of her owner.

"Damn," he whispered when he saw the broken circle marking that was completely unfamiliar to him.

Since he was already trespassing, Jarrett kept working his way through the milling cattle. Years of practice allowed him to keep from disturbing them very much as he got a look at as many as he could. The next few all bore a brand similar to the one Jarrett had already seen. A couple after that, however, bore another brand. This one was a lopsided *M* that was taller on the left. Three of them had brands that were too elaborate to be discerned without better light, and the next one he examined seemed much more familiar.

"What have we here?" he whispered as he touched the cow's flank to trace the brand. "Do I know you, girl?"

He stood up a little straighter to take stock of the cows he'd examined, only to see that he'd worked his way through more than half of the animals being held in the pen. When he got a look at the next animal in the group, he found another brand that struck a chord in his mind. There weren't many cows left in the pen that he hadn't already seen, but three of them bore a brand he recognized.

Jarrett crouched down low so he was just barely seeing over the rump of the nearest cow. While there might not have been enough light for him to spot brands from a distance, he could be certain enough that he was the only thing on two legs in that pen. Knowing how severely the owner of such a place might deal with intruders, he kept his body low and his steps as quiet as he could manage as he made his way to the nearby building.

The back wall had a set of barn doors leading into the pen, and Jarrett wasn't at all surprised to hear a lot more cows on the other side of that door. He tried to open it but could feel it was held in place by a latch on the other side. With a few harder pushes, though, the brackets holding that latch proved to have enough give in them to provide a narrow gap between the two doors. If he put some effort into it, he could possibly break the doors open. Rather than commit that particular crime after being in town for less than half an hour, Jarrett pulled the doors shut and took another quick look around.

There was still nobody else in the pen with him or anywhere in sight, for that matter. He could hear movement and voices from somewhere farther down the street, but the cattle were still relatively calm. Knowing better than to put too much stock in the mood of a bunch of dumb animals, Jarrett worked his way over to a small window left of the barn doors.

That window was positioned near the fence surrounding the pen. Several barrels were stacked nearby, most of them broken and on their side to form a heap of splintered wood and rusty hoops. Since getting close to that portion of the window would have been a noisy and possibly painful ordeal, he hurried to the fence and jumped over it to approach the other half of the window. He couldn't get as close as he would have liked, but at least Jarrett wasn't in a spot that would require so much explaining if he was discovered. For the moment, at least, that didn't seem to be a concern.

As Jarrett walked along the fence, he moved as if he were taking a stroll to enjoy a warm evening. He stopped short of whistling a tune so as not to draw any attention once he got close enough to the side of the building to get a look through the window. The glass was smeared with mud and had enough dust on it to form a gritty shell. After cleaning a small section in one corner, Jarrett leaned over to see what there was to see.

Inside, there was beef packed from one side of the building to another. As far as Jarrett could tell, the place was one big room with a few lanes sectioned off by low wooden rails. He could see plenty of movement, which wasn't much help. The glint of light coming through one wall, on the other hand, made Jarrett's heart skip a beat. On the opposite side of the building from where Jarrett was standing, toward the front wall, a door had been opened. He couldn't see the person who'd opened the door from his vantage point, but Jarrett had seen enough to know he'd overstayed his welcome. Even though the cows didn't seem to notice him being there any longer, he wasn't about to risk an introduction to the owner of that building. Having climbed onto the lowest rail of the fence so he could peek through the window, Jarrett lowered himself down and backed away.

Almost immediately, he was met by a stocky man holding a shotgun.

"What the hell are you doing there?" the man asked.

Jarrett smiled sheepishly. "I'm new in town. Must have come here by mistake. Sorry about that."

"Sorry, huh? Not half as sorry as you're about to be."

Chapter 21

"Keep your hands where I can see 'em," the man with the shotgun said.

Jarrett did as he was told and moved away from the window.

Balding and covered in dust, the man looked every bit like someone who'd spent the entire day working in a building full of cattle. His eyes showed anger, but no more than what was called for by the situation. "What are you doing here?" he asked. "And don't give me no talk about you making a mistake!"

"It is a mistake," Jarrett said. "Like I said, I'm new in town. When I got here, I was looking for a stable. This seemed to fit the bill, so I was just looking to have a word with someone who works here."

"You found him, but this ain't no stable where you can put your horse."

"Do you have any idea where I might find such a place?"

The man's eyes darted down to Jarrett's gun belt, and his hands tightened around his shotgun. "You lookin' to steal these cows?"

"What? No!"

"You a lawman?"

"Not hardly. I assure you, I'm just looking for a place to put my horse up for the night so I can get a hot meal and bed for myself. If you don't have any recommendations, then I'll be on my way."

When the man's shoulders came down from around his ears, Jarrett thought he might be in the clear. All too quickly, however, the man tensed once again. "Toss that pistol and let me get a look at you."

Just then, Jarrett saw Lem and Ackerman come down the street. He waved to both men before immediately extending his hands even higher above his head.

"Who are they?" the man asked.

"They came with me." Before either of the other two could say anything, Jarrett quickly added, "We're just passing through. No need for trouble."

Ackerman started to say something while reaching for the section of his jacket covering his badge, but Lem quickly stopped him with an extended arm. Once the deputy lowered his hand, Lem asked, "There a problem here?"

"They're my friends," Jarrett said. "And there's no problem. This is just a mistake."

Although Ackerman and Lem weren't at ease, they were willing to hold their ground and see what happened next.

The man with the shotgun shifted nervously like so many of the cows penned nearby.

"I'm going to put my gun on the ground," Jarrett said.

"Easy," the man warned.

Jarrett removed the Colt using just his thumb and forefinger and set it near his feet.

"Kick it over here."

Following the command he'd been given, Jarrett used one boot to shove the pistol away. His two partners became even more uncomfortable, especially when the man with the shotgun stepped forward to tap both barrels against Jarrett's belly. "I'm gonna have a look beneath that jacket," he said.

Jarrett nodded. "Be my guest."

The man's search was quick and when he was through, he stepped back. Lowering the shotgun slightly, he said, "Get out of my sight and don't let me catch you snooping around here again."

"I'm taking my gun back," Jarrett said.

After taking a few seconds to consider that, the man nodded once. "Then be on your way."

"Most definitely."

The man with the shotgun left the Colt where it lay and backed toward the fence. He then watched all three of them like a hawk guarding its hatchlings.

Jarrett picked up his pistol and eased it into his holster. He then kept his hands out to either side while backing away.

Unable to contain himself any longer, Ackerman asked, "You sure there's nothing I can do to help?"

The deputy was itching to assert his authority, but at least he knew enough to ask before doing so. Jarrett nodded and told him, "No need for any help. I'm just taking my horse to a stable. I'm sure I can find one nearby."

Some small part of Jarrett's mind thought he might get the recommendation he'd wanted from the man with the shotgun. That part would have been dead wrong, because the man grunted once under his breath and walked around the building to get back to the open door that Jarrett had spotted through the window.

Still keeping his movements nice and slow, Jarrett walked over to the spot where he'd put Twitch and loosened the reins so he could lead the gelding away from the post. After moving an acceptable distance from the cattle pen, Ackerman asked, "What in blazes was the meaning of that?"

"We're here looking for cattle," Jarrett replied. "There's a lot of cattle being kept here and it seemed prudent to have a look."

"Was it prudent to wind up on the wrong end of a shotgun?" Lem asked.

"No. That part wasn't very prudent."

"Before we take another step, you need to tell me how that came about," Ackerman demanded.

"Maybe I got a little anxious," Jarrett said. "I admit that much."

Lem shook his head. "That's real big of you."

The three of them walked along the side of the street. More people were appearing, but none of them cast a second glance at the town's newest arrivals. They were more interested in getting to one of the saloons that were growing louder with every passing second.

Jarrett kept walking and made sure not to speak too loudly when he said, "I've heard some things about this town from plenty of the men who've come to work on my ranch over the last few years. One of the things that have been said was that stolen cattle or horses could be found right out in the open. When I heard what sounded like a good number of cows nearby, I had to take a look."

"And why didn't you ask us to come along?" Ackerman asked. "Aren't we all supposed to be doing this together?"

"I thought I'd attract less attention if I went on my own."

Jarrett had fully expected Lem to say something to that. Instead of providing a sarcastic comment, Lem merely laughed.

Seeing the disapproval on the young deputy's face and not appreciating it one bit, Jarrett said, "You were content to follow our lead this far. If you think you can make better progress than us . . . go right ahead."

Lem raised an eyebrow.

"What is it?" Jarrett asked. He might not have spent years with Lem, but he'd ridden with him long enough to know when he thought he had an ace up his sleeve. "Don't make me ask twice."

Nudging Ackerman, Lem said, "Go on and tell him."

Jarrett scowled up at the young man. "Tell me what?"

Although he seemed mildly embarrassed, Ackerman couldn't help puffing his chest out a bit when he said, "I found Roland Gein."

"You met him already?"

"No. I said I found him," Ackerman clarified. "I know where to go and when to be there."

"Even better," Lem added, "he arranged a meeting."

"I could've done that," Jarrett said.

"But it's better coming from him," Lem said while hooking a thumb toward the deputy. "No real chance of him being recognized."

"I'm not exactly infamous, you know," Jarrett said.

"Right. You're just a successful rancher looking for stolen cattle. Considering how we just found you," Lem said, "I'd say you're doing real well with keeping from being noticed."

As the sun crawled toward the western horizon, Muriel grew louder and brighter. Not only were lanterns lit in most of the windows facing the main road, but an old-timer in a raggedy brown coat walked down one side of the pathway to light torches that were stuck into the dirt. Not wanting to be heard by that old man or anyone else in the vicinity, Jarrett led Twitch to a restaurant advertising a cheap steak dinner special and leaned against a rail that was to be used as a hitching post.

"How'd you manage to find Gein?" Jarrett asked one of the men who'd followed him.

Ackerman climbed down from his saddle and secured his reins to the rail. "I was arranging for a place to put the horses up and someone asked if I wanted to sell them. I asked who was interested in them and he mentioned Gein by name."

Now it was Jarrett's turn to laugh. "And here I thought you'd gone through some kind of investigation."

"Most of a lawman's work is done by keeping his eyes and ears open," Ackerman pointed out. "Did you have anything else better to go by . . . apart from knowing that Gein was somewhere in this town?"

"Yes," Jarrett said. "But not much."

"Hopefully you found something else. Otherwise we all just made a loud entrance into this town for no good reason."

"I did find something. Some cows from my herd for starters."

That brought the other two in a bit closer so they could speak in quieter tones. "You're certain they're yours?" Lem asked.

"I saw the brands myself."

Ackerman's eyes widened expectantly. "Then all we need to do is go back and get a few of them to prove they were stolen. By law, the owner of that stable will have to tell you where he got them."

"It's not that simple."

"It never is," Lem sighed.

"The brand's been altered," Jarrett said.

Ackerman shook his head. "For all you know, it could just be a brand that looks similar to yours. I've seen the

Lazy J's mark. There must be plenty out there close to it in some way."

"No. It's my brand. It's just been altered."

"You've got to be completely certain about that," the deputy warned. "Otherwise it won't stand up in court."

"I'm certain," Jarrett said with absolute confidence. "I've seen more than enough altered brands to recognize another one. Especially when it's mine in the first place."

"There's one man who'll either know the truth of the matter for certain or be able to find out quickly enough," Lem said.

Jarrett gave Ackerman a friendly pat on the shoulder. "And we've got an appointment to speak to him real soon."

Chapter 22

There were only two saloons in Muriel. Each was situated on opposite ends of town from each other to divide what seemed to be a lucrative liquor trade. Between the locals, cowboys, and unsavory types drifting through, there were plenty of business opportunities for both places to stake their claim. One of the saloons was MacGrearey's: a bar stuck in amid a collection of mismatched tables beneath a large canvas tent. Within seconds after stepping into the place, one big difference between that saloon and most others became plenty clear.

"No gambling?" Ackerman said as he read a sign posted behind the bar. "That's mighty strange for a saloon."

"You want to gamble, you go to the place on the other side of town," Jarrett explained. "You want to buy the attentions of a woman for the night, you come here."

"Sounds like you know a lot on the subject."

"I've heard plenty about this place from the hands that have drifted through the Lazy J looking for work. Not all of them think of stolen cattle when they talk about Muriel."

One of the many women in the saloon worked her way over to Ackerman. She was a tall redhead with ample hips and a dress that barely kept her covered. She smelled like vanilla and smiled with thick red lips. When she saw the nervous expression on the young deputy's face, she moved over to Lem, who snaked one arm around her waist. "I can see why," he said. "There seems to be a whole lot more to this place than the cows that come through it."

"You can say that again," the redhead purred.

"Time for that later," Jarrett said.

She looked over to him and asked, "You promise?"

It was a long time since Jarrett had blushed. Just having the voluptuous redhead look at him with her deep, hungry eyes was enough to do the trick.

Lem chuckled and swatted her on the backside. "He's right. Business first." Seeing the little pout she gave him, he added, "I don't like it either, darlin'. That's just the way it goes."

She shrugged and walked away. As she passed Ackerman, she brushed a hand against his cheek and puckered her lips to send him a kiss.

"I see you've found something to your liking," proclaimed a large man with a wide chest and an even wider belly. He was dressed in light brown clothes that seemed better suited to the desert than the rolling Wyoming trails. His head sprouted thick, dark curls from every possible angle starting at the chin, moving up to his ears and ending with a mop covering most of his scalp. As he approached the three new arrivals, he opened his arms as if he meant to embrace them all at once. "Welcome to MacGrearey's!"

"Are you the owner?" Jarrett asked.

"Part owner. I take it this young fellow here is Mr. Ackerman?"

"That's right," the deputy said.

"I'm Roland Gein," the wide man said. "I have a private table in back. Let's have a seat and discuss business."

When Gein turned to walk through the saloon, Jarrett followed him. Ackerman started to as well but was held back a few steps by Lem, who grabbed his arm and hissed, "You didn't tell me you gave him your real name."

"What name should I have given?"

"One that's not attached to a deputy."

"Too late now."

"Let's hope not," Lem said while letting go of Ackerman's arm. "For your sake."

As they made their way through the crowded saloon, several of the girls drifted over to touch the men's shoulders, brush against them, or even just smile in a way to let them know they were interested. As far as Jarrett could tell, every single one of them was interested. As soon as they made their presence known, they deferred to Gein and faded back into the crowd without otherwise disturbing the solidly built man.

The table at the back of the saloon was surrounded by smaller tables where armed men were seated. In a place that seemed to have been built more as an afterthought instead of a permanent fixture in that town, it was the closest thing Gein could get to sitting with his back to a wall. Lowering himself onto a chair that creaked loudly in protest, Gein set one hand on the table in front of him and let the other dangle off the backrest. "What can I do for you?" he asked.

Ackerman looked first to Lem. When he looked to Jarrett, he got a subtle nod and a wave to let him know he was free to lead the way. There were four other chairs situated around the table, so Ackerman sat down in one that put him more or less directly in front of Gein. Lem and Jarrett sat on either side of him but leaned back as if they were barely there at all.

"I heard that you buy horses," Ackerman said.

"That's true enough," Gein replied through a smile that could hardly be seen through his beard.

"I've heard you buy . . . horses that a man . . . may not be able to sell just anywhere."

Gein leaned forward. "Really? Is that what you've heard? And why wouldn't this man be able to sell these horses just anywhere?"

"Because . . ."

"Because they're stolen?" Gein asked. His eyes widened a bit, making him look as though his was mildly appalled by such a prospect.

"Well . . . yeah. Because they're stolen."

Gein's smile might not have grown any wider, but it appeared to be a lot more genuine as he eased back into his chair once more. "You can let out the breath you're holding, young fellow. We're in a town full of stolen horses, sitting in a place where women get paid to tell lies to men before taking them to their beds. If we can't speak freely here, then we can't speak freely anywhere!"

"All right, then. How much will you pay for my horses?"

"How many horses do you have? Just the three you men rode in on?"

"That's right."

"Do you know who I am?"

Ackerman blinked in confusion. The men on either side of him, however, were more disturbed than confused. Jarrett shifted in his seat, knowing better than to even think about moving his hand toward his gun. Lem, on the other hand, inched his arm back so that hand hung closer to his holster. As Jarrett had expected, some of the armed men at the nearby tables didn't take kindly to that at all.

"Let me ask that question again," Gein said. "Do you know who I am?"

"Of course I do," Ackerman said.

"Not you," Gein snapped with a dismissive wave. "Them two."

Lem's eyes narrowed, but he kept his mouth shut.

"Yes," Jarrett replied. "I know who you are, but we've never met."

"Is that why you sent your boy here to ask for me?" Gein asked. "So you three could get good and close while I just assumed you weren't anything more than a few simpletons looking to unload a few horses?"

"We came to Muriel to speak to you," Jarrett replied. "Time isn't on our side and we weren't certain we could just walk in and ask for a moment of yours."

"Well, let me tell you something," Gein snarled. "You would've been right. If I sat down to personally talk with every filthy bugger that came in off that trail, I'd never have a moment to think. While I don't like being lied to, I gotta admire your pluck. Sending that kid straight in here got me curious. Also," he added with a shrug, "you happened to catch me on a slow night. There's just one thing that bothers me, though, which is one of the bigger reasons I agreed to have this personal talk with you."

"What's that?" Ackerman asked.

"I wonder if you three think I'm stupid."

"Not hardly!" the deputy said.

But Gein clearly wasn't interested in Ackerman's opinions. In fact, he'd stopped responding in any way to anything the young man said. Gein's eyes darted back and forth between Jarrett and Lem while he drummed thick fingers on the table in front of him. "Tell me something, kid," Gein said without so much as glancing at Ackerman. "Do you know who you've got riding with you?"

"Of course·I do," Ackerman said. He was clearly getting tired of being treated like a child, which didn't make a dent in any of the men surrounding him.

Gein spoke in a tone that was bereft of all the hospitality he'd shown earlier. "I know who you are . . . Mr. Pekoe."

Jarrett nodded at Gein. He was surprised to hear his name spoken by the big man, but he did his best not to let it show. Judging by the confidence etched into Gein's face, he didn't need affirmation to know he'd struck a nerve.

"You're not here to sell any horses," Gein said. "We may not have met face-to-face before, but I've heard enough about you to know you thought you ran the Lazy J as aboveboard as possible."

"There wasn't anything below-board with my ranch," Jarrett said proudly.

Gein shrugged. "No man can watch every angle every moment of every day. But if it makes you feel any better, I know of your ranch mainly because it's one of the few that puts less money in my pocket than most. Every spread gets a few head of cattle taken every now and then, but some spring more leaks than others."

Jarrett wasn't overly familiar with the inner workings of acquiring stolen cattle, but in a strange way, Gein's words did make him feel a little better. At least his ranch had run almost as smoothly as he'd hoped.

Gein furrowed his brow. "What I'm asking myself now is why an upstanding rancher like yourself would come to me?"

"My ranch is gone," Jarrett said.

"Pardon?"

Jarrett nodded. "Burned to the ground by a bunch of murderous thieves who made off with my herd."

"I . . . hadn't heard that," Gein said. This time, he seemed completely sincere in his bewilderment. "You said . . . murderous?"

"I did. My family. My . . ." Jarrett took a moment to draw a deep breath. While the pain was still very close to the surface, it was more of a jabbing blade instead of the pressing weight it had been. "My men," he continued. "They were killed."

Gein's expression darkened. Without knowing what exactly was going through his mind, every man in the vicinity could only hope the powerful anger boiling within him wasn't directed at them. "All your men?" he asked.

"No. Some made it, but that's only because I could get to them before the fire did."

"That's a true shame, Mr. Pekoe. I pray you don't think I would have had anything to do with something like that."

"Honestly, I don't know for certain if you did or didn't. What I do know is that you're one of the first men those thieves might come to when looking to sell the cattle they stole from me."

Gein twitched, possibly at the fact that he hadn't heard exactly what he'd been hoping to hear. Rather than rush to his own defense, he nodded. "You could be right about that. What do you want me to do in that event? Turn them away on principle?"

"I want to find those men, plain and simple."

"And then what?"

"If you'd lost your family to a bunch of animals, what would you want to do after finding them?"

"We're not exactly cut from the same cloth, now, are

we?" Gein replied. "Wanting to extract a certain price from someone isn't quite the same as doing what's necessary to make certain that price is paid."

"I want to find those men," Jarrett growled.

"I heard you the first time."

"Then stop feeding me all this guff and tell me whether or not you'll help me."

A few of the men standing nearby started to move forward with painful intentions written on their scarred faces. Gein held them back with a simple gesture from one hand before setting his face into an expression that could have been forged in iron. "Don't mistake my good nature for weakness. I don't care who you are or what kind of tragedy has befallen you. I will not stand for anyone walking up to me and treating me with disrespect."

Jarrett could only hope he wasn't tipping his hand as far as his true nervousness was concerned. It was all he could do to maintain a hard-edged expression that could hold a candle to Gein's.

"It's in your best interest to help us," Ackerman said.

"Really?" Gein mused as if he'd only just taken the slightest interest in what the young man had to say. "How so?"

Before Ackerman could speak again, Jarrett said, "If you tell me where to find these men, I can pay you. Handsomely."

"No offense meant, but didn't you just get finished telling me how your spread was burned down?" Gein asked.

"I still own the property," Jarrett explained. "And I still have a bank account."

"How much are you offering to pay?"

"Five hundred dollars. Just for pointing us in the right direction."

Gein's eyebrows lifted slightly. "Not bad."

"It gets better. If you deliver those men to me, or at least the one leading them, I'll pay you even more."

"How much more?"

"You hand over that pack of dogs," Jarrett said, "and you can keep however many cattle are brought to you. I don't pretend to know how much you pay or how you make a profit in dealing with stolen beef, but I've got to imagine you'll earn a lot more if you don't have to pay for the initial purchase."

"You'd be right about that . . . if I didn't have to first get them cattle from whoever has them now."

"I know who's got them," Jarrett said. "I'm making it my business to find them, and when I do, they won't be able to sell, buy, or steal anything again. I'll reclaim my herd and then I'll sign them over to you straightaway. All you need to do is hold up your end of the bargain. Pure profit. Nice and legal. In your line of work, I'd imagine it doesn't get any easier than that."

"Legal ain't always as easy as you may think," Gein said. "Still . . . I like the sound of this deal."

"Good. So it's agreed, then?"

"There's one slight problem. What makes you so certain I'll even catch a glimpse of your herd or the men that stole it from you?"

"You're a resourceful man," Jarrett said. "I'm sure you'll come up with something."

"We'll just see about that, Mr. Pekoe," Gein said while pushing away from the table.

Jarrett and Lem stood up as well. Ackerman hopped to his feet so as not to be too far behind the rest.

"Let me see what I can find in regard to those men you're after or the cattle they might have along with them," Gein said. "In the meantime, why don't you have a drink on the house?"

"Just a drink?" Lem asked.

"If you're up for more," Gein replied with a wide smile while opening his arms to encompass the entire place, "you know where to get it."

"What about a card game?"

"If you want to piss away your money on cards, that's not my concern. Just as long as it's not done here. Me and the other saloon in town have what you might call an understanding."

"Understood."

Giving Lem a friendly slap on the back as he walked by, Gein headed for a corner of the large room where several doors were arranged in a row. They were so close together that the doors must have led to small rooms. Considering MacGrearey's specialty, Jarrett had no problem figuring out what those rooms were used for. Nobody followed Gein into the room he chose, however, and Jarrett wasn't about to knock on that door after it was shut.

Ackerman let out a relieved sigh after the armed men who'd been surrounding Gein's table found somewhere else to be. "That didn't go anything like I thought it would," he said.

"I thought it went pretty well," Lem said.

Looking over to Jarrett, Ackerman asked, "Was that the deal you had in mind when you wanted to come to this town?"

"No," Jarrett said. "I came up with it during the ride. It would have been nice to present it under slightly better circumstances, but Lem's mostly right. It went pretty well."

The deputy couldn't hide the fact that his attention was being pulled toward several of the ladies circulating throughout the room. Considering the high caliber of those ladies, nobody would have thought any less of him for it. "You think Gein will take the offer?"

"I can't think of why he wouldn't."

"Sure, as long as those rustlers come here to sell those cows."

"We already know they're in town," Jarrett said. "Some of those cattle being held in that pen I was sneaking around had my brand, and Gein is the man with the deepest pockets in Muriel. They'll want to meet with Gein, if they haven't already. Now we've got to see where this river's current takes us and try to keep from being pulled under."

Chapter 23

Gein didn't come out of that room for hours. At first, Jarrett thought he was thinking over the offer he'd made or possibly discussing it with a partner. While that negotiation was happening, Jarrett indulged in a few drinks of whiskey. He hadn't been much of a drinker until recently. For most of his life, he wanted to have all his faculties to deal with whatever might come his way. After everything that had come his way of late, he'd developed an appreciation for taking leave of his senses. Instead of feeling rowdy or giddy like some drunks, he felt calmer inside. The longer Gein remained in that little room, however, Jarrett's serenity began to wane.

He considered the possibility that Gein's office was just another little room used by the soiled doves who worked there. The very notion that Gein would spend so much time whetting his own appetites made Jarrett's temper flare. When looking back at the other section of the main room as he'd done so many times over the last hour, Jarrett found one of Gein's hired guns staring right back at him. Whether it was because of the whiskey he'd drunk or the sleep he needed, Jarrett lost his last remaining strand of patience. He slammed down the glass he'd just emptied and turned around to find Ackerman at a nearby table working on a plate of fried eggs.

Storming over to the deputy, Jarrett asked, "Where is he?"

Stopping with a fork poised halfway between his mouth and plate, Ackerman said, "You mean Lem? He mentioned something about finding a poker game at that other saloon."

"Not Lem. Gein. Where's Gein?"

"Last I saw of him, he went into one of those back rooms."

"Haven't you been watching for him to come out?" Jarrett asked,

Ackerman set his fork down and snatched up his napkin. "What are you shouting at me for? You're the one that's been over there drinking this whole time. Why haven't you been watching for him to come out?"

"It's getting late."

"Is it? I always lose track of time in places like this."

"Tell me something," Jarrett said in a much quieter voice. "Have you shown anyone around here that badge?"

"No." Ackerman's posture straightened, making him look like a plant that had just gotten a much-needed dose of water. "Should I march into that back room and demand Gein to—"

"No," Jarrett snapped. "If marching into that room doesn't get you shot, making harsh demands from Gein definitely will. As far as that badge is concerned, you need to keep it hidden as if your life depends on it."

"Why?"

"Because your life does depend on it. Haven't you noticed that nobody around here, from that man at the cattle pen to Gein himself, seems at all concerned with the law?"

"I doubt there's any law in this town," Ackerman pointed out.

"Or they've already got whatever law there is in their hip pocket. Either way, I can tell you've been itching to make an arrest, but you need to hold back on that for a while."

"Isn't that why we're here?"

"You can make an arrest once you're certain you can live to tell about it. For now," Jarrett said, "you're following me into that back room so we can figure out what's taking Gein so long to do a simple job."

Ackerman went back to cutting his eggs. "If it was so simple, we would've done it by now."

"If you truly think every job can be done quicker by the letter of the law, you're going to make a terrible sheriff someday."

"Why don't you just have a seat and wait awhile longer? Get something to eat. The girl working in the kitchen at this time of night only knows how to fry eggs, but she does it real well."

"Something tells me we've waited long enough already," Jarrett said.

"You're just being skittish. Too much whiskey for one night."

"Skittish, am I? What about that man with the shotgun back there who's looking at us like we were being served up on a plate?"

Ackerman shifted around in his seat to get a look at the man in question. "He's been there ever since Gein walked into that back room," he said while acknowledging the vicious armed man with a nod.

"What about the other ones by the bar?"

Looking in the other direction, the deputy spotted another couple of armed men. "Gein owns a part of this place," Ackerman said. "Why are you so surprised that he's got men here to look after it?"

"I'm not surprised. I just wanted you to get a look at all of the ones keeping an eye on us. That way, if any of them come after me, you can make sure they don't get very far."

"Why would they come after you?"

Jarrett answered that by leaving the table and walking straight over to the row of doors on the other side of the room. He didn't make it halfway before one of the armed men stepped up to block his path.

"Mr. Gein wants you to wait," the armed man said.

"I'm sick of waiting," Jarrett replied.

"Then go somewhere else."

"Only place I'm going is into that room right there."

The man had been keeping one hand resting on the grip of his holstered pistol, presumably as an implied threat. Since that threat wasn't helping him very much at the moment, he made good on it by drawing the pistol. "I've got my orders," he warned. "And so do you. Now make yourself scarce until someone comes to get you."

Jarrett wasn't quick on the draw, but he managed to pull the Colt from its holster without losing his grip or snagging the barrel along the way. Considering how much he'd drunk in such a short amount of time, he considered that to be fairly impressive. Even more impressive was just how quickly he sobered up once he found himself a hairbreadth away from getting shot.

"Now what?" Jarrett said in the toughest voice he could manage.

Fortunately the man in front of him was even more

surprised by Jarrett's actions than Jarrett himself. After taking a moment to weigh his options, the man nodded and slowly lowered his gun. Jarrett kept his Colt at hip level as he moved toward the door separating him from Gein.

Tensing, the man who'd just holstered his weapon started to bring it out again. "I still can't let you do that," he said. At least this time, it sounded less like a demand and more of a request. He wasn't alone when he spoke. The men Jarrett had spotted earlier at the bar were now moving closer to back his play.

"Stand aside," Ackerman said. Jarrett hadn't even noticed the deputy approaching the growing collection of armed men, but he was mighty relieved to hear the younger man's voice in such close proximity.

Even though Gein's men had a slight advantage in numbers, something kept them from pressing forward.

"No need to make a scene here, gentlemen," Jarrett said. "I was supposed to speak with Mr. Gein again and that's all I intend to do. Something tells me he won't appreciate a fight breaking out and driving all these customers away no matter what might have been the cause of it."

The man closest to Jarrett looked slowly about. So far, their little skirmish of words hadn't attracted more than a dozen curious stares from customers who were undoubtedly used to seeing much worse in the wee hours of any given night. Rather than lose any more face in front of his partners, the man who'd first drawn down on Jarrett circled around him with hands held slightly out to the sides. Jarrett let him pass but kept him in his sights.

"Mr. Gein," the man said while knocking on the door. "That rancher's here to have a word with you."

"Give me a second," Gein said from the next room.

Jarrett could sense that his standoff wouldn't remain peaceful for much longer, so he stepped forward and tried the door himself. It was locked. His fingers were still wrapped around the handle when the door was pulled open by Gein himself.

"What is it?" Gein snarled. When he saw who was in front of him, he recoiled a bit in surprise. Jarrett caught sight of another door on the opposite side of that room, along with a fleeting glimpse of a man hurrying through it. Although he couldn't see much of that man, Jarrett was able to make out straight black hair covering the back of his head and a set of sharpened spurs attached to the heels of his boots. Before he could try to get a closer look, Jarrett's view was obstructed by a large and angry part owner of MacGrearey's.

"You're trying my patience, Mr. Pekoe," Gein snarled, "and it was still thin from the last time we spoke."

"Who was that?" Jarrett asked.

"What business is it of yours?"

"Was he one of the men trying to sell you my cattle? Or maybe he was one of the men trying to change the brand on the ones that are already here."

Gein took hold of Jarrett by the front of his shirt and pulled him into the small room with so much force that he nearly tossed him through a wall. "I don't appreciate you or *anyone* coming into my place to give me orders."

"Tell me who that man was and don't try to tell me it was something involving another order of business. I doubt you conduct much important business at this hour."

"You gonna use that pistol or just hold it and expect me to quiver in fear?"

Jarrett looked down as if to remind himself that the Colt was still in his hand. A quick glance over his shoulder was enough to tell him that Ackerman was still nearby and keeping an eye on the other gunmen. Holstering his weapon, Jarrett said, "We can talk like men without armed guards."

"Agreed," Gein said with a polite nod. The look he gave to the men who'd allowed Jarrett to enter the room wasn't nearly as polite when he closed the door in the closest one's face.

Chapter 24

Once they were alone in the room, Gein turned to Jarrett and said, "Now, what's gotten into you?"

"I don't like being ignored."

"I wasn't ignoring you. I was just collecting as many facts as I could before deciding on a course of action. It's called looking before you leap. You might want to try it sometime."

"Not tonight," Jarrett said sharply. "What facts did you collect?"

"Some cattle from your herd are here," Gein said. "And before you make another accusation, I hadn't been told about it yet. Only a few were brought in to see if I was interested. I would have had a look at them in the morning."

"What else were you talking about?"

"I asked how they were acquired. It's usually not a concern of mine, but I've found it to be quite beneficial for the bigger picture if I'm no longer so closely associated with killings. He didn't say much, but I got enough to be comfortable that the story you gave me is mostly the truth."

Suppressing the urge to squabble over being accused of telling "mostly" truths, Jarrett said, "The deal was for you to hand them over to me."

"I realize that. He's only one man and you damn near lost him by charging in the way you did. You're lucky he didn't catch a look at you or things could have taken a turn."

"Why didn't you keep him here? I would have dealt with him."

Gein approached Jarrett so he could place a heavy hand on his shoulder. Leaning in close to stare directly into his eyes, the large man explained, "There are more of them here in Muriel. He was already suspicious enough and if he was given one more thing to worry about, he would have warned the others. They would have cleared out of town faster than you could collect those other two friends of yours."

Now that the whiskey haze had been burned from his head and his breath had slowed to a normal pace, Jarrett was thinking a lot clearer than before. Gein's words made sense, which went a long way in making him feel even more grounded. "You said those rustlers are nervous. Why?"

"On account of that deputy you brought along," Gein replied.

"Someone recognized him?"

"No, but he reaches for that badge pinned to his chest more often than a gunfighter itching to skin his revolver. Plenty of men caught a glimpse of tin under his jacket, and one of those rustlers must've done the same."

"Damn it." Jarrett sighed.

"It's not a complete loss. It may have hurried the process along since that man I spoke to was all too happy to have our talk at this hour instead of waiting for me to have a look at those cattle."

Jarrett ran through several options in his mind. While most weren't as bad as they could have been, none of them inspired much confidence. "You think that man will be willing to come back here?"

"Only if he wants money for them cows. Since rustlers don't care about much else, I'd say the odds of him coming back to see me are pretty good."

"Are you going to hand the men over or not?"

Gein took his hand from Jarrett's shoulder, only to put it back again with a solid yet friendly slap. "I give you my word and it's good as gold. Besides, that man who just left here tried to lie to me about a few things to swing a better deal for himself. That, piled on top of everything else they've done, will make it a pleasure to see them get what they deserve. I deal with thieving scum out of necessity, Mr. Pekoe. Thieving, lying scum who'd kill an innocent family is something else. Even a man in my line of work needs to be able to look at himself in a mirror."

Jarrett didn't know whether he should fully trust Gein or not. His instincts pointed him very clearly toward taking him at his word, which confused him even more.

"The man that left here was Sol Carter," Gein said. "That name mean anything to you?"

Jarrett didn't need much time before he said, "Never heard of him. Of course, those men didn't exactly take time to make proper introductions before burning my ranch to the ground."

"Of course they didn't. I'd say that, between the two of us, we've done enough for one day. Why don't we both get some rest and reconvene here at noon tomorrow?"

"Noon? I thought you said you were meeting with them in the morning."

"I am," Gein replied. "But these men are suspicious by nature. I'll need time to let them get comfortable before trying to detain them." Gein scowled as he dropped his voice to something closer to a snarl. "This isn't the sort of thing I do very often, so it's got to be done right. If word gets out that I treated one of my customers this way, things will get difficult for me. Considering the men who are my customers, you don't want to know how difficult that is."

"Right."

"Now you and your friends will stay somewhere other than here for the night," Gein said while pushing Jarrett toward the door through which he'd entered. "I'd recommend the Wheatley Inn. It's just down the street from here next to a pair of dry wells. You can't miss it. Keep your heads down and for the love of God, keep that deputy on a short rope before he finds himself at the end of a long one."

Shaking loose of the big man's grasp, Jarrett asked, "What should I expect when I get back here? More posturing from your men?"

"You stepped too far tonight and I let you get away with it. Don't put me to the test again."

Taking full advantage of the advice he'd been given, Jarrett thought better of the threat he was about to make and nodded in agreement instead. Gein opened the door and all but shoved him through it.

Outside, things were much closer to normal that Jarrett had been expecting. Although Ackerman and Gein's men were all still within close proximity of the door, they sat at their own respective tables and none of them looked as though they'd been scrapping with the other. Ackerman stood up a bit too quickly, which prompted the others to stand as well.

"Everything all right?" the deputy asked.

"Yeah," Jarrett said. "Or it will be once we get out of here."

"We're leaving?"

"Just this saloon." Looking over to a table where two of Gein's men sat, Jarrett added, "And we're coming back tomorrow."

The man in Jarrett's sights seemed less than thrilled about that, but he wasn't going to do anything at the moment. Gein's men all kept their eyes on Jarrett and Ackerman as they headed for the front door and allowed them to leave without further incident. None of the customers were inclined to do much either. They were too busy drinking or laughing with the working girls to be anything to Jarrett other than elements of a backdrop.

"What happened in there?" Ackerman asked once they were outside. His face was thin enough already, but his worried expression and pale color made him look even slighter than normal.

"Those men were just trying to do what Gein pays them for," Jarrett said in what was supposed to be an assuring manner.

"That's not what I meant. What happened with you? I mean . . . one moment I was sitting there eating my eggs and you were at the bar drinking your whiskey. The next second, you were worked up into a lather and picking a fight with armed men."

"I guess it could have seemed that way."

"That's how it was! What were you thinking?"

Giving Ackerman a shove to get him moving faster, Jarrett walked beside him down the street. "I should ask you the same thing," he said. "Everyone in there knows you're a lawman. Everyone that matters anyway. And before you try to defend yourself, think about how many times you started to show a damn tin star in a town that's home to one of the most prosperous outlaws in three counties."

Ackerman winced, started reaching for his badge as if to make sure it was still hidden, and then winced again. "Point taken."

"It's all right." Jarrett sighed. "We both made a few bad decisions, but someone's looking out for us because we're making progress despite ourselves. Where'd you say Lem got off to?"

"Playing cards down the way," Ackerman replied while nodding toward the only other spot in town that didn't look like a dead lump of shadows.

"I'll go get him and you find us someplace to sleep. I heard there's a hotel down by a couple of dry—"

"Found you," Lem said as he crossed the street.

Ackerman finally relaxed now that the other two were present and accounted for. "We were just going to try to find you," he said. "Let's get some sleep and put this night behind us."

"Not yet," Lem said. "There's still a thing or two that needs to be done."

"What are you talking about?" Jarrett asked. "And why are you smiling like that?"

Lem's only response was to turn his back on them, walk to the other side of the street, and motion for the other two to follow him. Jarrett did so reluctantly and Ackerman came along only because he wasn't about to let them out of his sight. Lem took them down the street, around a corner, and to a small storefront that was dark and closed up tight. He circled around to a side door and eased it open.

"What is this place?" Jarrett asked.

"Don't know," Lem replied. "Some sort of store, I think. Doesn't matter."

"Doesn't matter?" Ackerman whispered. "How could it not matter? Where's the owner of this place?"

Lem shrugged. "Couldn't tell you."

"Couldn't or won't?"

"What the hell difference does it make? If you don't like it so much, you can wait outside. Just try not to make a spectacle of yourself."

The door led into a small, narrow room. Inside that room, light from a single lantern cast just enough of a glow to show them the way farther into the building without running into anything along the way.

"I'm just doing my job," Ackerman said while nearly avoiding walking into the doorframe. "And since I am the ranking member of this group, it's high time for me to lay down a few rules. Before we go any farther—"

Jarrett was already in the next room and stopped dead in his tracks. "Stop," he said. "Just . . . stop talking. I need to think."

Being the first one to get through the door, Lem walked ahead a couple of steps to circle around a chair positioned near a table where the single lantern was resting. Tied to that chair was a slender man with straight black hair. A bandanna was tied around his mouth to muffle his screams, and blood was caked on his chin. One of his eyes was swollen shut. The other was filled with a mix of panic, desperation, and rage.

Ackerman might not have appreciated being told to shut up, but he wouldn't have been able to say a word at that moment anyway.

Chapter 25

"What . . . what is this?" Jarrett stammered. "Who is that?"

Lem circled the chair like a bird of prey that had already spotted its next meal on a canyon floor. "Don't you know who this is?"

He did know, but Jarrett couldn't be certain. Not until he got a closer look. As he approached, the man tied to the chair thrashed as much as he could. Considering how well he'd been bound by those ropes, it wasn't much.

Finally Ackerman found his voice again. "You're holding this man prisoner? You can't do that!"

"Looks like I already did," Lem replied while gesturing toward the chair.

"Is he . . . under arrest?"

Stepping back while crossing his arms, Lem said, "You're the lawman, not me. If it makes you feel any better . . . go ahead and arrest him."

Ackerman studied the prisoner from head to toe. "Why is he here?" the deputy asked.

Lem kept his eyes on Jarrett as he said, "I couldn't exactly have him running around loose. Besides, he's the reason we're in this cow town. Well, one of the reasons anyway."

Hunching over to get a closer look at the prisoner's boots, Jarrett reached out with one hand to scrape a finger against the sharpened spurs attached to one heel. "This really is him."

Lem nodded. "I was walking to that other saloon when one of Gein's boys pointed him out to me. Said I should keep an eye on him if I was looking for those rustlers. I followed him for a short spell and he eventually came back to MacGrearey's. Didn't have to wait long before he hurried out a back door. He was in such a rush he didn't know I was there until it was too late."

Jarrett straightened up and looked down at the prisoner in disbelief. Since Ackerman looked as if he was about to burst, Jarrett told him, "This is one of the rustlers we're after."

"Are you serious?" the deputy gasped.

"Yeah. He was having a word with Gein and left as soon as I got there. His name's Sol . . . Carter. Isn't that right?"

Upon hearing that name, the prisoner stopped struggling. Jarrett stepped around to stand directly in front of him. Bending slightly at the knees, Jarrett put himself mostly at the seated prisoner's eye level.

"You're sure that's him?" Ackerman asked.

"I got a quick look at him when he was on his way out of Gein's place. He was wearing the same spurs. Gein told me he's one of the men looking to sell off my herd."

"Spurs?" Ackerman scoffed. "That's all? A place like that saloon must have plenty of side doors. We've got to be absolutely certain that this here is the same man that—"

"They're distinctive spurs," Jarrett said. "And he knows he's the one we're after. Look at him right now. He recognizes me. Don't you, you son of a bitch?"

Every word that Jarrett said was more venomous than the last. And as he spoke, he glared at the prisoner as if he were burning all the way through his very soul. The man tied to the chair stopped squirming. The recognition in his eyes was unmistakable. More than that, he seemed genuinely spooked by what he saw.

"He's the one all right," Lem said. "I'd swear to it on every Bible you could find."

Ackerman stood beside Jarrett, stared at the prisoner, and obviously didn't see the same thing as anyone else. "Why did you snatch him up and stash him away like this?" the deputy asked.

"Isn't that why we're here?"

"We're here to bring these outlaws to justice," Ackerman replied calmly. "This wasn't done the way I would have expected, but I suppose it falls within our jurisdiction to capture a fugitive by any means necessary."

Those words were barely out of Ackerman's mouth when Jarrett drove his fist straight into Sol's face. He put all of his weight behind that punch and followed through as if his knuckles would continue onward through the wall behind the back of the prisoner's skull. Sol's head snapped back and his body sailed in the same direction. He and the chair were overturned and his legs pointed toward the ceiling.

"Keep still," Jarrett said as he grabbed hold of one of Sol's boots. "I told you to keep still, damn it!"

Ackerman surged forward to try to grab Jarrett but was quickly grabbed himself. "What're you doing, kid?" Lem asked as he held on to the deputy the way he would restrain an overeager child.

"I can't allow this," Ackerman said.

"It's like the man said. This is why we're here."

Although Jarrett heard the other two men talking

about him, he was too busy to respond. Sol kicked and thrashed in a fairly impressive manner considering how well he was tied to that chair. Eventually Jarrett got a firm grip on Sol's boot and pulled it off in one strong tug.

"What are you doing?" Ackerman asked.

"Help me set him upright," Jarrett said.

Since Ackerman was still too flustered to do much of anything, Lem pushed him aside so he could lend Jarrett a hand. Between the two of them, they quickly got all four of the chair's legs on the floor. Blood poured from Sol's nose to soak into the bandanna acting as a gag. Whenever he pulled in a breath, Sol coughed and hacked it right up again.

Unable to get a response from Jarrett so far, Ackerman shifted his focus to Lem. "What's he doing?"

"Not quite sure yet," Lem replied. "Just keep back and let him do it."

Jarrett tore off Sol's spur and then tossed the boot away. Holding the spur so the sharpened end protruded between his first two fingers, he said, "In my years of riding and working on ranches, I've found there's a certain kind of man who uses spurs like these." Raising his fist so the corner of the sharpened square spur was less than an inch away from Sol's cheek, Jarrett used his other hand to grab hold of the prisoner's hair. "They're the sort of men who know they're hurting their horse, making it bleed, and don't give a damn."

Sol shook his head as much as he could without jamming his own cheek into the spur.

"They're the sort of men," Jarrett continued, "who are cruel and small. They don't mind spilling blood or inflicting pain just so long as none of that blood and pain is their own."

As the spur drew closer, Sol became very still. His

eyes widened, staring down at the spur that was now close enough for him to see every fleck of dried blood on it. When the sharpened metal touched his skin, he reflexively tried to pull away. Thanks to the grip Jarrett had on him, he didn't get very far.

"I won't stand here and watch this," Ackerman said.

"Then step outside," Lem said.

The deputy moved to push Jarrett back but was pulled away by Lem. This time, Ackerman wheeled around to push back. "Get your hands off me!" he said.

Although Lem did release him, he remained planted between the deputy and Jarrett. "They deserve this," Lem said quietly. "Both of 'em."

"You hear that?" Jarrett snarled. "Ain't no one going to come and save you. How do you like that?"

Sol tried to maintain a brave front but wasn't doing a very good job. The couple of words he attempted to spit out were soaked up by the bandanna over his mouth. Although relieved, he was clearly surprised when Jarrett pulled that bandanna away.

"You got something to say?" Jarrett asked. "Go ahead and say it."

"You're dead," Sol sputtered. "All of you."

"Is that a fact?"

"I ain't alone here, you know."

"I realize that," Jarrett said. "Which brings me to the first thing I wanted to tell you. Well . . . actually . . . the second. First I wanted to say you've got a debt to pay with me and my family." With that, Jarrett leaned his shoulder forward to push the sharpened spur into Sol's cheek. As Sol squirmed and grunted, Jarrett pressed the spur in deeper.

Chapter 26

"That's enough of that!" Ackerman said. Instead of trying to push by Lem, he stepped around to the other side of the chair and grabbed hold of Jarrett's sleeve.

Jarrett smiled and allowed his arm to be drawn aside. "Think about all the blood you spilled, the pain you caused, and think about how much blood I'll be taking from you in return."

"Jarrett," Ackerman said sternly. "I want to have a word with you."

Sol smiled up at him through the steady flow of blood spreading down his face. "That's right, rancher. You had your fun. Time to crawl on back to—"

"Shut up!" Ackerman snapped. "We're not through with you yet. Just sit there and be quiet if you know what's good for you."

Even though he shut his mouth, Sol still met Jarrett's eyes with a smug expression. Jarrett wiped that expression clean away with a left cross that put the prisoner once more flat upon his back on the floor.

After taking Jarrett to the other side of the large room, Ackerman dropped his voice to a whisper while doing his best to also keep an eye on Lem, who remained with the prisoner. "What do you think you're doing?" Ackerman asked. "This is a posse, not some kind of lynch mob."

"I'm questioning him," Jarrett replied. "You think he'll tell us what we need to know just by asking him politely?"

"No, but there are ways to do things. Civilized ways."

"That's right. And that man gave up his chance to be civilized when he put my ranch and family to the torch."

"We're not here for revenge."

"Speak for yourself."

Ackerman stood his ground, waiting for a few seconds while taking a hard look at the man in front of him. As he watched, Jarrett's heaving breaths slowed to a pace that didn't take such a toll on him. Sweat trickled down Jarrett's face, cooling him and granting a couple of much-needed seconds.

"There," Ackerman said. "I know you must want to kill that man for what he did, but it won't help get the rest of them."

"I told you . . . I was questioning him."

Ackerman shook his head. "You may have eventually gotten around to asking a question or two, but you meant to kill him sooner rather than later. In that state of mind, if you heard one or two more things you didn't like, it would have been sooner and we wouldn't have learned a thing. Tell me I'm wrong."

When Jarrett pulled in his next breath, he'd intended to use it to put the deputy in his place. When he released it, however, he didn't say a word. The only thing worse than being talked to that way by a man as young as Ackerman was having to admit that the same man was absolutely right.

"All right," Jarrett said. "You did your job. I've got myself under control. Let's get on with this."

Reluctantly Ackerman stepped aside. When Jarrett started walking past him, the deputy held out an arm to stop him. "I'll be keeping an eye on you."

"I've guessed as much. And if you want to keep that arm," Jarrett added, "I'd suggest you take it back right about now."

There was no way for the deputy to avoid a fight while also keeping the illusion that he was in control of Jarrett. Instead of trying to do so, he simply did as he was told and got out of Jarrett's path.

As he stalked across the room, Jarrett took a few more deep breaths to calm himself down a bit more. When he'd cut Sol's face, it was almost as though he'd been several paces away watching someone else put the fear of God into that prisoner. His actions hadn't come as a complete shock, but Jarrett had been overtaken by them without a moment to try to rein himself in. He felt the sobering ache that had become his normal state of mind return and could only vow to do his best to keep the beast inside him at arm's length for a while longer.

While Jarrett and Ackerman had been having their talk, Lem hadn't exactly been twiddling his thumbs. As Jarrett crossed the room, Lem stood to the left of the chair where Sol was tied. His arms were crossed, his head was angled down to stare directly at the prisoner, and he spoke in a tone that Jarrett couldn't hear.

Jarrett stopped before getting too close. Sol turned his head toward him but was unable to peel his gaze away from Lem. "What were you talking about?" the prisoner asked. "What are you gonna do to me?"

"I've got some questions to ask," Jarrett said to him.

Instead of taking any comfort from Jarrett's more controlled tone of voice, Sol became increasingly more nervous. "What questions?"

"How many came with you into Muriel?"

Before uttering another word, Sol glanced over to Lem, who only nodded back at him. "Two," Sol said.

"Just two?" Lem asked.

Hearing the other man's voice impacted Sol almost as much as a punch to his ribs. He flinched and said, "Yes."

Although he wasn't certain what had happened between Lem and Sol when he stepped away, Jarrett was grateful for the shift in tone. "What were you doing here?" he asked.

"We brought a few cattle in to the Brander to see if they could be fixed up."

"The Brander?"

Sol nodded. "He's the one that changes the brands. Does real good work. The quicker and better that job gets done, the better price them cows will fetch."

"Where are the other two now?" Lem asked.

"Probably long gone by now," Sol replied. "I was supposed to meet them after I talked with Gein about a few things. Since I haven't shown up, they could've skinned out of this town to bring back ten more to burn this place to the ground." Locking eyes with Jarrett, he added, "You heard me! Burn it down . . . just like we burned your place till there weren't anything left but ash!"

Jarrett felt the cold touch of hatred cinch in tight around his heart, choking him from the inside. His hand slapped against the grip of his Colt. His finger slipped around the trigger. He even started to lift the gun from its resting place before he regained his composure. Ackerman was nearby, but Jarrett extended a hand toward the deputy to keep him from getting any closer.

"Go ahead, Lem," Jarrett said. "Seems you may have something to add."

Judging by the look on Sol's face, he would rather have heard a gun being fired at him than those words. When he slowly looked away from Jarrett, Sol was greeted by Lem's unwavering stare.

"Them other two," Lem said. "They're not gone. You and I both know that much for certain."

"I don't know where they'd be. How would I know?" Sol groaned. "I've been here for . . . I don't even know how long."

"It hasn't been that long. And before you try to pass it off that I knocked you senseless to drag you in here, I barely gave you a solid punch. You sure ain't a delicate flower, Sol, so drop the act."

Sol's mouth hung agape. One corner flinched when some of the blood trickling from the cut Jarrett had given him dripped toward his chin. "There's a cathouse on the north side of town," he said.

Lem was shaking his head before that sentence was fully formed. "Gein runs the only whores in Muriel."

"It's a small place. Just a couple of girls working there. Too small for Gein to worry about. Or maybe they got an arrangement with him to keep operating. I don't know. You asked me where I was to meet the others and that's it. I swear!"

Watching Sol squirm, watching him bleed, Jarrett couldn't scrape up an ounce of pity for him.

"What do you think?" Lem asked. "You believe him?"

"Not yet," Jarrett replied. All he needed to do from there was walk slowly around the chair, pick up the spur that had been dropped, and fit it once again between his fingers to elicit a response.

"That's the truth," Sol yelped. "I swear!"

Standing like a statue near the chair, Lem said, "There's something he's not telling us."

"How do you know?" Jarrett asked.

"I can see it in his eyes."

"Maybe I should get a look at those eyes for myself. Well," Jarrett added as he brought the spur up, "at least one of 'em."

"That's all I got to say!" Sol said. "What else do you want from me?"

"The other men that came with you to Muriel," Jarrett said. "Is one of them Clay?"

"No."

"What about Dave?" Jarrett asked. "He was one of the others with Clay at my ranch. Is he here?"

Sol's eyes widened. "Yes! Dave Massey! He's here. He's the one you want. More than Clay, he should be the one you want!"

Ackerman stepped forward. He knew better than to get directly in front of Jarrett or Lem, but he stood so he couldn't be ignored by either man. "That's it," the deputy said. "He told you what you wanted to know."

"Let him talk," Jarrett said.

Sol was squirming like a worm on a hook and Jarrett was inclined to keep it that way, especially since he was in a mood to talk. Just to grease the wheels a bit, he placed a finger on one of the spur's points and set it to spinning.

"You asked him your question and he answered," Ackerman insisted. "We're through."

"Through?" Jarrett said. "Not by a long shot."

When Sol glanced in his direction, Lem shrugged. "Don't look at me. Even if I could rein him in, why would I?"

"Because I can still help," Sol said in a hurry. "If you kill me, I won't be able to do anything."

"Nobody's going to kill anyone," Ackerman said nervously.

"Right," Jarrett said. "I wasn't planning on killing you. That would be way too quick."

"Hold on, now," Ackerman said as he tried to pull Jarrett aside as he'd done before. "This is getting out of hand."

Lem grabbed the deputy's arm and dragged him away from Jarrett. "It ain't out of hand just yet, but we may be getting close to there before long."

That was more than enough to further stoke the panic that was evident on Sol's face.

"You hear that?" Jarrett asked his prisoner. "Seems like things for you are about to go from bad to worse."

"What do you think you're doin'?" Lem snarled in an angry whisper.

Having been dragged several paces away from the other two men in that room, Ackerman tore free from Lem's grip. "I am not to be pulled here and there like some damn kid!"

"Would you have come along with me without a fuss?"

"I should be over there before—"

"Well, there you go." Lem sighed. "He's about to make some progress, so let's not gum up the works."

"I'd say they're plenty gummed up already," Ackerman said. "Starting from the point when you dragged a man off the street. That doesn't strike me as fully legal, you know."

"Really? And if we all caught sight of him, knowing he's one of the men we're after, what would we have done?"

"Brought him back with us."

"Sounds a lot like taking him prisoner to me," Lem pointed out.

"This isn't the same and you know it!"

"Yeah, yeah," Lem replied as he looked over to try to gauge how much more time he needed to buy for Jarrett. "I know it."

Chapter 27

When he'd started this, Jarrett was concerned that he might not be able to pull it off. He'd never before set out to scare someone into giving him something, and the biggest fear was that his efforts might come across as pathetic or even humorous. The longer he stood there, however, the less Jarrett needed to do to make Sol more uncomfortable. Instead of shoving the spur up to where Sol could see every dent in the beveled metal, he simply kept it in a loose grip and allowed his arm to hang at his side. Sol's eyes remained glued to the spur anyway, so there was no reason for Jarrett to wear his arm out.

"It seemed to me like you had more to say," Jarrett said.

"What do you want to know?"

"I want to know how you think you can still be useful enough for us to consider allowing you to remain in this world for a while longer."

"Your partner over there seemed to be feeling charitable," Sol said.

Jarrett looked back to Ackerman and then returned his eyes to Sol. "You really want to gamble on that?"

Sol's last, desperate attempt to talk his way out of that room ended just as quickly as it had begun. "Before I tell you anything more," he said, "I want your word that you'll set me free afterward."

"You're not in any position to make a deal, Sol."

"Then at least don't kill me," he pleaded. "Promise you'll let me live."

Jarrett would never feel sorry for this man or any of the others who had anything at all to do with what had happened to his family. Even so, watching Sol grovel without any attempt to keep a shred of pride or dignity brought Jarrett as close to pity as was possible. Studying him like a bug under a magnifying glass, he said, "You must have something really good to tell me."

"I do!"

"What is it?"

"Promise me," Sol said. "Promise me you won't kill me."

"All right. I promise."

Sol looked relieved, but only for a moment. His eyes took on a desperate intensity as he quickly said, "Promise me you won't let either of them other two kill me either."

"What could you possibly have to say to me that's valuable enough for me to make so many promises just to hear it?"

"It's worth it," Sol vowed. "I swear."

Finally curiosity mixed with that little granule of pity to get the better of him and Jarrett said, "All right. Tell me your big secret or whatever it is and I promise none of us will kill you."

"Or hurt me again. Like . . . with that spur or—"

"That's it," Jarrett grunted as he reached for the Colt.

"That woman we captured at your ranch is still alive!" Sol spat.

Jarrett froze with his hand on the pistol's grip. Whatever he'd intended to do with the gun after it had been drawn was now forgotten. He almost forgot how to stand upright since Jarrett's entire world had suddenly gone off-kilter. "What did you just say?"

For a second, Sol couldn't move.

"If you think that's some kind of joke," Jarrett warned.

"It's not a joke."

"Why would you even think to say such a thing?"

"Because," Sol replied, "I saw her. She was coming out of your house when it was set on fire. I thought Clay was gonna leave everyone in there, but she came right out."

As a test to see if Sol was making something up to save his skin, Jarrett asked, "What did she look like?"

Not only did Sol describe Jen's face, hair, and general stature, but he also described what she'd been wearing on that terrible night. The picture that was drawn in Jarrett's mind was vivid enough to make his heart ache.

"Clay took her outside before the house collapsed?" Jarrett asked.

"Not . . . as such. She came out on her own. Just her and a baby."

Suddenly Jarrett was brought one half step closer to being the man he'd once been. "She had the baby with her?"

"Yes. She called it . . . called it . . ." After thinking for a few moments, Sol snapped to attention and said, "Autumn! She called the baby Autumn."

"Oh my God." When he focused on Sol again, Jarrett lunged forward to grab the prisoner by the collar and pull him with enough force to bring him and the chair off the floor. "Where are they? Tell me!"

At first, Sol was terrified by Jarrett's sudden loss of restraint. Once he saw he had something the other man wanted, he found a little of the confidence he'd so recently lost. Before Jarrett could knock him down a few pegs, he was being pulled away from the prisoner by two sets of hands.

"Take it easy, there," Lem said. "Don't want to rattle the little fellow too much."

"But I'm not through with him yet," Jarrett said.

"I think you are," Ackerman said. "At least for a few moments. Why don't you let one of us take a run at him?"

Having dragged Jarrett a few paces back, Lem stepped in front of him and said, "That may not be a bad idea. Could give you a chance to catch your breath."

"Did you hear what he just told me?"

Lem backed up a step as a flicker of concern crossed his face. "What did he tell you?" he asked.

"He said my brother's wife and her baby girl are alive."

"Do you believe him?"

"I was about to get to the bottom of it when I was dragged off," Jarrett said. "Let me finish what I started."

"Why don't you let us have a crack at him?" Lem said. When Jarrett started to protest, he added, "I'm not asking you to leave. Just stand over there and watch."

"I want to do something to help."

"You'll be helping plenty. Just try to look menacing."

Jarrett wasn't exactly sure what Lem meant by that or how he could pull it off. He thought he could use a moment to catch his breath, so Jarrett took a few steps back and watched to see what would happen from a distance.

In the few moments it took for Lem to get back to the chair where Sol was tied, he shifted into a whole new skin. Instead of the soft-spoken man Jarrett had come to know, Lem took on the bearing of a predatory animal with his shoulders squared, head leaning slightly forward, and a nasty snarl on his lips. "What do you know about that man's family?"

"Like I told him," Sol said. "I'll only say what I know if I'm to be cut loose afterward."

Lem's hand snapped out to grab hold of Sol's chin. Making sure at least one of his fingers was digging into the fresh wound on Sol's cheek, Lem turned him to face Jarrett while asking, "You see that man there?"

"Y . . . yes," Sol replied.

"You think I can keep him from killing you in the worst way possible after what you and Clay did to his kin?"

"But . . . the deal was to—"

Lem used his free hand to slap Sol across the face. It would have been an inconsequential blow if not for the bloody gash that was Lem's main target. Sol grunted and tried to turn away but wasn't very successful. While Ackerman wasn't comfortable with this any more than he was with what Jarrett had been doing, the deputy wasn't as eager to interfere with Lem.

"You'll answer the question I ask and only that question," Lem snarled. "Got it?"

"Yeah."

"What do you know about that woman and her little baby?"

"Just what I already told him," Sol replied. "I saw them leaving the house before it burned down."

"What about the rest of his family?" Lem asked. "You know anything about them?"

"I want—"

"Look over at that man," Lem said while jabbing a finger in Jarrett's direction.

Sol looked over at Jarrett, who stood nearby like a

coiled snake that could lunge at any second to bury its fangs into his flesh.

"Do you think that man gives a damn about what you want?" Lem continued.

"No," Sol said. With that single word, all hope drained from his eyes.

"Your only hope is to deal with me. But you already knew that, didn't you?"

Sol nodded. He then sighed and said, "I saw a little girl as well. But that was after the fire. I don't know for certain whether she came out of that house or not."

"Did Clay have any little girls with him before you all got to the Lazy J?" Lem asked.

"No. We were to meet up with someone afterward, though. Someone who might be bringing along a prisoner or two."

"Where did these prisoners go after the fires were started?"

"Clay took them," Sol said.

"Where?"

Sol shook his head. Upon seeing that, Jarrett took a step forward and then stopped from going any farther. Before Jarrett could get any closer, Sol quickly said, "I don't know what Clay has in mind for them. They were taken off the ranch and I didn't see them again after that."

"How could you not have seen them?" Jarrett asked as he came forward a bit more.

"Because I was sent here with some of the cattle to arrange for a buyer. Why don't you ask him what Clay has in mind?"

Jarrett's mind was moving through several paces at once. "What about a boy?" he asked. "Was there a boy with them as well?"

Sol didn't have to think for very long about that. "I didn't see no boy, but that don't mean there wasn't one. After the fires were set, things were crazy. The herd had to be rounded up and we had to get moving quickly. Most of my job was to keep an eye on the ranch hands and keep an eye out for any law that might come along to check on the fire. I only got a quick look at the house and such and I already told you what I saw!"

Listening to Sol talk about gathering up that herd after setting those fires, Jarrett had all he could do to keep from killing him right then and there.

"I'm betting Clay took a different route than the others driving that herd," Lem said.

"That's right," Sol replied. "He did."

"Where's he going?"

"Due north into Canada."

Lem's scowl took such a narrow focus that it made Sol recoil from it. "Last chance," Lem said. "Whatever you got to say that might save your miserable hide, this is the time to say it."

Jarrett watched closely without expecting a single peep to come out of Sol's mouth. After how scared the prisoner had been at so many different points during their questioning period, surely there wasn't much else for him to say. Jarrett was quickly proven wrong.

"I still don't know about any boy," Sol said, "but them two ladies . . . the woman and the girl . . . they'll be traveling with Clay."

"You're sure of that?"

Sol nodded, keeping his head hung low as he added, "He mentioned something about sellin' them off."

"You mean, selling off the herd?" Jarrett asked.

"No," Sol said. "The ladies. He wants to sell off the ladies."

"Good God," Ackerman said.

Lem moved closer to Sol, but the prisoner was done flinching. He'd been put through the wringer so many times in one night that there wasn't much else to be done to him apart from putting a bullet through his skull.

"Sell them to who?" Lem asked.

Shrugging, Sol replied, "I don't know. Someone at the Canadian border. Could be sellin' them as . . ." His eyes darted up to Jarrett as he picked some more tactful words than what he had in mind. "Could be sold to work for a Frenchman by the name of Jacque. I don't know his last name. He buys women and takes them to work all over the country. Sometimes they're ransomed for a few quick dollars. To be honest, I was glad to get away from that sort of thing so I could bring these cows in for their brand. I don't want any part of the rest."

"What's the best way for us to find Clay?" Ackerman asked.

"Should be a trail about seven miles west of Flat Pass that heads due north."

"I know it," Lem said.

"Then you know what I know," Sol said. "There ain't more for me to say. If'n you're gonna kill me, just get it over with."

"You two," Jarrett said to Lem and Ackerman. "Get out."

Ackerman shook his head but was taken from the room by Lem. Despite the deputy's protests, he was overpowered and had no choice but to step outside for the moment.

"What now?" Sol asked. "You gonna shoot me?"

"No," Jarrett said.

"Cut my throat?"

"I'm handing you over to that deputy. Unless you

want to help us round up the other men that came to
Muriel with you."

"I already told you more than enough. If you can't get
them with that, then you don't have a prayer against
Clay."

Jarrett stepped closer to the prisoner. Although he
kept his hand on his Colt, he didn't have any intention of
drawing it. "Answer me one more question."

"Sure. Why the hell not?"

"Why'd you do it?"

"Do what?"

"Burn my ranch," Jarrett said. "You had what you
needed. Everyone was tied or knocked out or shot. Clay
and the rest of you could have taken the herd just as
easily without setting any fires. You could've gotten away
even sooner, in fact. Why take the time to do all of that?"

Sol swallowed hard. For a moment, he seemed ready
to keep his silence. Whether he was afraid of further
questioning or just too tired to resist any longer, he said,
"Clay wanted to send a message."

"A message? To who?"

"I don't know," Sol replied with a weary shake of his
head. "Clay just wanted to hit that place hard and leave
nothing behind. Nothing."

"And now you say he's headed north?"

Sol nodded. "If you're gonna kill me, just do it and get
it over with. There ain't anything else I can tell you."

Every bone in Jarrett's body told him he could believe
what he was hearing. Still, there was another part of him
that wasn't satisfied. Placing a hand on his Colt was the
first step to scratching that itch.

Jarrett looked over one shoulder and saw Ackerman
watching him intently. The young deputy was tensed and

ready to act. He gave Jarrett a stern glare that was unmistakably a warning that said, *Back off.*

When Jarrett looked over his other shoulder, he caught sight of Lem standing a few paces behind him wearing a much different expression. Lem was quiet and unmoving, but his eyes reflected more than just understanding. There was a hint of approval there as well that said, *Do it.*

Jarrett's grip tightened around his Colt as he brought the gun up. Stopping just short of clearing leather, he dropped the pistol back into its holster. "Get this piece of trash out of my sight," he snarled. He didn't have to look to see which of the two other men in that room would be the one to take custody of the outlaw.

As Ackerman went to the chair where Sol was tied, Jarrett approached Lem. "It's not too late, you know," Lem said to him. "We can put a bullet into that murderer anytime we choose."

"I know that. We've still got two others to deal with. Ackerman's going to need some breathing room to get a prisoner out of here. Why don't you check to make sure the street's clear and I'll help get him to his feet?"

"All right."

After Lem turned and left the room, Jarrett stalked toward the other two. Even though he'd already made up his mind, there were still plenty of demons rustling around inside him trying to be heard. Locking eyes with Sol, he drew his pistol and held it at hip level. "I've got him covered, Ackerman," he said. "Get him untied."

The deputy hurried to cut the ropes keeping Sol connected to the chair while leaving the ones binding his wrists and ankles intact.

"What the hell are you looking at?" Jarrett asked.

Sol hardly moved. There clearly wasn't enough steam in his engine to mount an escape. There was barely enough for him to say, "Best keep your eye on that friend of yours."

"You don't know a thing about it."

"Is that a fact, now? Why don't you enlighten me?"

Chapter 28

The cathouse had no proper name but was known well enough throughout Muriel. All Jarrett had to do was ask someone at the closest saloon about it and he was told exactly where to look. When he stepped out of that saloon again, Jarrett crossed the street to where Lem was waiting.

"You know where we're headed?" Lem asked.

Jarrett nodded. "It's a house with two floors and three lanterns along the porch. Just down that street and right at the corner."

Lem glanced over to where Jarrett was pointing and nodded. "Might as well get going before them other two get nervous."

"I imagine they'll find a way to amuse themselves while waiting for Sol."

"You're right about that."

Both of them headed down the street. It was so late that time no longer mattered and Jarrett was so exhausted that he was no longer tired. He knew he'd collapse as soon as he gave himself a moment to rest, so he just had to keep moving.

After rounding the corner, Lem said, "I trust the kid got away without incident."

"He did."

"You think he can handle Sol on his own?"

"He'll have to," Jarrett replied. "If he can't ride with one man that's tied as tight as Sol was, he'll be pretty useless as a deputy."

"Very true." They walked another fifty yards or so before Lem asked, "So, what's the plan for these other two?"

"We find them at that cathouse and drag them out by their ears if necessary."

"And then what?" When he got a sideways glance from Jarrett, Lem added, "I don't mean to sound ignorant, but it might be wise for us to be thinking along the same lines when we get in there. Once the lead starts to fly, there won't be a lot of time to discuss things like there was with Sol."

"You think I made a mistake keeping him alive?" Jarrett asked.

"Doesn't matter what I think. These men just need to get dealt with."

"And why is that so important to you?"

Lem looked over at him with half a tired grin on his face. "What's gotten into you? I signed up for this posse and I've been doing my best to see the job through to its end."

"I know you have. My question is why."

"Because what those men did wasn't right. You think you're the only one who sees it? If that sort of thing is tolerated, then it'll only get worse from there. Besides, there was a payment being offered and I need the money."

With a town as spread out as Muriel, all anyone needed to find a particular spot was a general direction. The farther they went from the center of town, the easier it became to navigate. Jarrett could see a short row of small houses not too far away. The one at the far right end was marked by a trio of flickering lanterns.

Unlike the gaggle of beauties to be found at Mac-Grearey's, one lady was sitting quietly alone on the porch of that house. She was dressed in a white slip and wore a shawl over her shoulders. When she saw the two men walking toward the house, she crossed one leg over the other and hiked the slip up just enough to give them a peek at her thigh.

Lem took his hat off and waved it at her. Now that she knew the men were definitely coming to pay her a visit, the woman on the porch got up and went in through the front door. Judging by the shadows moving behind the front window, the other girls inside were all getting ready for a night's work.

"This way," Jarrett said as he took a sharp turn to the left and headed for the neighboring house. Once he and Lem were able to keep an eye on the house with the lanterns without standing in the open, Jarrett drew his Colt and pointed it at Lem.

Recoiling more out of surprise than fear, Lem asked, "What's this about?"

"What's your angle?"

"That's what I was trying to figure out before we got here!"

"Not in regard to those men," Jarrett said. "In regard to me. Whatever you got in mind, I want to get it out in the open right now."

Lem squinted at Jarrett. "I already told you all this. If you don't believe me, then I don't know what to tell you."

"How about you tell me if you're one of Clay's men? Why don't we start right there, huh?"

Lem's reaction was barely noticeable. He hardly seemed to move as he snarled, "Where'd you hear that?"

"Sol told me, just as he was about to be taken away by Ackerman."

"And you put any faith in what that man had to say on the matter?"

"The only thing I have any faith in anymore is what I can see and hear for myself," Jarrett said. "Some things with you didn't seem quite right, but I went along with them because my whole damn world was turned on its ear. Now that I've had a bit of time to catch my breath, things are clearing up a bit. If I didn't believe what Sol had to say about where to find them others he came to Muriel with, we wouldn't be alive. And if I didn't believe what he told me about you, I wouldn't have this gun in my hand. So now it's your turn to tell me something, and if you know what's good for you, you'd better make certain I believe it."

"First things first," Lem said. "Sol got it wrong."

"Did he?"

Lem nodded. "I'm not one of Clay's men. I used to be one of his men. That's an awfully big difference."

"Strange, but it doesn't seem so big from where I'm standing."

"Well, it is. I don't want a thing to do with Clay Haskel," Len said. "Not after what happened to your family."

"Oh, so now you go from killer to saint?" Jarrett scoffed. "All on account of some pang of guilt you're supposed to feel?"

"I wouldn't put it in such theatrical terms and I sure wouldn't use the word *saint* when talking about me," Lem said. "But apart from them things, that's about right."

Jarrett shook his head. "Sorry. I don't buy it."

"I've killed plenty of men. I've stolen from plenty more. I've taken horses, money, cattle, and any number of things that didn't belong to me and called it all a part of the business I'd chosen."

"Business? Is that what you call it?"

"Yeah," Lem replied. "That's all it ever was for me. Business. Just a way to earn a living."

Jarrett's face darkened as his thumb began to apply pressure to the hammer of his Colt.

Before that hammer could be cocked back, Lem said, "I'm not about to apologize for the things I've done. It's too late for that. It's also too late to make amends to you or any of the others out there who deserve that and more from me. When Clay took the job he was given, most everyone else who rode with him thought it was going too far. Speaking for myself, I guess I thought Clay would treat it like any other job and tell the man who hired us to go to hell if he didn't like it. Wouldn't be the first time such a thing happened."

"What man hired you?" Jarrett asked.

"John Brakefield. He's some Kansas cattle baron who wants to put as many competitors out of business as he can. Your spread was one of a dozen names on a list that was split up and doled out to Clay and others like him. The instructions were to tear the ranches apart, burn them down, and leave nothing behind. It was meant to be as ugly as possible so nobody would consider taking over in your place. We'd keep the cattle and anything else we could carry, all for a bounty that was paid for every spread brought down."

"I've . . . never even heard of this man," Jarrett said. "Why would he single me out for something like this?"

"You and the other men on that list are other ranchers who proved to be competition to him in some way or other. All he cared about was clearing you out and making sure nobody was left to stand in his way once he came around to buy up what Clay and the others left behind. Just business."

"If you use that word to describe murder one more time, I'll shoot you on principle."

Lem nodded while keeping his hands where they could be seen. "At first, I thought Clay and the rest of us would just go and steal some cows. Maybe rob whoever owned the spread. Same as always. When I saw that Clay meant to follow through on the craziness that Brakefield wanted us to do, I couldn't be a part of it. At first, I thought it would be enough to leave Clay and the others to fend for themselves without any more help from me. But none of the others followed my lead and your place was burned anyway."

Jarrett's trigger finger reflexively tightened, but not enough to send a bullet down the barrel.

"When I saw the flames from a distance," Lem continued, "I came back and, to be honest, wasn't really certain what I could possibly do. But then I saw you riding away from that spread and knew you must have killed at least one of Clay's men to get that far. I couldn't believe anyone could get away from there, but . . . there you were."

Lem lowered his hands and turned to face the wall directly behind him. The wind had picked up and there was enough rustling nearby mixed in with noise from the raucous part of town to keep their voices from drifting very far. Jarrett took a quick look around the corner of the house to see what was happening at the place with three lanterns. The woman wearing her slip was back on the porch, leaning on a rail and looking out at the shadows nearby. Not seeing much of anything, she took her seat to rock back and forth on the chair's rear legs.

Placing his hands on his hips, Lem shook his head. "At first, I thought I'd follow from a distance just to make certain you arrived safely to wherever it was you may be headed. But that wasn't going to be enough. Not if you were headed after Clay instead of going somewhere safe. I didn't have to think about it too long to know that I would've done the same thing in your place."

"So you're trying to reform," Jarrett said in a terse voice. "Is that it?"

Lem shook his head while turning around. "No. It's too late for that. What Clay did to you was . . . I don't even have the words for what it was, but he can't get away with it. We never did nothing like that before."

"Did he ever mention something about selling women prisoners to some fella in Canada?"

"Yeah. He did."

Jarrett surged forward and had his hands around Lem's throat before he even knew what he was doing. Although he loosened his stranglehold once he got his wits about him, he didn't relax it by much. "You knew about that?" he asked.

Lem took hold of Jarrett's wrists without making an attempt to pull the hands away from his neck. "Clay talked about a lot of crazy things," he said after making just enough room for him to get some air into his lungs. "That didn't mean he was going to follow through on any of it."

"Those are my brother's children," Jarrett snarled. "My family!"

"I know. That's why I'm doing this. We're already heading after Clay. You need all the help you can get, and knowing this would have only sidetracked us."

"Sidetracked? It's done a hell of a lot more than that. I can hardly think of a good reason not to shoot you right now."

"Simple," Lem replied. "I may be the only man capable of helping you to save them."

"I heard enough from Sol to know where to look. Why should I trust you?"

"Because I had no reason to go this far in the first place," Lem pointed out.

"Maybe you're just waiting for a moment to shoot me in the back."

"I could've done that a dozen times by now. What possible good would that do for me?"

Unable to come up with an answer for that, Jarrett asked, "What happens when you meet Clay again?"

"Clay used to work by a set of rules. Now he's just a mad dog and there's only one thing to do to a mad dog."

Staring straight into Lem's eyes, Jarrett said, "That's right. It's the same thing I'll do to you if I get the first notion that you're gonna double-cross me."

If Lem was at all uncomfortable by having a pistol pointed at him, he kept that fact very well hidden. He didn't so much as look at the Colt in Jarrett's hand as he took another look at the house with three lanterns. "So it seems like we're right back where we started."

"Except now anyone inside that cathouse probably knows we're coming," Jarrett said.

"It's too dark out here for that girl to have seen much of anything other than two strapping young men approaching the front porch. She probably just thinks we lost our nerve. As far as anyone else in there besides the girls is concerned, they'd be on the lookout for one man on his own."

"They might be taken off their guard if we got close enough to get the drop on them."

Lem nodded. "Possibly. They're probably still wound pretty tight. We gotta figure they'll see us. We could've tried sneaking in, but—"

"No," Jarrett interrupted. "If we snuck in, we'd have to go in there to face them down."

"Wasn't that the reason for coming here?"

"If there's to be a fight, I don't want it to happen in that house. Too much of a risk of someone else getting caught in the cross fire. I want to bring them outside."

"I suppose we could pay that girl to fetch them," Lem offered.

"When they take a look outside, it might be best for them to see a familiar face."

It didn't take long for Lem to catch on. "I haven't been gone for long, but they might have already figured I left the gang. Either way, I suppose they'll want to have a word with me. There's always the chance that I was seen in your company by one of Clay's men before now. If that's the case, things won't go very well for either of us."

"All I need is to get them outside. Whatever happens after that don't matter. Just as long as I bring them animals down with me."

"You don't strike me as a man who wants to die."

"Then you haven't been paying attention."

Lem shook his head. "There are much easier ways to get yourself killed. Besides, Clay is still out there."

"Do you have a point or are you just trying to waste time?"

"My point is that we can get this job done, but not if one of us is distracted by watching the other instead of the men pointing guns at him."

"Exactly," Jarrett said. "That's why you're going to give me your gun."

"What use would I be to you without it?"

"Your use for now is as a distraction. Also, if we're to continue this job together, we need to trust each other."

"Trust isn't a problem with me," Lem pointed out.

"But it's a mighty big one for me," Jarrett replied. "Handing over your gun will go a ways in settling that problem."

Lem let out a long, grating sigh as he slowly reached for his pieced-together pistol. Skinning it with a quick motion, he flipped it around to hand it over butt-first. "There," he said. "Feel better?"

"Not all the way," Jarrett said as he took the gun, "but it's a start." After tucking Lem's weapon under his gun belt, he reached into one of his pockets for something else.

"What've you got there?"

"Sol's bandanna. Let's see how quick these two can think on their feet."

Chapter 29

Lem and Jarrett approached the house again. This time, when the woman on the porch saw them, she stood up without moving toward the door. Wrapping her shawl around her shoulders without covering too much, she asked, "You coming in this time or are you just out for a stroll?"

"Actually we're meeting someone here," Lem said. "Should be two men inside. One's about my age with beady eyes. Both will be armed."

"We get a lot of men through here," she said. "They all look the same after a while."

Lem reached into one of his pockets. "I just bet they do," he said while taking out a small wad of dollar bills. As he approached the porch, she came to meet him at the steps. Holding out the cash, he asked, "This make it easier for you to tell us menfolk apart?"

She took the money and smiled. "They're inside. Want me to get them?"

"That'd be splendid."

Jarrett was sweating profusely beneath the bandanna he wore. Even though he was doing nothing more than standing in one spot, his heart thumped against his ribs as if he'd run there all the way from Flat Pass. The hammering sound filled his ears, growing worse the more he thought about it. All he could do at that point was try not to think too much.

Lem, on the other hand, couldn't appear any calmer unless he was asleep. "This may be hard to believe," he whispered, "but I kinda wish Ackerman was still here."

"So we can arrest these two?" Jarrett asked.

"No, so he could draw some gunfire away from both of us."

Jarrett's laugh was a small one, but it felt good all the same. That single bit of air he let out was enough to calm his nerves so they at least weren't jangling in every corner of his skull.

The front door swung open, allowing two men to step outside. One of them wasn't familiar to Jarrett. He was tall and had a face that would make him look perpetually ten years younger than his true age until the day he sprouted gray whiskers from his chin. The other was Dave Massey. After both men were on the porch, the woman who'd summoned them stood in the doorway with her shawl wrapped even tighter around herself than before. The worried expression on her face gave Jarrett an inkling of what had been said inside the house.

"I'll be damned," Dave said. "That you, Lem?"

Lem stepped forward to place one foot on the edge of the lowest step. "It sure is. Fancy meeting you here."

"Where you been hiding?"

When Jarrett looked at Dave, his mind became flooded with memories of that man and Clay dragging him through his house to get one last look at Jen and those children. One last look. The finality of that turn of phrase had never hit him harder. Feeling a pain in the side of his face, Jarrett realized he'd been clenching his jaw so tightly that he could have bitten through a leather strap.

"Hiding?" Lem said with just enough of an edge in his voice to put a look of concern on the second gunman's face. "I wouldn't exactly call it that."

"Isn't that what you're best at? Hiding in the bushes like a snake, waiting for Clay to give the signal for you to shoot a man from a hundred yards without him ever getting a look at your face?"

"Why, Dave . . . you don't seem pleased to see me."

"Why the hell would I be?" Dave growled as he came to stand at the top of the steps. "You ran off like a yellow dog."

"That ain't what happened."

Dave took one step down so he was lording down at him from a scant couple of inches away. "Yeah? Well, why don't you tell me what happened?"

"How about I buy you a drink?" Lem offered. "Or do you still prefer to discuss business matters in front of whores? I'd think after what happened in Fresno, you'd try to be more careful."

Whatever had happened in Fresno, the mention of it put a sour look on Dave's face. He pushed Lem aside and stomped down the steps while setting his gaze on Jarrett. Lem looked to the gunman with the baby face and said, "Good to see you, Brian. I thought you were killed back at that ranch."

"Does it look like I'm dead?" Brian spat.

"No," Lem replied as he raised his eyebrows. "Surprising."

Brian attempted to assert himself by shoving Lem in a manner similar to what Dave had done. He would have had more success in trying to push down the house behind him. Not only did Lem remain where he was, but he immediately shoved Brian with enough force to send him stumbling back toward the house's front door.

Jarrett stood several paces away from the steps leading to the front porch. As Dave approached him, he fought the urge to make a move right away. Dave still had his hackles up when he asked, "That you, Sol?"

"Yeah," Jarrett replied in what he hoped was a passable impression of Sol's voice.

It must have at least vaguely resembled Sol's tone, because Dave's features relaxed somewhat as he asked, "You get what we were after?"

Jarrett recalled just enough of what Sol had told him to reply, "The Brander's all set."

Jarrett's impersonation must have passed muster, because Dave was all too anxious to turn back to Lem and say, "You see, Brian? Some men can be counted on to do their jobs while others run at the first sign of trouble."

"Perhaps you weren't there that night," Lem said, "but there wasn't much trouble at that ranch. Not on our end anyways."

"Then why the hell did you scamper away like a rat? Tell me!"

"I'll tell it to Clay. He's the only one I owe any explanation to, and if you want to be there to listen, you're more than welcome."

Dave's hand snapped out like a rattler sinking its fangs into a mouse. Grabbing hold of Lem's jacket, he gave him a shake and said, "You owe an explanation to *all* of us! Clay wasn't the only one you were covering with that rifle and eagle eye of yours. And Clay sure as hell wasn't the only one covering *you* at one time or another."

"You through ranting?" Lem asked.

"Not yet. Where have you been? Tell me, if you got an ounce of self-preservation in you."

Lem looked down at the hand that was holding his jacket. He swatted that hand aside with a motion that was so quick it could hardly be seen. Although he'd barely shifted his weight, the difference between how he carried himself now compared to before was like night and day. "Clay's getting into the slave trade. Isn't that right?"

Dave scowled and took half a step back. "He told us what he had planned for any prisoners, but you know Clay. He ain't the sort who takes prisoners."

"That's right. He also talks about a lot of plans that never see the light of day. But I had a word with Paxton after he tried to kill me and a few others back in Flat Pass."

Grinning, Dave mused, "Ol' Pax found you after all, did he? When he didn't come back, we thought he was either killed or decided to follow your example."

"He kicked down a door and opened fire while I was having a bath," Lem said.

"Pax was a good tracker, but he never was very subtle."

"He told me that a few prisoners presented themselves to Clay after I left. Seems Clay decided to follow through on one of them plans after all where selling folks to the Canadian was concerned."

"That's right," Dave said with a slow nod. "He did."

Jarrett kept still and quiet as those two spoke to each other. Although Dave wasn't paying him any mind for the moment, Brian was studying him carefully. Jarrett tried to look annoyed by being under such scrutiny. By the third time he looked in Brian's direction, the act was already wearing thin.

"We're robbers," Lem continued. "Killers, when necessary, and rustlers to be certain. That's what we do. What we know. Do you have any idea how differently we'll be treated now that we're slavers?"

Dave let out one snorting laugh. "Selling a few women to a Canadian don't make us slavers."

"One woman. One girl. How many other children were there?"

"I saw a baby," Dave replied.

"And what's to become of that littlest one?" Lem asked. "Do you know? Do you even care? Because I do!"

Instead of looking over at Brian directly, Jarrett checked on him using just the corner of his eye. He was still being watched. Jarrett eased his hand over to his holster, getting as close as he dared to the Colt.

"You hearing this, Brian?" Dave sneered. "Our sharpshooter's grown a conscience. Ain't that just quaint?"

"It's got nothing to do with a conscience," Lem said. "Every man's got one. Either he works around it or he don't. My concern is about Clay making our jobs and our whole lives harder than they need to be. If you had the wits God gave a mule, that would be your concern as well."

"Weren't you listening when Clay told us how much we could stand to make from selling off them women?"

"So are you looking to find some safe little hole to crawl into and curl up with your money? Because that's what you'll have to do to avoid all the heat that'll come our way once word gets out that Clay and his gang have started stealing people instead of cattle."

Dave scowled at him. "You don't think Clay will pay us our cut when he gets back from Canada? He's never cheated us before."

This time, it was Lem who grabbed hold of Dave by the jacket and shook him. "No!" he said after jostling him and letting go. "This isn't about the money. Even if Clay does pay us everything he promised, things will be different. The law will come after us harder than ever before. Bounty hunters will be hired by grieving family members looking to extract revenge. Our tracks will be harder to cover."

"We know how to cover our tracks well enough," Dave said.

"That'll change real quick when bounty hunters and lawmen find other witnesses to question. Who knows what they'll be told when they have a word with them women that were sold off? Rustling cattle is a whole lot easier. Cows can't do much of anything to point back at us."

Dave's eyes narrowed into a squint. "You always did plenty of thinking, Lem."

"I'm the one that's always lying in a bush a hundred yards away from everyone else. That gives a man plenty of time to think."

"Maybe too much time." After a long second or two, Dave asked, "What did you do to Pax?"

"I found him after he made a mess of his attack on me."

"It was a mess?"

"I'm still alive, ain't I?" When Dave shrugged, Lem continued. "He told me about the prisoners and that Clay sent him to put an end to me since he knew I didn't already agree with selling them off. After that . . . I shot him."

"Just as simple as that, huh?" Dave said with disgust. Before long, he shrugged. "Can't say I'm surprised. Pax always was hotheaded. One of us was gonna kill him sooner or later. Still . . . that don't excuse you turning your back to the rest of us."

"You honestly think everything would have been rose petals and fat bags of money once Clay drug us into the slavery business?"

"I wouldn't call it slavery as such," Dave said. "Whores get sold back and forth all the time."

"And you don't call that slavery?"

"I call that a bad contract."

"Those folks that were taken from Jarrett's ranch didn't sign any contract," Lem said. "And even if they did, they don't deserve to be dragged away and put into the hands of someone who'll . . . well . . . God only knows what that Canadian will do to them. I'd rather not find out."

"Since when did you become so soft when it came to conducting business?" Dave asked. "I know this is new territory, but still . . ."

"If you recall, I voted against the idea when Clay brought it up the first time. I voted against this sort of thing every time, as a matter of fact."

"Yeah, I recall. Clay was never too happy about it. You weren't the sort who would skin off in the middle of a job, though. And you were never the one to call folks by their proper names until you knew them. I believe one time you told me it was so you wouldn't get too close. Come to think of it," Dave said suspiciously, "how did you know that rancher's name was Jarrett?"

"I heard it somewhere along the line."

"Hey, Sol," Dave said as he turned toward Jarrett. "Do you recall Lem being within earshot when we heard that rancher's name?"

Jarrett shook his head and Brian was all too quick to throw in as well. "I didn't hear you, Sol," the gunman said while storming down the porch steps. "Why don't you take that bandanna off?"

"Yeah, Sol," Dave said. "I can never hear you when you wear that thing."

Jarrett had waited too long. He knew that now. But it wasn't too late. Dave looked at him with more annoyance than suspicion and Brian wasn't convinced enough to draw his pistol. That meant the window of opportunity was still open, even if it was about to slam shut.

Taking a step back, Jarrett took hold of the Colt at his side. Before he got it free of its holster, things had already gone straight to hell.

Chapter 30

In a short span of time, Jarrett's proficiency with a firearm was definitely improving. It wasn't, however, improved enough to beat the likes of the experienced gunmen in front of him. His only remaining advantage was the element of surprise, and Jarrett hoped that would be enough to keep him alive for the next couple of seconds.

Dave reached for his pistol and brought it up in a smooth, practiced motion. Before he could squeeze his trigger, he was knocked backward by Lem, who threw himself at the outlaw. Snarling a litany of profanity, Dave staggered toward the house until he knocked into Brian, who then tripped on one of the lower steps directly behind him.

Jarrett now had his gun in hand and the hammer cocked back. Taking quick aim, he fired a shot that burned through the air to shred away a large piece of Brian's elbow. The impact spun the gunman to one side and sent him to his knees. Inside the house, women screamed and hurried to find suitable cover.

"I knew it!" Dave snarled as he wrestled with Lem. "The second you turned up missing, I knew you couldn't wait to sink a knife into all our backs. Pax was one thing, but this!"

Lem's response to that was to drive a knee into Dave's stomach. The impact doubled the outlaw over, setting him up for another knee that caught him on the jaw. Dave staggered back until he hit the railing along the front of the porch. Behind him, Brian had just gotten back to his feet so he could fire a shot at Jarrett.

That round hissed past Jarrett's head, causing him to drop to one knee. From that lower stance, he needed to lift the Colt a bit more so he could fire at something other than the ground. His arm trembled with the effort and the trigger suddenly felt almost too stiff to be pulled.

"I was glad when you left," Dave said as he drove an upward punch into Lem's chest. When he heard Lem suck in a wheezing breath, Dave stood tall and slammed his knuckles against Lem's gut. "Showed everyone your true colors," Dave continued. "But some of us already knew what them colors were."

Brian sidestepped on the porch until he could take a shot that wasn't blocked by Dave or Lem. His sights were fixed solely on Jarrett and he fired before he had his feet firmly set. The bullet whipped past Jarrett's left side, scraping the meat of his arm without giving him more than a brief twinge of pain and a scratch. As the outlaw lined up a proper shot, Jarrett unleashed his remaining bullets in a torrent that chipped away at the porch rail as well as the man standing behind it. Brian's entire body convulsed and was tossed against the house's front window before sliding down the glass.

"You . . . stupid . . . son of a bitch," Dave growled. "Should've stayed in whatever rat hole you slunk into the first time."

Lem put all of his weight behind his left fist as he hit Dave with a chopping blow across the face. As he spoke, he followed up with one punch after another delivered to

Dave's head. "I . . . *never* . . . liked . . . you!" he said until he barely had enough wind to get another word out.

Although Dave had reeled back from the punches, he wasn't knocked very far. One heel was braced against the bottom steps for support and he remained standing purely through force of will. When he lifted his head to look Lem in the eye, Dave's face was a bloody mess. One eye had absorbed most of the damage and his nose was skewed at an awkward angle. Running the tip of his tongue over a split bottom lip, Dave hacked up a mouthful of blood and spat it at Lem's feet. "Aw," he said in a mocking tone. "Ain't that just a shame?"

Jarrett pulled the bandanna off all the way and threw it to the ground. "What's the quickest way to find Clay?"

"You're that rancher, right?" Dave asked.

"Yeah. Now answer my question."

"Don't bother waving that gun at me, rancher. You emptied your cylinder."

"You're still outnumbered," Jarrett said fiercely. "And I can reload plenty quick enough."

"He's got nothing else to say, Jarrett," Lem said. "Even if he knew anything worth hearing, he wouldn't tell either of us."

"You never were stupid, Lem," Dave said. "A yellow-bellied coward, maybe, but not stupid."

"We all have our faults," Lem said. "Care to guess what yours may be?"

"Do tell."

"Overconfidence."

Scowling distastefully, Dave reached for his holster. He recoiled slightly when his hand found nothing but leather at his hip. Dave even looked down to make absolutely certain that he was feeling in the right spot for his weapon, only to come up empty once more.

"And your other fault," Lem said as he showed Dave the pistol he'd lifted from his holster during their scuffle. "You're easily distracted."

"And you're not long for this world," Dave replied. "Once Clay finds out that you're a traitor as well as a coward—"

"He won't find out anything," Lem said. "Not until it's too late." With that, he squeezed the trigger of the gun he'd stolen. The pistol barked twice in quick succession and then, after a pause, once more.

Dave remained standing for a moment, blinking as his mouth moved to form words. His lungs couldn't put enough wind behind them to get those words out, so Dave wound up taking them to his grave.

Looking up, Lem found Brian on the porch, took aim, and fired two more rounds into the unmoving body.

"What was that for?" Jarrett asked after reloading his Colt. "He was already dead."

"Had to be sure," Lem said. "Dave was right about one thing. If Clay finds out how many men he's lost, it won't bode well for us."

"How long had you ridden with them?"

Lem was already taking the gun belt from around Dave's waist. "What's that matter?" he asked.

"Because you just gunned him down without a thought."

"I thought about it plenty," Lem said. "Starting with all the times I watched this animal kill folks without good reason and every time he threatened to kill me just because I didn't agree with every little thing that came out of his stupid mouth. Last time I thought about it was when I saw he'd become an even worse animal than before. Why? You feeling sorry for him?"

"Not one bit. Just . . . if you could do that to men you used to call friend . . ."

"I called them partners. Not friends."

"I guess it just surprises me, is all," Jarrett said. "Especially after all that talking between you and Dave before a shot was fired."

"The only reason I was talking to him for so long was that I was waiting for you to make a move. Took you long enough."

By now, the front door of the house squeaked open so a woman could take a peek outside. Lem and Jarrett both froze like a couple of boys who'd been caught trying to sneak into a circus tent without paying for a ticket.

The woman opened the door all the way. She was a bit older than the one who'd been sitting on the porch earlier and spoke with a distinctly authoritarian sharpness in her voice. "So, I take it the four of you aren't partners after all?"

"Not anymore, ma'am," Lem said.

After taking a quick look at the state of her porch and window, she said, "You left us a mess."

Lem knew exactly where to look when he dug into one of Dave's shirt pockets. The wad of cash he found there seemed to be a bit more than he was expecting, but he handed it over all the same. "Here you go," he said while picking up Dave's body. "That should cover the damages with some to spare. For that extra, I'd like to ask that you forget we were here."

The woman sifted through the money and nodded. "Far as I'm concerned, you're just a couple men who came along to collect your friends that were passed out on the porch. Guess these two must've shot each other in some sort of argument."

"Much obliged," Lem said as he carried Dave across the street.

Jarrett picked up Brian's body and slung it over one

shoulder. Following Lem across the street, he dropped the body next to the spot where Dave had been propped against a building. The spot was thick with shadows at the moment, but even that didn't fully hide the two gunmen.

"Come morning, they'll be spotted easy enough," Jarrett said.

Lem hunkered down over Brian so he could perform a quick search of the younger man's pockets. "Come morning, we won't be here. Besides, I'm sure these won't be the first corpses to be found after a particularly eventful night."

"I suppose you're right. If that had been a rare event, someone would've come running to investigate these gunshots."

"This place belongs to men like Roland Gein. Plenty of nights around here are eventful."In the third pocket he searched, Lem found a wad of cash roughly the same size as the one that had been in Dave's possession. "They must've divvied up some money while they were in there."

"You think that'll keep us in supplies for the ride north?" Jarrett asked.

"All the way to Canada?"

"That's where Clay's headed. That's where we need to go."

"What about Sheriff Rubin? Didn't you want to meet up with him again?"

"Something about him never seemed quite right," Jarrett said. "I still don't think it was just bad timing that he never went out to my ranch when the herd was being moved out of there. After all, he did say he'd seen smoke from the fire."

Lem took the gun belts off both dead outlaws and

draped one over each shoulder. "Yeah," he said while leaving the bodies behind him. "The sheriff did say something about that."

"He's crooked, right?"

"No," Lem replied. "He's just lazy and his deputy couldn't give a damn about doing his job."

"Ackerman?"

"Tom."

"Good," Jarrett said. "I was beginning to like Ackerman." He and Lem walked down the street a short ways before either of them spoke. Once the house with three lanterns was well behind them, Jarrett asked, "So, is this how outlaws settle things when they have a parting of ways? Someone starts shooting and someone else winds up dead in an alley?"

"Occasionally. If it makes you feel any better, these are the first partners I ever killed."

"Somehow I doubt that."

"You talking about what happened between me and Paxton back in Flat Pass?" Lem asked.

The image of Lem shooting the man who'd stormed into the bathroom at that fancy hotel was still burned into Jarrett's head. "Yeah," he said. "I was."

Lem nodded. "I knew someone was there watching us. Since I wasn't grabbed up and tossed into jail, I figured it wasn't a lawman. There were no screams, so it probably wasn't a fainthearted girl or young fella. I'd ask how you knew to look for me there, but I suppose it really doesn't matter now."

"What matters is that issue of trust that keeps cropping up."

"I suppose so." Lem stopped and turned to face Jarrett. Holding open his jacket to reveal the holster that now held the gun that had once belonged to Dave, he said, "If it makes you feel better, you can take this gun as well."

"When you met that man outside Annie's, the two of you spoke for a short spell."

"Damn, you were standing there longer than I thought. Ain't too many men can sneak up on me like that."

Ignoring the peculiar compliment, Jarrett asked, "What were you two really talking about?"

"It was a short conversation and the first bit was pretty much the same as what you heard from Dave. Where did I go? Why am I such a traitorous dog? That sort of thing. The rest was what I already told to Dave as well as me trying to find out where Clay and the rest had gotten to. He didn't tell me much, but he never was very bright, so he let a few things slip. Told me that if I wanted him to help me I might as well shoot him. After that," Lem said without a hint of emotion, "you know the rest."

"That's why you killed him?"

"I had to make certain he didn't get around to letting anyone know I was riding on this posse."

"So I didn't find out?" Jarrett asked.

"Partly," Lem replied. "But mostly I wanted that to be a surprise for the others that we rounded up. Catch them off guard and such. Seems to be working out pretty good so far, wouldn't you say?"

Just then, Jarrett didn't quite know what to think. Although Lem had most definitely lied to him, the reasons he gave as an explanation made fairly good sense. Also, with two more of Clay's men sent to meet their Maker, the arrangement definitely was working out pretty well. If Lem had been sent as a spy or to get in close enough to eradicate the posse coming after Clay and his gang, the effort was so poorly executed that it was no threat at all.

Only one question remained. It was an obvious one,

but Jarrett needed to see Lem's eyes when it was answered.

"Should I expect the same treatment as what you gave to your other partners?" Jarrett asked. "Not right now, but after this job is finished."

"We've still got a ways to go before this job is done," Lem said good-naturedly. "Even so, I doubt you'll pose the same problem as my former associates did."

"Which is?"

"Being an obnoxious ass."

Jarrett reached for the pieced-together pistol he'd taken from Lem earlier and handed it back to its owner. "Here you go," he said. "I need to keep my sights set on the task at hand instead of fussing with details."

"The possibility of being gunned down is more than a detail," Lem said as he took his pistol and holstered it.

"Even so, considering what's ahead of us, the odds are we'll both be killed within the next day or two anyway."

"What's worse, after what happened here and at Annie's, we won't be able to show our faces near any cathouse in the county for quite a while."

Chapter 31

Not only did MacGrearey's serve a hearty breakfast, but it was brought to Lem and Jarrett's table by some of the most attractive servers either man had ever seen. Not long after their steak and eggs were placed in front of them, they were joined by Roland Gein, who looked just as alert as he had when they last met only a scant number of hours ago.

"I trust you two had an eventful night," Gein said.

Using his fork to stab some steak, Jarrett asked, "You heard about what happened?"

"I did. This meal and anything else you might need for the remainder of your ride is on me."

"That's mighty generous."

"Generous, my ass," Gein said. "Having two men gunned down on that place's front porch will scare away their customers for at least a couple days. Customers, I am pleased to add, that will come here. That profit is because of you."

"Surely," Lem said, "something like that is worth more than a few meals and some supplies?"

Before Gein could give voice to whatever had caused his brow to furrow, Jarrett said, "The meal and supplies will be just fine. Thanks."

"You're welcome," Gein said. "Is there anything else you might need?"

"Not that I can think of. We plan on riding out as soon as our food settles, so we'll let you know if anything comes to mind."

"You do that." Gein shifted as if he was about to stand up, but then settled back into his chair. Leaning forward, he folded his hands on top of the table and said, "That just leaves the small matter of our arrangement. Since those two won't be leaving town, I doubt the rest of those rustlers will be coming by. At least, not with the herd anyway."

"I suppose not," Jarrett said.

Lem winced. "One or two may come around looking for the men that we got last night. They may come straight to you since you're the one they were dealing with."

"I can handle a few rustlers trying to assert themselves," Gein said. "If not, I would've been out of this line of work a long time ago. I was thinking more along the lines of that herd. Our previous arrangement was for me to keep it. Since I am one of the largest buyers of what I like to call . . . creatively acquired cattle, they still may come my way. What shall I do in that event?"

"Whatever cattle come here will most likely be stragglers or less than a dozen head that were skimmed from the rest," Jarrett said. "Do with them as you please. From what I gather, you're the one who delivered Sol to us."

"You are correct," Gein said.

"Then keep whatever you get from the Lazy J. It's worth it to me not to have to come here again and collect them. No offense, of course."

"Don't be silly," Gein replied. "Muriel may suit my purposes, but it's a wart on the back of Wyoming and I'll

be pulling up stakes at the soonest opportunity myself."
He got to his feet this time and extended a hand across
the table. After Jarrett shook it, Gein said, "Pleasure doing business with you."

"Likewise."

As for Lem, he and Gein merely nodded to each
other to represent a civil, if not amicable, parting.

There was one more hunk of steak on Jarrett's plate,
which he cut in half and dipped into the spilt yolk of his
fried eggs. "You two barely seem to tolerate each other."

Eventually Lem said, "He's a broker. I don't like brokers. They get fat off the sweat of other men and profit
from the work they do. Brokers are just a bunch of damn
leeches."

"I understand," Jarrett said. "Although I found Gein
to be much more agreeable than I expected, there are
plenty of men like him who make their profit by shaving
off pieces of ranches like mine."

"Just don't get too comfortable on account of Gein
being so agreeable," Lem warned. "Men like him pat
someone on the back just to look for a good spot to sink
a knife."

"Which is why we're leaving here as quickly as possible. Let's get our supplies, saddle the horses, and get on
with it."

"No arguments here."

Leaving Muriel was just as simple as that. One of
Gein's men rushed over to their table as soon as they
stood up to leave and told them where to pick up the
supplies they'd been promised. The horses were ready to
go and so were their riders. Lem and Jarrett put the cow
town behind them and were well on their way to meeting
up with Sheriff Rubin after less than five hours of gallop-
ing over a whole lot of flat terrain.

As they rode, Jarrett's thoughts cleared considerably. While his spirit was still scarred by the fire that he could still smell and hear as if the embers were still hot, he'd taken several steps away from being a helpless prisoner. He knew what needed to be done and who was left to do it to, and he had a good idea of where to find them. That day, all there was for him was to ride. And so he rode.

The sun had spent the better part of the day lost behind a bank of clouds that stretched in the sky for as far as the eye could see. Sometime between late afternoon and early evening, Lem pulled back on his reins, which prompted Jarrett to follow suit. Pointing to the north, Lem said, "Looks like someone's taken an interest in us."

Jarrett squinted to see a shape in the distance that hadn't quite caught his attention yet. It had all but blended in with a staggered row of trees and a few boulders wedged in between some low hills. He dug into his saddlebag for his field glasses and placed them to his eyes.

"Whoever it is, they're headed this way," Lem said without the need of any lenses to magnify what he saw.

After gazing through the field glasses for a moment, Jarrett said, "I think it's Ackerman."

"How can you tell from here?"

"Whether it's up close or from a distance, that gangly kid looks like a scarecrow tied to his saddle," Jarrett said as he dropped the field glasses back into his bag. "We should meet him before he starts hollering at us like a damn fool."

Both of them snapped their reins and rode straight at the oncoming horseman. Ackerman pulled back on his reins when he was about thirty yards away from crossing paths with the other two men and shouted, "Come along! This way!"

Lem chuckled at Jarrett's prophetic statement and soon the three of them were all headed back along the trail from which Ackerman had come.

"Where's Sol?" Jarrett asked once the three of them fell into a quick and steady pace.

"He's with the sheriff," Ackerman replied. "Safe and sound."

"Pity," Lem grunted. "Would've been easier if he'd fallen from his horse."

The deputy had his hand on his holstered pistol and tightened his grip on the weapon as he said, "Considering what he had to say about you, I'm not surprised to hear that."

"Relax, kid," Jarrett said. "I know all about it."

"You know that Lem used to ride with Clay Haskel and those rustlers?"

"Yeah."

Ackerman first looked over to Lem and then to Jarrett. Settling back into his saddle with his eyes facing front, he said, "And here I thought breaking that news was going to be messy."

"You don't seem very happy that it wasn't," Jarrett said.

It was obvious that Ackerman was uncomfortable. He gnashed his teeth and continued to tighten his grip on his pistol as if he was engaging in a silent tug-of-war between keeping it holstered and drawing it. "I . . . it's just . . . ," the deputy stammered.

Before the young lawman squirmed out of his skin, Jarrett said, "Lem, why don't you ride on ahead?"

Lem looked over to Ackerman and said, "I take it the others aren't far from here."

"Right," the deputy replied. "Just follow that trail about a mile or two. You won't be able to miss them."

After Lem had gone, Jarrett asked, "What's bothering you, kid?"

"First of all, I'm not a kid."

"Fine. What's bothering you, Deputy?"

Straightening up like any kid who felt he'd just proven himself, Ackerman said, "How can you still want him around, knowing who he is?"

"Lem's proven to be a valuable man to have along. Considering the animals we're after, he may also be the *best* man to have along."

"If you say so."

"I'm guessing the sheriff doesn't share my opinion."

"He's on the fence," Ackerman said. "When he first heard about who he was, there was talk about stringing him up right along with the others."

"Sol told him?"

"Him and anyone else who'd listen. We had to stuff another bandanna in his mouth just to get some peace and quiet."

"Sounds about right. What's the sheriff thinking now?"

"He's in a much better mood after the easy victory we had today."

"Easy victory?" Jarrett asked. "You caught up with the herd?"

Ackerman nodded. "Just like you said, it wasn't much of a chore to track a herd of cattle. Sheriff Rubin and Tom caught sight of them the day after we split off to go to Muriel. Took a bit of time to scout them out and see how many gunmen had to be dealt with, and we rode in on them at first light this morning."

"Sounds like it went well."

"There were hardly any shots fired. One of the rustlers got anxious and tried to take a run at the sheriff, but he didn't make it very far. The rest gave up real quick after that."

"How many were there?" Jarrett asked.

"Four," the deputy said. "It was barely enough to keep the herd in line. Then again, rustlers aren't as concerned about rounding up strays as someone who paid for the cattle properly. The whole bunch is tied up and being dragged back to Flat Pass along with Sol. Your herd is on its way back to your land. Sheriff Rubin meant to ask if you'd rather it was steered somewhere else."

"Let's send half to Muriel for Roland Gein. The rest can keep going back to my property."

"You sure about that?"

"Yeah," Jarrett replied. "Gein earned that much."

"Shouldn't be a problem. We might lose a few head along the way, but you don't seem overly concerned about that either."

"I'm not." Jarrett sighed. "Think I'm out of the ranching business for now."

"I suppose this job is mostly done, then," Ackerman said proudly.

"Not yet," Jarrett said. "Between the two men killed in Muriel, the one that was captured there, the one that was killed in Flat Pass, the ones captured along with the herd, and the ones I got the night of the fire, there can't be many more to contend with. Clay himself wasn't with the herd, was he?"

"No."

"Actually I'm surprised there were as many men as you say guarding them cattle."

Ackerman shrugged. "Sheriff Rubin thinks one or two of the men we caught were brought on along the way. Probably hired by the rustlers for a few dollars just to wrangle the herd as best they could since they were so shorthanded and all."

"Still," Jarrett said, "job well done."

"The sheriff is happy with how things went, but he won't much like it when Lem comes back. He'll ask some questions and he may not like the answers."

"How much did you tell him about what Sol said back in Muriel?"

"Not a lot," Ackerman replied. "Sol was a handful, even with all the ropes that were tied around him. When I got him back, he did all that talking about Lem and then I had to do some explaining myself."

"What have you got to explain?" Jarrett asked.

"Sheriff Rubin just wanted to know my impressions of Lem and you as for how well you handled those rustlers we found in Muriel."

"What did you tell him?"

"The truth. Not like there was anything to hide. There wasn't much time before we had to scout ahead to find the herd. Once we found it, we had our work cut out for us."

"And after that was done, I'm guessing nobody cared about much else other than celebrating," Jarrett said.

"More or less. Now that I think about it," Ackerman said, "it doesn't seem as impressive as it was before."

"Oh, it's worth a celebration."

"You did a good amount of work yourself, Mr. Pekoe. You and Lem."

"That's right and there's more ahead of us."

"You going to tell the sheriff about the rest of what Sol had to say back in Muriel?" the deputy asked. "I mean, as far as what was said about that Canadian fella goes?"

"No point," Jarrett replied. "It seems they're all too busy patting each other on the backs."

"I was gonna tell him myself and I'm not about to keep anything from Sheriff Rubin. I'm surely not going to lie to him either. It just seemed proper to wait until you got back."

"I wouldn't think of asking you to hide anything from the sheriff. Something tells me I know exactly what he's going to say, though."

Chapter 32

"Canada?" Sheriff Rubin said after Ackerman led Jarrett and Lem back to the rest of the posse members. "That's a long ways from my jurisdiction."

Jarrett stood near the spot where Twitch and a few other horses were drinking from a stream. The herd was a stone's throw away being tended by Tom and one other posse member. When the deputy looked to him out of frustration, Jarrett gave Ackerman a shrug that screamed *I told you so* without actually saying it. The deputy wasn't happy to see it from him and was even more annoyed when he saw a similar look from Lem. Turning to Rubin, Ackerman said, "But Clay is the leader of the gang we're after. Isn't this posse supposed to go after the entire gang?"

"Not if it involves crossing jurisdictional boundaries," Rubin said. "Especially not if we have to ride out of our own country! Besides, we can't stay away from Flat Pass for much longer. We're already taking the time to drop off some of them cows to that friend of yours in Muriel. We'll keep our eyes open and if any of them remaining rustlers show their faces near us again, we'll make them wish they hadn't."

"Clay might be the only one left."

"Well, then . . . all the better."

Although Jarrett and Lem seemed ready to be done with the lawmen, Ackerman wasn't ready to give up just yet. "But we almost got him!" the deputy said. "We can't just give up before finishing what we started."

Rubin was already pulling on his gloves and approaching his horse. "It seems you forgot what our duty is here. A posse is formed to deal with a threat posed by a dangerous man or men who have attempted to escape. As lawmen, we need to see to it that the threat is answered. Most of those rustlers are dead and the rest are right here with us," the sheriff said while sweeping a hand to the outlaws that had been captured. The rustlers formed a short train, linked at the wrists by a length of rope. "The threat is contained," Rubin concluded. "Just because one of the weasels managed to wriggle away doesn't mean we failed. I'm sure another lawman farther north will get the chance to hang him. For us, it's time to finish up and go home."

Ackerman might not have been a deputy for very long, but he knew when the sheriff had made up his mind. He walked back over to where Lem and Jarrett were standing. Sighing, he said, "Looks like that's that."

"Sure does," Jarrett said.

"The sheriff's right, though. Clay's the only one left as far as we know and he doesn't even realize all of his men have been either killed or rounded up."

Lem nodded. "Yep."

Most of the lawmen were preparing to commence the ride back to Flat Pass. Tom and another man tending to the animals started to get some of the cattle moving, which would eventually set the entire herd into motion.

"You should probably get back with them," Jarrett said. "Don't want to be left behind."

"What about you?" Ackerman asked. "Don't you want to get a look at your herd? Count up how many head may be missing? Make certain they all get safely back to where they need to go?"

"No."

"Where are you going?"

"Do you really need to ask?"

"The sheriff's right, you know," Ackerman said. "Going after Clay will take you outside the jurisdiction of this posse."

"Does your sheriff honestly consider us to be members of this posse anymore?" Lem asked.

"At least come with us back to Flat Pass," Ackerman said to Jarrett. "More than likely, Sheriff Rubin will change his mind about going after Clay. We've got the whole ride back to make sure he does."

Jarrett shook his head. "I don't think he will and neither do you. Rubin is more than happy to drag in the men he's already got and call it a day. He'll look like the big lawman when he returns to his office, where he can prop his feet up and read his newspapers again."

"If you ride north from here to go after Clay," Ackerman warned, "you won't have the law on your side."

"If the law doesn't back a man who rids the world of scum like Clay," Jarrett said, "then I don't want any part of it."

"What about your land? Your home?"

"You must not have been paying attention, kid. My home is a pile of burned rubble and my land is a graveyard."

"You can start over. Plenty of men do, you know."

"I'll think about that sort of thing when I come back from Canada," Jarrett said.

"You mean if you come back."

Jarrett let that sink in for just over a second before saying, "Yeah."

Realizing that he wasn't making a dent in the rancher's resolve, Ackerman said to him, "I learned a lot riding with you. Both of you."

"That's strange," Jarrett said with a slight laugh. "Didn't think I was teaching anything."

"Doesn't matter." Looking between Jarrett and Lem, the deputy said, "I'll do what I can to explain what you two are doing to the sheriff."

"Probably best if you don't explain anything," Lem said. "Just tell him you don't know where we went or why."

"I suppose that's mostly the truth. There's a lot of ground between here and the border. If the sheriff presses the matter, I won't lie to his face," Ackerman warned. "A head start is all I can guarantee."

"That's all we need," Jarrett said. "Much obliged."

"Don't thank me. Feels like I'm not doing you any favors."

Jarrett made it easier for the younger man by nodding once, turning the other direction, and walking away. Not long after that, the deputy climbed onto his horse and rode off to join the others.

"You think we should worry about that one?" Lem asked.

"Nah. He means well and he's got a lousy face for lying. He'll do what he told us he would. Even if he doesn't do a very good job of sidestepping any questions that come his way, he should be able to stall for a spell."

Lem was watching the deputy ride away. His eyes also wandered back and forth to take in the sight of the rest of the posse splitting the herd and driving most of it back along the same tracks they'd put down when leaving Flat

Pass. "I imagine them lawmen will be bragging about whatever bit of nothing they did to round up the dregs we left behind. If the kid said those men put up hardly any fight, they must have been a bunch of cross-eyed pups that couldn't hit the broad side of a barn."

"Probably. Let's get going before anyone notices we're not joining them."

As they skirted along the outer edge of the herd, they were spotted by a couple of posse members. The men weren't proper deputies, but volunteers who were more comfortable wrangling beef than firing a gun. They waved at Jarrett and he waved back. Tom spotted them as well and didn't even do that much.

"The kid had his heart in the right place," Lem said through a smile that was about as genuine as a wooden nickel, "but I'm not gonna miss the rest of these idiots. At least I don't have to look at them again."

Twitch was especially nervous around the cattle, even though they were the same animals he'd lived with on the Lazy J for years. Jarrett calmed the horse without even thinking about it. His hands pulled the reins just right and he nudged the gelding with his knees to keep Twitch moving along in a mostly straight line. "I know what you mean," he said.

"Yeah, but you'll have to deal with them again."

Jarrett had nothing to say to that.

"You didn't really mean what you said about not going back home, did you?" Lem asked.

"Why wouldn't I mean it?"

"Because we're headed after Clay. He should be with your brother's wife and at least one of those children."

Jarrett winced as if he'd been shot in the chest. "Maybe he's got fewer along with him than that."

"Even if he's only got one of your family along for the ride, that's more than you've got right now."

"Yeah," Jarrett said in a voice bereft of even the slightest trace of humanity. "That's right."

Lem leaned over to give him a shove. It wasn't enough to push Jarrett off Twitch's back, but it did a good job of rattling the other man. Having regained his balance in the saddle, Jarrett asked, "What're you trying to do? Break my damn neck?"

"I'm trying to see if you're still in there," Lem replied while tapping a finger against Jarrett's head. "You can't be drifting like this when we find Clay, because he'll have no qualms about killing a man who isn't up to snuff."

"I'll be fine when that time comes."

"And what about after?"

"I don't know," Jarrett said. "I hadn't thought about it."

Lem shook his head and let out a tired sigh. "Great. That's just great."

"What's your problem?"

"My problem is that I gave up riding with one bunch of shortsighted fools just to ride with another one."

"And what's that supposed to mean?" Jarrett asked.

Without looking over to him, Lem said, "It means you could have saved everyone some time if you had just put a bullet through your own skull and been done with it."

"Trust me, I thought about it."

"But you didn't do it. Instead you decided to ride out and shove all your pain down the throats of those who deserve it! And when you heard about your kin still being alive, you jumped at the chance to get them back. What happened between now and then to make you into such a sorrowful lump?"

"I just get the feeling that there's more misery waiting for me if I find Clay," Jarrett said. "More for you, to be certain. There's been enough misery already."

"So you intend to let your family fend for themselves? I don't believe that."

Jarrett shook his head. "I'm still going after Clay. I just . . . don't know what I'll find."

"You're not a fortune-teller. Neither am I. Hell, neither are the folks who tell you they're fortune-tellers!"

"I don't know what you want from me."

"What I want is to hear that there's a good reason for what we're doing. You've got to have a plan. Otherwise we're just riding out to kill a man. That don't make us any better than another outlaw or some piece-of-trash bounty hunter. If that's all this is about, then I'd rather ride in another direction to take my chances with a new life and a new name in some other part of the world."

They rode for a while longer. Neither man felt like saying much of anything. They left the herd behind and then turned toward the north before picking up their pace. On more than one occasion, they discussed the route Clay would take to get to Canada. Between Lem's familiarity with how Clay would travel with at least one prisoner in tow and Jarrett's knowledge of the terrain itself, they narrowed their options down considerably. For the rest of the day, however, there was only one option.

The trail they used wouldn't meet up with any others that would lead to Canada for quite a while. There were ample watering holes and even a few small trading posts along the way where they stopped for food or merely to stretch their legs. If they made it into Montana before dark, they stood a chance of catching up to Clay in a few days. Of course, there was always the possibility that

Clay had taken a different route or was on a schedule that meant he'd already met the Canadian slaver and was on his way back with a pocketful of cash. Jarrett couldn't let himself think about that.

He did allow his mind to wander in other directions, though. Mostly he thought about what Lem had said to him when they were back at the herd. He'd been right about one thing. Whether it was because of the dark turn his life had taken or all the blood that had been spilled in such a short amount of time, Jarrett had allowed himself to be drawn down into darkness. Quite simply, that could not be allowed. If the darkness sank its claws in too deep, Jarrett would lose sight of why he'd started fighting so hard in the first place.

After crossing the Montana border, they rode for several more miles and made camp in a clearing. A fire crackled beneath a pot of beans while Twitch shifted from one hoof to another a few yards away. Using a branch to stoke the flames a bit, Jarrett said, "Peach cobbler."

"What was that?" Lem asked.

"You asked about my plans before."

"And you plan . . . peach cobbler?"

Jarrett nodded and smiled. "My brother's wife makes some peach cobbler that's one of the best things I've ever tasted. It's a Pekoe family recipe, but she does it better than anyone else. When this is through, I figure I'll have a plate of Jen's peach cobbler."

Now Lem smiled too. "That sounds damn good."

Chapter 33

They kept riding north and when they came to the spot where they had to make a decision as to which trail to follow from there, fortune smiled upon them.

Lem rode back along the trail he'd followed wearing a big smile on his face. "River's washed out an entire stretch of road just over a mile up ahead," he said while pointing in the direction from which he'd come. "Ain't nobody getting through that way unless they're fish, and by the looks of it, that's how it's been for a good long while."

"That's usually bad news," Jarrett mused.

"Not this time. That just leaves one of the trails we meant to try."

Both men looked at the trail stretched out in front of Jarrett. "That is," Jarrett said, "if either of them is the right one."

"Only one way to find out, and it ain't by talking." With that, Lem snapped his reins and galloped northward.

Jarrett didn't let him get more than a few paces ahead before racing to catch up.

Once they were committed to their decision, the only thing to do was ride that trail all the way to the Canadian border and hope they would find something promising before getting to Alaska. It was just past eight o'clock in the evening on the second day of riding when Lem motioned for them to stop.

"It's too early to make camp," Jarrett insisted.

"Quiet!" Lem hissed. Keeping his eyes fixed on a point in the distance, he reached back with one hand and whispered, "Give me them field glasses."

Jarrett dug in his saddlebag, found the glasses, and handed them over. Leaning forward as if that would help him see any more without the use of any equipment, he asked, "What is it?"

"Don't know yet," Lem replied as he stared through the glasses. "Could be nothing."

"Or it could be something."

"Stands to reason." Lem climbed down from his saddle, tied off his horse, and hurried through some brush alongside the trail. Not far behind him, Jarrett mimicked the other man's movements by moving swiftly while keeping his head down.

"Where are you going?" Jarrett asked.

"I've got to get to a better spot so I can get a clearer line of sight."

"To what?"

Jarrett guessed they were headed for higher ground. Instead Lem picked a spot in a clearing and shifted his gaze skyward. Looking up there as well, Jarrett didn't see much of anything apart from a few lazily drifting birds and a few clouds.

Undoubtedly sensing he was drawing close to being pestered with more questions, Lem nodded at the clouds and asked, "See that?"

Jarrett squinted and looked again. The only other thing he saw this time was that some of the clouds formed a straighter line than others. Blinking away a few bits of dust that had gotten into his eyes, he said, "Is that smoke?"

"Sure is."

"Probably from a cooking fire."

"That's what I was thinking," Lem said.

"Could it be Clay?"

Lem gnawed on one cheek as he watched the smoke trail closely. "Maybe."

Jarrett jumped to his feet. "Let's get down there to see. If it's not him, perhaps whoever it is has seen him."

"And if it is Clay, he might get spooked if we come barging in on him. Spooking a man with prisoners is a good way to get them prisoners hurt."

Reminding himself that Lem must have had plenty of experience in dealing with prisoners, Jarrett said, "All right, but we'll have to get closer if we want to find out who made that fire. We can't exactly see much from here."

Pointing the field glasses at the smoke trail, Lem followed it up and down as he said, "We can see enough."

Jarrett gave him some time to see whatever he thought he could see. After a minute or so that felt a whole lot longer than that, he said, "You can sit here. I'm going for a closer look."

"Does that smoke look broken to you?"

Freezing where he was, Jarrett felt like a confused mutt as he angled his head to get another look at the sky. "What do you mean?"

"The smoke trail. Does it look broken?"

Now that he had something on which to focus, Jarrett hunkered back down in his spot and stared upward. "It does. Toward the top, right where it all starts to dissipate."

"That's what I thought as well," Lem said.

"Does that mean something or are you passing the time by asking strange questions?"

"Clay always liked to learn whatever he could about Indians. He used to say that any group of men who gave the soldiers and law alike such big headaches must have a whole lot to offer to outlaws. In some respects, he was right. Foraging for food, hunting, even some raiding practices he liked to use came from what he gathered from the Indians. Another trick he liked to use was smoke signals."

Jarrett looked at the smoke trail and scowled. "I don't think that looks like any sort of signal."

"I said Clay liked to think he'd learned from the Indians," Lem said. "That doesn't mean he was a good student. As far as the signals go, he would use them when he was waiting for someone to let them know where to find him. It wasn't anything too complicated. Just an occasional break in the smoke." Smirking, Lem added, "Kind of like that one right there."

At first, Jarrett couldn't see what Lem was talking about. As he followed the smoke trail toward its base, he saw a sliver of skylight cut between it and the tree line. That sliver slowly grew as the smoke continued to rise. It took a couple of minutes, but it soon became clear that the column had been cut off at its source. Then the smoke appeared again in a wider shape that would have come if more smoke had been trapped and then released. Jarrett looked up higher and saw a similar swelling in the smoke trail. The break wasn't nearly as easy to see, but it had been there some time ago.

"That's Clay all right," Lem said.

"Or," Jarrett added, "an Indian with very little to say."

Chapter 34

The campsite was situated on the edge of a small clearing partly surrounded by trees and bushes. A few boulders were scattered in the area, but only enough to create a quarter circle away from the flickering flames. A blanket lay near the fire, which was probably used to make the crude signal. Sitting with her back against one of the trees was a slender female figure. Jarrett couldn't see much more than that since her head was covered by a dirty sack and her arms were tied behind her.

"Grace?" Jarrett whispered as he inched closer. "Is that you?"

The figure lifted her head and looked from side to side.

"It's all right, darlin'," he said.

Before Jarrett could take one more step toward the clearing, another voice cut through the air like a knife.

"That's close enough," Clay shouted as he took half a step out from behind one of the boulders at least forty to fifty yards away from the fire. He had a rifle in hand and held it to one shoulder. "I got you in my sights and I know there ain't no more of you on their way."

"You're done, Clay," Jarrett said. "I'm taking this girl along with any other prisoners you have with you and we're going home."

Clay moved a few steps farther from the boulder. Squinting at Jarrett, he asked, "That you, rancher?"

"The name's Jarrett Pekoe and yes. It's me."

"Now, this is a surprise! I figured there'd be a posse comin', but I guessed that sheriff in Flat Pass was lazy enough to give me a bigger head start."

The outlaw's words barely registered in Jarrett's head. All he could think about was the slender figure tied to the tree. "This ends here," he said. "Your men are all dead or in jail."

"Well, that still leaves me," Clay said. "And that's all I ever needed."

From somewhere nearby, a baby's voice rose to a shrill cry.

"You want that little brat," Clay snarled, "you're welcome to it. I only kept it alive this long to keep the womenfolk busy."

"Where's the rest of the people you're holding?" Jarrett asked.

Even from a distance, Clay's leering smile could plainly be seen. "You mean that brat and its mother? They're close. You harm a hair on my head and I'll put an end to both of 'em real quick. You kill me, and I swear you won't never find that woman."

"Tell me where they are!" Jarrett roared. He already had his pistol drawn but didn't have a clear shot. When he heard movement beside him, his finger twitched against the Colt's trigger.

"Take a breath," Lem said from directly beside Jarrett. "Let me handle this."

"Lem?" Clay shouted. "No matter how many times I heard that you ran off and no matter how many told me it was true, I didn't want to believe it. I never had you pegged as a coward."

"I'm not a coward, Clay."

"Stop right where you are!" Clay snapped as he pressed the rifle's stock even tighter against his shoulder and set his feet in a firing stance. "Show me them hands!"

Lem raised his hands and opened his jacket to reveal the gun belt at his side.

Shifting to a more casual posture, Clay asked, "Where's that rifle of yours?"

"Didn't think you'd let me get far if I was carrying it."

"You're right about that. I'm surprised you even showed your face. Ain't it more like you to hide somewhere and try to pick me off from a distance?"

Lem shrugged. "Couldn't get a clear shot from a distance. I imagine that's because you believed what those others were saying about me a bit more than you just said."

"Maybe that's so. Did you come all the way out here to prove yourself to be something other than a dog that scurried away with its tail between his legs?"

Taking a step forward, Lem said, "I've already heard the insults from Dave and the others. They were the last things they said to anyone on this earth."

"Not another step!" Clay said.

"Maybe we can rush him," Jarrett whispered.

Keeping his eyes on Clay, Lem said, "He's ready for that."

"But if we both start shooting . . ."

"He's keeping his distance for a reason," Lem said in a louder voice. "He likes to stay outside effective pistol range, which means our shots will go wide while his stay nice and level. Ain't that right, Clay?"

"I learn from the best," Clay replied. "Hanging back does have its advantages after all."

"Let me take the baby, at least," Jarrett said. "You told me I could—"

"That was before I saw who was with you," Clay cut in. "The brat's here with me where I can reach her with the back of my hand, the butt of this rifle, or even my bootheel if I'm so inclined."

"Get away from her, damn you!" Jarrett roared.

Clay laughed. "I was told I might be able to get a price for this little nuisance, but didn't think it would be much. Now I see it was worth dragging this brat along just for the show I'm getting."

The more the men shouted back and forth, the more the baby cried. As the noise grew, Grace struggled against her ropes. She tried to shout as well, but her cries were muffled by what must have been a gag hidden beneath the sack covering her head.

"So, what now, Clay?" Lem asked. "We just stand here and yell at each other?"

"I've got business to conduct," Clay replied. "Even if what you said about the others is true, that just means more cash for me. The two of you can either turn around and ride away now or I can pick you off. Doesn't much matter to me."

"I can get to Grace," Jarrett whispered.

"No," Lem quickly said. "Clay wasn't bluffing about what he might do to the baby."

"Could anyone do something that vile?"

Lem glanced over at him with a look that told him everything he needed to know. Even after what he'd seen and been through, Jarrett realized he hadn't fully experienced how dark another man's soul could be.

Even with Grace and Autumn so close, he felt more desperate and hopeless than ever. If Jen was stashed somewhere else entirely, that made things even more complicated. "What do we do, then?" Jarrett asked.

"Go on and leave," Clay said. "Get on your horses and ride away. I'm feeling generous."

"We can retreat now and regroup," Jarrett offered. "If we come at him some other time from some other angle—"

"No," Lem said in a quiet and oddly calm voice. "He'll put a bullet into us once we're clear. We walk away and he'll only have more time to line up a shot. Even if he just wounds us, there'll be less places for us to scatter."

"Then what do we do?"

"I suggest you take what I'm offering," Clay said. "Before I decide to cut my losses, starting with this particularly annoying one that just won't stop crying."

"Step back, Jarrett," Lem said.

"Listen to your friend there," Clay shouted. "He may be a coward, but he's not stupid."

Dropping his voice until it could barely be heard even by Jarrett, Lem said, "If you're ever going to trust me . . . even for an instant . . . do what I say and step back."

Jarrett's mind raced through all that he knew about Lem and everything he'd done in the short time they'd known each other. All of those things, combined with the fact that he didn't have any other viable options, brought Jarrett to one conclusion. He let out a slow breath and stepped back.

"Your turn," Clay said.

"Is that how you want to finish this? We part ways?" Lem asked. "I would have thought you'd prefer something a bit more final."

Clay shook his head. "You take one more little step and I'll start cutting those losses." For good measure, Clay took a step back himself. "This is a hard life we've chosen and I haven't made it this far by being stupid. We live and die by knowing the tools of our trade. You and I both know you can't hit me with any accuracy from where you're standing. Not without your rifle."

Lem's hand flashed down to his side to draw the pistol, bring it up, and fire a shot in one fluid motion. That first shot blasted through the air and knocked Clay back. Lem fired again and knocked Clay back a second time. He then sighted along the pistol's barrel and squeezed his trigger to put Clay flat on his back.

As the roar of those three shots rolled through the air to dissipate like the smoke still hanging over the camp, the baby's cry rose to a terrified pitch.

Rushing over to Lem, Jarrett said, "What on earth? I thought Clay was too far for an accurate pistol shot!"

"He was," Lem replied as he reloaded with fresh rounds from his gun belt. "But not for this pistol. The inside of the barrel I chose is filed in such a way that improves performance. The mechanism and cylinder can hold a bullet packed with more powder than most and—"

"That gun you put together on the day we first met," Jarrett marveled. "All those pieces you took from other pistols and put together into that one. It was all for this?"

"Yeah. Clay was right. We live and die by knowing the limits of our weapons. Ain't no other pistol would have made that shot. Seems this one worked out even better than I'd hoped."

Jarrett kept his Colt in hand as he ran to the spot where Clay had fallen. The outlaw wasn't moving and the front of his shirt was so bloody that it was clear he wasn't getting up. After kicking the outlaw's rifle away just to be safe, Jarrett turned his attention to the source of the crying. The instant he picked the baby up, she began to settle.

"There you are, Autumn," Jarrett cooed. "I thought I'd lost you, girl."

"Uncle Jarrett?"

He turned around to see that Lem had cut the ropes tying the older girl to the tree and had removed her mask and gag. As soon as she was able, she rushed straight to Jarrett. Tears streamed down her face and she wrapped him up in a hug that brought a tired smile to his face.

"Thank you, Uncle Jarrett," she said. "Thank you so much. I thought . . . I thought . . ."

"I know," Jarrett said as he embraced her with one arm while cradling the baby in the other. "I thought so too."

Jarrett took a few moments to look both girls over. He checked them from head to toe, looking for wounds, bruises, cuts, scrapes, anything at all that needed tending. Apart from some scuffs and bumps that could be expected on anyone making a hard journey, the girls appeared to be fine. He asked Grace if she was all right and she nodded timidly.

"What about the others?" Jarrett asked.

"What others?"

"Your mother and brother. Are they here as well? Did Clay stash them somewhere?"

Grace shook her head. Although there was sadness in her eyes, she didn't have any more tears to shed at the moment. "They're gone," she whispered.

"What happened to them?"

"Scott got loose somehow back at the house. The fire had already started," she said. "Those men had left. Scott got free and went to Mother first. When she came for me, Scott moved on to Autumn and carried her to try to find a way out. We tried windows and the back door just because they were closer, but we had to get to the front door." Blinking as if she were looking at something very far away, Grace wiped away a few tears that poked through at the corner of her eyes. "Mother helped me and Scott carried Autumn all the way. I was almost outside when Scott fell over. There was so much fire . . . so much smoke . . ."

Jarrett held on to her tightly. Before he could tell her she didn't need to say any more, Grace started talking again as if she absolutely needed to expel the words from her lungs.

"Scott just . . . fell down," she said. "Mother tried to drag him a ways, but she bent down and shook him and he was just gone. He was gone. I could tell. So could she. She still tried to carry him out, but she was starting to fall over too. I started to get dizzy, so Mother grabbed me and the baby and pushed us outside to get out of that smoke. She said she just had to catch her breath and that she was going right back in for Scott. Before she could, the roof fell in. Beams started to fall. The door was blocked. It was so terrible."

"It's all right, honey," Jarrett said. "There was nothing you could have done. You were so brave."

Grace shook her head. "I didn't do anything. I just ran."

"That's not true. You survived. That's no small feat."

"Mother . . . stayed with us for a while," she continued. "The men took her and me and the baby. They said they were going to sell us. One night, after that man took the three of us away, Mother tried to escape. She tried to get us all away from him. She got loose somehow and was untying my ropes, telling me we were going to run and be safe again when . . . he killed her. That man," Grace said as she looked over to Clay's body. "He stabbed her in the back."

Recognizing all too well the hatred brewing in the girl's eyes, Jarrett took hold of her and spoke firmly. "This is a terrible thing," he said. "It's over now. We'll all miss your parents and brother, but we need to honor their memories, not turn them into something ugly inside you. Understand me?"

Some of the rage in her eyes dimmed as Grace nodded but didn't go out completely. It was a good start.

"Come on," he said. "Let's go."

"Where?" she asked. "To get back the rest of what Clay stole from us?"

"You don't worry about that. It's just money. There're more important things. Your aunt Catherine has a real big house and I'm sure she'll love having you and Autumn as guests. It'll be good for you to be with family again."

"Will you stay there too?"

"I don't know just yet," Jarrett replied. "There's still some things that need to be taken care of."

Lem remained quiet until Jarrett approached him and asked, "You knew about Jen when you killed Clay? That she was . . . gone and he wouldn't have been able to get her back?"

Lem nodded. "Clay wouldn't have let her out of his sight if he was going to trade her."

Deciding to trust Lem enough to let the matter drop right there, Jarrett introduced him to Grace. All of them wasted no time before starting their ride back south toward Nebraska.

Clay Haskel was left to rot where he'd fallen. It was better than he deserved.

Chapter 35

One month later

It was dawn and the approaching summer could be felt from the dew in the grass to the growing thickness of the air. When the men had first ridden through the gate surrounding the impressive spread that was the Triple Diamond Ranch, their numbers were smaller. Like snow rolling downhill, the group had gathered mass from its surroundings until it became something more than what it had originally been. The original members of that group were easy enough to distinguish from the rest. They were the ones carrying torches and wearing burlap masks over their heads.

The owner of the spread stepped out onto the wide porch surrounding his three-level house. He pulled his suspenders over his shoulder and ran a hand through the rumpled hair on top of his head. When he'd first seen the masked riders, he scowled as if they were nothing but a nuisance. Once he spotted the additional men that had been collected along the way, his expression became much more serious.

"What the hell is going on here?" the man on the porch asked.

One masked man separated from the rest by riding a few paces forward. He carried a torch in his left hand and used his other to continually tug at the reins of his nervously fretting horse. "John Brakefield?" he said.

"You know damn well who I am," the man replied. "This is my ranch, my land, and my home. You're trespassing, so I suggest you leave."

"You'll come with us and answer for what you've done."

Brakefield cast his eyes at the crowd of men, most of whom stared right back at him through square holes cut into their masks. The rest shifted in their saddles, trying to keep their balance even though their hands were either tied behind their backs or bound to the horns on their saddles. "What I've done?" Brakefield replied. "You're the ones who've come onto my land, taken my men prisoner, and made threats."

None of the men said a word to that. The quieter they became, the eerier they appeared.

"Who sent you?" Brakefield demanded. "What right do you have to take my men hostage?"

Although the men who were tied up didn't appear to be hurt, they obviously weren't free to do much more than sit where they were and look frightened.

"We know about the men you hired," announced the lead masked rider. "The men sent to put those ranchers out of business."

"If some ranches burned down, that doesn't have a damn thing to do with me," Brakefield said.

"How did you know they were burned?"

"Release my men."

"I don't think so. Not until you tell them what kind of man they're working for."

Brakefield stomped to the edge of his porch. As he clenched his fists, his hands shook with the desire to take a swing at any or all of the men in front of him. "You want to know what kind of man I am? I'm the kind who's got the law in this county and every surrounding one eating from the palm of his hand! Those men you've got there are just the ones on this ranch. When I call down the rest of my group, they'll bury every last one of you!"

"You're a killer," the masked man said.

"You don't know the half of it. I'm also rich enough to pay to have your families strung up in front of you and there's not a judge within twenty counties that will make me spend so much as a single night in jail! How do you think some bunch of ignorant vigilantes will survive once I call down some *real* killers?"

"You mean like Clay Haskel?"

"Him and worse," Brakefield snarled. "Now get the hell out of my sight before I burn your houses down too."

The riders shifted in their saddles and looked at each other anxiously. The man next to the one who'd done all the talking thus far asked tentatively, "You're the one who hired Clay Haskel?"

"You're damn right I am!"

Turning to the rider beside him, the second masked figure peeled off his burlap sack. "You see?" Lem said as he tossed his mask aside. "I told you it would be easy to get him to confess."

The man at the head of the group took off his mask as well. Jarrett dropped the sack and said, "Good enough for me. How about you?"

Brakefield scowled down at them. "None of this means a thing." When he pointed to the house behind him, armed men appeared in the windows and a few stepped out to flank him on the porch. "You fire a shot at me and it'll be the last thing you do."

"I don't think so, John," said one of the other masked men. When he took off his mask, the rest of the riders did the same.

Now Brakefield was truly flummoxed. "Marshal Vernon?"

The marshal nodded. "And it's too bad I'm not one of the lawmen you have in your pocket. You could sure use a friend like that right about now."

"Come on inside, Marshal," Brakefield said in a voice dripping with honey. "Let's talk this over."

"You've said more than enough, John. Let's talk in my office."

"No. We can—"

"Now, John," the marshal snapped.

One of the gunmen at Brakefield's side got anxious and started to bring up his gun. That was enough to cause Jarrett, Lem, and every lawman present to raise their weapons and prepare them to fire. After that, Brakefield decided to go along quietly.

Sometime later, Jarrett and Lem were riding away from the Triple Diamond Ranch. "You think the marshal's got enough to put Brakefield away?" Lem asked.

"That rich man back there better hope it is," Jarrett replied. "Because jail is the safest place for him. I'm fairly certain a man like that has partners who'll lose faith in him once it gets out that the law is onto him."

"There's bound to be a few other gunmen he hired that're still out and about," Lem added. "Once they learn Brakefield is in custody and spelling out everything he's done and who he did it with to the marshal, those men will come around to silence him real quick."

"Even if Brakefield would do such a thing, how would those men find out about it?"

"I know plenty of ways to spread the word among some men in bad circles," Lem said. "They'll be more likely to put Brakefield down than gamble on him actually showing a spine and keeping his mouth shut."

"That just makes business sense."

"Now you're thinking straight."

They rode for a few more minutes, headed into town where a bottle of whiskey was waiting for them. Before their horses could hit their stride, Jarrett asked, "How did you know Brakefield would confess?"

"Men like him are itching to show how smart or tough they are. All they need is a little nudge and half an excuse. Besides, if he didn't feel like talking, one of his men we captured would have given up enough to spur the marshal along until they all wound up in jail anyway."

Jarrett nodded, finally feeling the weight from his shoulders ease up a bit. The cool pain in his heart, on the other hand, wasn't going anywhere anytime soon.

"There's another batch of men who worked with Clay not too far from here," Lem said. "Most likely, they're the ones Brakefield was bragging about hiring."

"How long do you think it'll take to track them down?"

"If we go in with guns drawn, it shouldn't take long."

"What about if we want to live through the experience?" Jarrett asked.

"Oh, so now you're thinking past the next day or two?"

"How long?"

After a moment's consideration, Lem said, "After some scouting and talking to some old friends who might be able to get me in close to them, I should be able to convince a few of them that I'm still on the wrong side of the law. It ain't as if Clay is around to tell anyone any different. I tread lightly enough, I imagine the both of us could get in real good with them and then bring down the lot of 'em real easy. Give me a few weeks to build the foundation and we should figure out a way to contact that Canadian slaver to see about arranging a meeting."

"Good," Jarrett said. "That gives me enough time."

"For what?"

"To pay my nieces a visit at my sister's place. I need to teach Grace how to make her mother's peach cobbler."

Read on for an excerpt from

SHOWDOWN AT TWO-BIT CREEK

A Ralph Compton Novel by Joseph A. West.
Available now from Signet in paperback and e-book.

"Seems to me a man who has so much mought want to spare some for poor folks like us, who have so little."

Buck Fletcher sighed, sensing the danger even as he recognized an old, familiar pattern that he'd experienced more times than he cared to remember in the clamorous saloons of dusty cow towns from El Paso to Dodge.

He was being set up, backed against the wall, and only his death in a sudden, roaring blaze of gunfire would satisfy the two men facing him.

The men stood tense and eager in a dugout that passed for a saloon in the Bald Mountain country of the Dakota Territory. They were rough, dirty and bearded, buffalo hunters by the look of them, and Fletcher recognized their stamp. These were men who would rather steal than work, and they would kill without hesitation or a single moment's remorse.

Both wore filthy sheepskin coats that were buttonless and tied around with string, moccasins to their knees and shapeless, battered hats that looked like they'd once belonged to other men. Fletcher figured these two shared maybe six rotten teeth between them, and even at a distance of eight feet he could smell their rank stench.

The man who'd spoken was the younger of the two, a mean-eyed towhead with a Sharps .50 caliber cradled in the crook of his arm, his loose mouth grinning, confident of his gun skills.

The two were on the prod, hungry to take what was Fletcher's: his guns, horses and the three hundred dollars in hard gold coins he carried in his money belt.

Fletcher was well aware that what he had was little enough. It wasn't much for a man to show for four years of war, another four as a ranch hand, two as a cow town marshal and then five rakehell years as a hired gun.

During those years, Fletcher had learned his profession well—the difficult way of the Colt's revolver, the draw and fire that took so much time and patience to master. The years had honed him down to six feet of bone and hard muscle, and he was lean as a lobo wolf and dangerous beyond all measure.

That Fletcher had now and then stepped lightly across the line that separates the lawful from the lawless goes without saying. It was the curious way of the gunfighter, a man who was part outlaw, part honest, upstanding citizen.

He had little enough, to be sure. But still, too much to be so easily parted with. A man should be allowed to keep what is his and not be expected to give it up without a fight.

Buck Fletcher had known men like these two before.

Huge, uncurried and wild, they had the look of dry-gulchers and back-shooters. They were men completely without honor, living by no code except that of the wolf. They were bullies who would meet face-to-face only the old, the weak, the timid and afraid.

The men didn't know it then, though they should have as their lives ticked down to a few final moments, but Buck Fletcher was none of these things.

But he was a man who had already seen more than his share of killing, and now he tried his best to walk away.

"Boys," he said, "I've been on the trail for a month,

and all I want is a bottle to cut the dust in my throat and a quiet hour to drink it in. I've never seen you men before, and I mean you no harm." He reached in his pocket and laid a gold double eagle on the rough plank that served as a bar. "That's yours. Now, drink up and welcome."

The men grinned, and the younger man shook his head. "You don't get our drift, rube, do you?" he asked. "Let me fill you in—we want it all. Every damn thing you got, including them boots an' fancy jinglebob spurs of yourn."

"Now, there's no need to rush your drink." The older man smiled. "Take your time, feller. Me and my boy here, we'll strip what we want from you after you're dead."

Fletcher turned to the man behind the bar. He was as dirty and unkempt as the other two, his eyes sly and feral.

"Can you do something?" Fletcher asked softly. "I mean, can you make it go away and let a man drink in peace?"

The man shook his head, a gleeful, knowing glint in his eyes. "It ain't my problem, feller," he said. "It's yours."

Fletcher nodded. "Figured you'd say something like that." He'd been standing belly to the bar. Now he turned slowly and faced the two grinning men. "You two have been pushing me mighty hard," he said wearily. "I'm not a man who likes to be stampeded, not by trash like you. So let's haul iron and get it over with."

Fletcher carried a seven-and-a-half-inch barreled Colt low on his right hip, its mahogany handle worn and polished from much use. Another revolver, its barrel cut back to four inches by an Austrian gunsmith in Dodge, hung in a crossdraw holster to the left of his gunbelt buckle.

In that single sickening instant as Fletcher turned to face him, the older man knew he'd made a big mistake.

He looked at Fletcher more closely and thought he saw something—something that ran an icy chill through his body and made him think he'd lost his reason. The tall, hard-eyed man wasn't afraid like others he'd known. He stood calm and ready, as if repeating a ritual he'd gone through many times before.

It came to the older man then that he should back off, call the whole thing an unfortunate misunderstanding and get drunk on the twenty dollars lying on the bar. Besides, there might be a better opportunity later, somewhere on the trail when they could use the Sharps big .50 and get a clean shot at this man's back.

That the young man facing him was a practiced gunfighter, there was no doubt, and the realization chilled the older man even deeper, all the way to the bone. There was danger here. Cold death was hovering very close, and he knew as the moments ticked by that he was fast running out of room on the dance floor. Now was the time to walk away from this. Now, before it was too late.

He opened his mouth to speak, planning to smooth things over, make what was happening stop before it went any further.

He never got the chance.

His son, meaner but less intelligent and not so perceptive, brought up the muzzle of his Sharps. He was lightning fast.

Fletcher was faster.

He drew his long-barreled Colt in a blur of motion that had long since become instinctive to him and slammed a shot into the younger man's chest. The towhead screamed and staggered a couple of steps backward. His father roared, gripped by both fear and anger, and drew from the waistband. His gun never cleared the top of his pants. Fletcher fired, the bullet crashing into the bridge of the man's nose. Blood splashed in a scarlet cloud around his head.

The older man's eyes curled back in his head, showing white, and he fell, shaking the foundations of the dugout.

The towhead, badly hurt, screamed something unintelligible and tried desperately to bring the Sharps into play. Fletcher shot him again. The man's face showed stunned surprise, an utter inability to comprehend that he'd caught a fighting scorpion by the tail and that he was the one doing the dying.

He gasped. "I thought . . . I thought . . ." Then he was falling headlong into black nothingness, the rifle dropping from his lifeless fingers.

Out of the corner of his eye, Fletcher saw the bartender come up with a double-barreled Greener. The man fired, but Fletcher was already diving for the dirt floor. Buckshot hissed like a striking snake past his head. He rolled, then came up on one knee and slammed two shots very fast into the man's chest. The bartender crashed against the sod wall behind him, dislodging a shower of bottles from the shelf, then sank to the floor, the light already fading from his eyes.

The air in the poorly ventilated dugout was thick with acrid gray powder smoke, and the concussion of the firing guns had extinguished the oil lamp above the bar.

In the gloom, Fletcher thumbed fresh shells into his Colt, then shoved it into the holster. He looked at the two men on the floor. They were both dead, the older man's twisted face revealing the stark horror and disbelief of his last moments.

The bartender was sprawled behind the bar . . . if a rough plank laid across two barrels can be described as such. A framed motto had fallen off the sod wall of the dugout and lay across the dead man's chest. It read:

HAVE YOU WRITTEN TO MOTHER?

Fletcher shook his head. "Mister, she must be right proud o' you."

He left the twenty dollars lying on the bar. It would pay to bury the dead, should some charitable soul pass by. Otherwise, they could rot for all he cared.

A sick, bitter emptiness in him, Fletcher took one last look at the three men, then stepped outside, gratefully gulping in drafts of cold fresh air.

He stepped into the saddle of his big American stud and caught up the rope of his mustang packhorse just as a small black-and-white-speckled pup ran around the corner of the dugout. The pup stopped and looked up at him, whimpering.

"You go on home," Fletcher said. "Find your mama."

The pup, his eyes wide and sad, stayed right where he was and whimpered even more.

Fletcher nodded. "Little feller, I think maybe you don't have a mama."

The pup was obviously a stray who'd been hanging around the saloon. Judging by his slatted ribs, the animal had missed his last six meals and then some.

"Where I'm headed, I got no place for a pup," Fletcher said sternly. "So just go on about your business. I want no truck with you."

He swung his horse around, preparing to ride out. The pup stood and immediately started to howl, then lay down again, resting his head on his oversized front paws, and crying softly.

"Oh hell," Fletcher swore. He dismounted, picked up the pup and set him on the saddle in front of him. "You piss on me, boy, and you and me will part company right quick."

The pup made happy little yelping noises and began to lick Fletcher's hand. The big man smiled. "Well, maybe not."

He turned his horse again and rode away from the dugout and its three dead men without a single backward glance.

Buck Fletcher was going home, riding north with the long winds that stirred the buffalo grass of the Great Plains into a restless sea of green and brown.

Fifteen years of wandering lay bleak behind him, and ahead . . . he had no idea.

There was little hope in him, no dream of a better life with a wife and tall sons and girls as pretty and fresh as bluebonnets in the spring. Such thoughts were for other men: ranchers, farmers, storekeepers. They were not for the likes of him.

He knew only that he was going home. As with the ragged *V*s of the wild geese in the sky over his head, it was an instinctive thing, unplanned, the action of a man who had reached the end of his rope and was now hanging on by a thread.

A rootless, violent past lay dark behind him, and he firmly believed all that was left to him now was to die well. The closing act of a famed gunfighter's life was remembered and remarked upon where men gathered, and Fletcher fervently hoped his final curtain would be drawn with dignity.

Yet he feared that when death came for him, it would come as it so often did for his kind—on the filthy sawdust of a barroom floor, where he would meet it with a gun in hand, hot blood filling his mouth with a taste of woodsmoke.

That fall of 1876, Buck Fletcher was twenty-nine years old, a tall, heavy-shouldered man with a long hatchet blade of a face honed sharp by sun, wind and hard times. Even so, women did not turn away from him, for his features were saved from irretrievable homeliness by a wide, expressive mouth that in times long past had been quick to smile and eyes that sometimes revealed a faint, self-mocking humor and a well-hidden but nonetheless inherent kindliness.

But those eyes could change in an instant from blue to a cold, pitiless gray when the six-gun rage rose in him. Now, for eleven men, that gray had been the last thing in this life they ever saw.

Fletcher had ridden out of the Badlands and into the Dakota Territory astride his long-legged stud, leading the mustang packhorse.

Some packhorses pony willingly, keeping up with a rider and his mount so that the lead rope is mostly loose. But the mustang, mouse-colored and evil-tempered, was a reluctant traveler and held back constantly, pulling on the rope so that Fletcher feared his arm would be ripped right out of its socket.

He turned in the saddle and yanked on the rope for maybe the hundredth time that morning. The mustang, resentful, unforgiving and sly, shook his head indignantly and sidestepped to his right, stretching the rope even tighter.

"I swear, hoss," Fletcher said bitterly, wincing against the wrench on his arm, "keep this up and before too long you and me are going to have a major disagreement."

The mustang, instinctively made wary by the tone of the human's voice, once again dutifully fell into line behind Fletcher's stud. But the big man knew by the crafty look in the pony's one good eye that he was just lying low for the moment, planning further deviltry. As he rode, Fletcher pondered the sheer cussedness of the mustang breed and shook his head more in sorrow than in anger.

Fletcher was tired, tired beyond his years. It was the tiredness he'd seen in men when they were old and full of sleep, seeking only a rocker in the shade where they could doze away the long, empty days.

But such a life was not for him. He had thought to head for Deadwood and the gold fields, where mine shafts were boring deep into the Black Hills and the precious orange metal was being ripped from the earth.

Where there was gold, there were miners, and where there were miners, there were those who preyed on them: gamblers, loose women and the sellers of bad whiskey. It was a combustible mixture that led to violence, gunplay and dead men. It was a place for a man like Buck Fletcher.

Somewhere back on the trail from Montana, he'd heard that the Denver gambler Colorado Charlie Utter was in town, and Charlie owed him a favor or three. And Wild Bill was there. If Hickok was in Deadwood, then there was work for top gun hands. Buck Fletcher lacked even the smallest shred of false modesty. The years had taught him that he was one of the best with a gun around, maybe the best there ever was. Deadwood, wide-open and roaring, could use a man with his flashing draw and steady nerves in the face of fire.

As he followed the path of the wild geese, Fletcher didn't know it then, but very soon that rare gun skill would be a thing he would have to prove and prove again.

He had embarked on a journey that would take him to the edge of hell—and there would be no going back.

Also available

The Dangerous Land:
A Ralph Compton Novel

by Marcus Galloway

Frontier life is hard enough without having kids to worry about—especially for a widower like Paul Meakes. So when his daughter is hit by a poisoned arrow during an Indian raid, Paul is determined to track down the Comanche villains who hurt his little girl—and bring them to justice with the help of Indian hunter Hank Adley, a hired gun who's got business of his own with the tribe.

But when the trail leads to a close call with Indian warriors and on to deadly intrigue, Paul discovers that the dangers of the West are far greater and more varied than he ever imagined. And to save his family, he has no choice but to take a stand against them all....

S0553